W9-BHY-697

Also by Jonathan Lethem

Jonathan Lethem

THE WALL OF THE SKY, THE WALL OF THE EYE

A Harvest Book • Harcourt, Inc.

Orlando Austin New York San Diego Toronto London

Requests for permission to make copies of any part of the work should be submitted
online at www.harcourt.com/contact or mailed to the following address: Permissions
Department, Harcourt, Inc., 6277 Sea Harbor Drive, Orlando, Florida 32887-6777.

www.HarcourtBooks.com

"The Happy Man," "Vanilla Dunk," and "Forever, Said the Duck" appeared, in slightly
different form, in *Asimov's Science Fiction*. "Light and the Sufferer" appeared, in slightly
different form, in *Century*. "The Hardened Criminals" appeared, in slightly different
form, in *Intersections: The Sycamore Hill Anthology*.

The Library of Congress has cataloged the hardcover edition as follows:
Lethem, Jonathan.
The wall of the sky, the wall of the eye: stories/
by Jonathan Lethem—1st ed.
p.   cm.
Contents: The happy man—Vanilla dunk—Light and the sufferer—Forever, said the
duck—Five fucks—The hardened criminals—Sleepy people.
1. Fantastic fiction, American.   2. Horror tales, American.   I. Title.
PS3562.E8544W35   1996
813'.54—dc20   95-32093
ISBN: 978-0-15-100180-4
ISBN: 978-0-15-603248-3 (pbk.)

Printed in the United States of America
First Harvest edition 2007
K J I H G F E D C B A

"The Happy Man" *is for Stanley Ellin*
—otherwise, for Blake Lethem

Without Whom

Michael Kandel, Richard Parks, Gardner Dozois, the Sycamore Hill Writers' Conference 1992 and 1994, and Charles Rosen and Christian K. Messenger, inspirers of *Dunk*.

The book's title is taken from a description of Fritz Lang's films in Geoffrey O'Brien's *The Phantom Empire: Movies in the Mind of the Twentieth Century*.

CONTENTS

CONTENTS

THE HAPPY MAN

THE HAPPY MAN

1.

I left her in the bedroom, and went and poured myself a drink. I felt it now; there wasn't any doubt. But I didn't want to tell her, not yet. I wanted to stretch it out for as long as I could. It had been so quick, this time.

In the meantime I wanted to see the kid.

I took my drink and went into his room and sat down on the edge of his bed. His night light was on; I could see I'd woken him. Maybe he'd heard me clinking bottles. Maybe he'd heard us making love.

"Dad," he said.

"Peter."

"Something the matter?"

Peter was twelve. A good kid, a very good kid. He was

3

just eleven when I died. All computers and stereo, back then. Heavy metal and D and D. Sorcerers, dragons, the flaming pits of Hell, the whole bit. And music to match. After I died and came back he got real serious about things, forgot about the rock music and the imaginary Hells. Gave up his friends, too. I was pretty worried about that, and we had a lot of big talks. But he stayed serious. The one thing he stuck with was the computer, only now he used it to map out real Hell. My Hell.

Instead of answering his question I took another drink. He knew what was the matter.

"You going away?" he asked.

I nodded.

"Tell Mom yet?"

"Nope."

He scooted up until he was sitting on his pillow. I could see him thinking: *It was fast this time, Dad. Is it getting faster?* But he didn't say anything.

"Me and your mother," I said. "There's a lot of stuff we didn't get to, this time."

Peter nodded.

"Well—" I began, then stopped. What did he understand? More than I guessed, probably. "Take good care of her," I said.

"Yeah."

I kissed his forehead. I knew how much he hated the smell of liquor, but he managed not to make a face. Good kid, etc.

Then I went in to see his mother.

It was while we were making love that I'd had the first inkling that the change was coming on, but I'd kept it to myself. There wasn't any purpose to ruining the mood; besides, I wasn't sure yet. It wasn't until afterward that I knew for sure.

But I had to tell her now. Another hour or so and I'd be gone.

I sat on the edge of the bed, just like with Peter. Only in this room it was dark. And she wasn't awake. I put my hand on her cheek, felt her breath against my palm. She murmured, and kissed my hand. I squeezed her shoulder until she figured out that I wanted her to wake up.

"Maureen," I said.

"Why aren't you sleeping?"

I wanted to undress again and get back under the covers. Curl myself around her and fall asleep. Not to say another word. Instead I said: "I'm going back."

"Going back?" Her voice was suddenly hoarse.

I nodded in the dark, but she got the idea.

"Damn you!"

I didn't see the slap coming. That didn't matter, since it wasn't for show. It rattled my teeth. By the time I recovered she was up against the headboard, curled into herself, sobbing weakly.

It wasn't usually this bad for her anymore. She'd numbed the part of herself that felt it the most. But it didn't usually happen this fast, either.

I moved up beside her on the bed, and cradled her head in my hands. Let her cry awhile against my chest.

But she wasn't done yet. When she turned her face up it was still raw and contorted with her pain, tendons standing out on her neck.

"Don't say it like that," she gasped out between sobs. "I hate that so much—"

"What?" I tried to say it softly.

"Going *back*. Like that's more real to you now, like that's where you belong, and this is the mistake, the exception—"

I couldn't think of what to say to stop her.

"Oh, God." I held her while she cried some more. "Just don't say it like that, Tom," she said when she could. "I can't stand it."

"I won't say it like that anymore," I said flatly.

She calmed somewhat. We sat still there in the dark, my arms around her.

"I'm sorry," she said, but evenly now. "It's just so fast. Are you sure—"

"Yeah," I said.

"We hardly had any time," she said, sniffling. "I mean, I was just getting the feeling back, you know? When we were making love. It was so good, just now. Wasn't it?"

"Yes."

"I just thought it was the beginning of a good period again. I thought you'd be back for a while . . ."

I stroked her hair, not saying anything.

"Did you know when we were fucking?" she asked.

"No," I lied. "Not until after."

"I don't know if I can take it anymore, Tom. I can't

watch you walk around like a zombie all the time. It's driving me crazy. Every day I look in your eyes, thinking *maybe he's back,* maybe he's about to come back, and you just stare at me. I try to hold your hand in the bed and then you need to scratch yourself or something and you just pull away without saying anything, like you didn't even notice. I can't live like this—"

"I'm sorry," I said, a little hollowly. I wasn't unsympathetic. But we'd been through it before. We always ended in the same place. We always would.

And frankly, once I'd absorbed the impact of her rage, the conversation lost its flavor. My thoughts were beginning to drift ahead, to Hell.

"Maybe you should live somewhere else," she said. "Your body, I mean. When you're not around. You could sleep down at the station or something."

"You know I can't do that."

"Oh no," she said. "I just remembered—"

"What?"

"Your uncle Frank, remember? When does he come?"

"Maybe I'll be back before he shows up," I said. It wasn't likely. I usually spent a week or so in Hell, when I went. Frank was due in four days. "Anyway, he knows about me. There won't be any problem."

She sighed. "I just hate having guests when you're gone—"

"Frank's not a guest," I said. "He's family."

She changed the subject. "Did you forget the medication? Maybe if you took the medication—"

"I always take it," I said. "It doesn't work. It doesn't keep me here. You can't take a pill to keep your soul from migrating to Hell."

"It's supposed to help, Tom."

"Well it doesn't matter, does it? I take it. Why do we have to talk about it?"

Now I'd hurt her a little. We were quiet. I felt her composing herself there, in my arms. Making her peace with my going away. Numbing herself.

The result was that we came a little closer together. I was able to share in her calm. We would be nice to each other from here on in. Things were back to normal.

But at the time, we'd backed away from that perilous, agonized place where to be separated by this, or separated at all, even for a minute, was too much to bear; from that place where all that mattered was our love, and where compromise was fundamentally wrong.

Normal was sometimes miles apart.

"You know what I hate the most?" she said. "That I don't even want to stay up with you. You'll only be around for what? A couple of hours more? I should want to get in every last minute. But I don't know what to say to you, really. There's nothing new to say about it. I feel like going to sleep."

"It's coming fast," I said, just to set her straight. "I think it's more like half an hour now."

"Oh," she said.

"But no hard feelings. Go to sleep. I understand."

"I have to," she said. "I have to get up in the morning. I feel sick from crying." She slid under the covers and hugged me at the waist. "Tom?" she said, in a smaller voice.

"Maureen."

"Is it getting faster?"

"It's just this one time," I said. "It probably doesn't mean anything. It's just painful to go through—"

"Okay," she said. "I love you, Tom."

"I love you too," I said. "Don't worry."

She went to sleep then, while I lay awake beside her, waiting to cross over.

If Maureen hadn't still been in school when I died, that would have been the end of it. If she hadn't been in debt up to her ears, and still two years away from setting up an office. As it was I had to sit in cold pack for three months while her lawyer pushed the application through. Eventually the courts saw it her way: I was the breadwinner. So they thawed me out.

Now she was supposed to be happy. I kept food on the table, and she had her graduate degree. Her son grew up knowing his dad. It wasn't supposed to matter that my soul shuttled between my living body here on earth, and Hell. She wasn't supposed to complain about that.

Besides, it wasn't my fault.

2.

In Hell I'm a small boy.

Younger than Peter. Eight or nine, I'd guess.

I always start in the same place. The beginning is

always the same. I'm at that table, in that damned garden, waiting for the witch.

Let me be more specific. I begin as a detail in a tableau: four of us children are seated in a semicircle around a black cast-iron garden table. We sit in matching iron chairs. The lawn beneath us is freshly mowed; the gardener, if there is one, permits dandelions but not crabgrass. At the edge of the lawn is a scrubby border of rosebushes. Beyond that, a forest.

Behind me, when I turn to look, there's a pair of awkward birch saplings. Behind them, the witch's house. Smoke tumbles out of the slate chimney. The witch is supposed to be making us breakfast.

We're supposed to wait. Quietly.

Time is a little slow there, at Hell's entrance. I've waited there with the other children, bickering, playing with the silverware, curling the lace doily under my setting into a tight coil, for what seems like years. Breakfast is never served. Never. The sun, which is hanging just beyond the tops of the trees, never sets. Time stands still there. Which is not to say we sit frozen like statues. Far from it. We're a bunch of hungry children, and we make all kinds of trouble.

But I'm leaving something out.

We sit in a semicircle. That's to make room for the witch's horse. The witch's horse takes up a quarter of the table. He's seated in front of a place like any other guest.

He's waiting for breakfast, too.

The witch's horse is disgusting. The veins under his eyes quiver and he squirms in his seat. His forelegs are chained and staked to keep him at the table. He's sitting on his tail, so he can't swat away the flies which gather and drink at the corners of his mouth. The witch's horse is wearing a rusted pair of cast-iron eyeglass frames on his nose. They're for show, I guess, but they don't fit right. They chafe a pair of raw pink gutters into the sides of his nose.

If I stay at the table and wait for breakfast, subtle changes do occur. Most often the other children get restless, and begin to argue or play, and the table is jostled, and the silverware clatters, and the horse snorts in fear, his yellow eyes leaking. Sometimes a snake or a fox slithers across the lawn and frightens the horse, and he rattles his chains, and the children murmur and giggle. Once a bird flew overhead and splattered oily white birdshit onto the teapot. It was a welcome distraction, like anything else.

Every once in a while the children decide to feel sorry for the horse, and mount a campaign to lure him forward and pluck the glasses from his nose, or daub at his gashes with a wadded-up doily. I tried to help them once, when I was new to Hell. I felt sorry for the horse, too. That was before I saw him and the witch ride together in the forest. When I saw them ride I knew the horse and the witch were in it together.

Seeing them ride, howling and grunting through the trees, is one of the worst things I experience in all of

Hell. After the first time I didn't feel sorry for the horse at all.

Whatever the cause, disturbances at the garden table are always resolved the same way. The activity reaches some pitch, the table seems about to overturn, when suddenly there's a sound at the door of the witch's house. We all freeze in our places, breath held. Even the horse knows to sit stock-still, and the only sound that remains is the buzzing of the flies.

We all watch for movement at the door of the witch's house. On the slim hope that maybe, just this once, it's breakfast time. The door opens, just a crack, just enough, and the witch slips out. She's smiling. She's very beautiful, the witch. The most beautiful woman I've ever seen, actually. She's got a great smile. The witch walks out across the lawn, and stops halfway between her door and the table. By now we're all slumped obediently in our seats again. My heart, to be honest, is in my throat.

I'm in love.

"Breakfast will be ready soon," sings the witch. "So just sit quietly, don't bother Horse, and before you know it I'll have something delicious on the table—"

And then she turns and slips back through her doorway and we start all over again.

That's how Hell begins. Maybe if I were a little more patient—waited, say, a thousand years instead of just a hundred—breakfast would appear. But then, knowing Hell, I'm not sure I'd want to see what the witch has been cooking up all this time.

But I don't wait at all anymore. I get up and walk away from the table right away.

Time in Hell doesn't start until you get up from the garden table.

3.

The Hell in the computer starts out the same way mine does: in the garden.

Peter laid it all out like Dungeons and Dragons, like a role-playing computer game. We entered a long description of the scene; the other children, the witch's horse, the witch. It was Peter's idea, when I came back with my first tentative reports of what I'd gone through, to map it out with the computer. I think he had the idea that it was like one of his dungeons, and that if we persisted we would eventually find a way out.

So Peter's "Dad" character wakes up at the garden table, same as I do. And when Peter types in a command, like GET UP FROM THE TABLE, WALK NORTH ACROSS THE LAWN, his "Dad" goes to explore a computer version of the Hell I inhabit.

I don't soft-pedal it. I report what I see, and he enters it into the computer. Factually, we're recreating my Hell. The only thing I spare him are my emotional responses. I omit my fear at what I encounter, my rage at living these moments again and again, my unconscionable lust for the witch . . .

4.

When I crossed over that night, after fighting with
Maureen, I didn't dawdle at the garden table. I was bored
with that by now. I pushed my chair back and started in
the direction Peter and I call north; the opposite direction
from the witch's house. I ran on my eight-year-old legs
across the lawn, through a gap in the border of rosebushes, and into the edge of the forest.

The north was my favored direction at the moment,
because I'd explored it the least. Oh, Hell goes on forever
in every direction, of course. But I don't always get very
far. I explored the territories nearest the witch's garden
most thoroughly, in any direction; as I get farther out it
gets less and less familiar. I just don't always get very far
out.

And the nearby territories to the north somehow
seemed less *hackneyed* to me at the moment.

The forest to the north quickly gives way to an open
field. It's called the Field of Tubers, because of the
knuckled roots that grow there. Sort of like carrots, or
potatoes, or knees. Like carrots in that they're orange,
like potatoes in the way the vines link them all together,
under the ground. Like knees, or elbows, in the way they
twitch, and bleed when you kick them.

The first few times I came to the Field of Tubers I tried
to run across. Now I walk, slowly, carefully. That way I
avoid falling into the breeding holes. The holes don't
look like much if you don't step on them; just little cir-
cular holes, like wet anthills in the dirt. They throb a

14

little. But if your foot lands on them they gape open, the entrance stretching like a mouth, and you fall in.

The breeding holes are about four feet deep, and muddy. Inside, the newborn tubers writhe in heaps. They're not old enough to take root yet. It's a mess.

Sure, you can run across the field, scrambling back out of the breeding holes, scraping the crushed tubers off the bottom of your shoes. You get to the other side of the field either way. It's not important. Myself, I walk.

Time, which is frozen at the witch's breakfast table, starts moving once I enter the forest. But time in Hell takes a very predictable course. The sun, which has been sitting at the top of the trees, refusing to set, goes down as I cross the Field of Tubers. It's night when I reach the other side, no matter how long it takes me to cross. If I run, looking back over my shoulder, I can watch the sun plummet through the treetops and disappear. Of course, if I run looking back over my shoulder I trip over the tubers and fall into the breeding holes constantly. If I idle in the field, squatting at the edge of a breeding hole, poking it with my finger to watch it spasm open, the sun refuses to set.

But why would I ever want to do that?

5.

When I first came back, when they warmed me up and put me back together, they didn't send me home right away. I had to spend a week in an observation ward, and on the fourth day they sent a doctor in to let me know where I stood.

"You'll be fine," he said. "You won't have any trouble holding down your job. Most people won't know the difference. But you will cross over."

"I've heard," I said.

"It shouldn't affect your public life," he said. "You'll be able to carry on most conversations in a perfunctory way. You just won't seem very interested in personal questions. Your mind will appear to be wandering. And you won't be very affectionate. Your co-workers won't notice, but your wife will."

"I won't want to fuck her," I said.

"No, you won't."

"Okay," I said. "How often will I go?"

"That varies from person to person. Some get lucky, and cross over just once or twice for the rest of their lives. It's rare, but it does happen. At the other extreme, some spend most of their time over there. For most, it's somewhere in between."

"You're not saying anything."

"That's right; I'm not. But I should say that how often you cross over isn't always as important as how you handle it. The stress of not knowing is as bad or worse than actually going through it. The anticipation. It can cast a pall over the times when you're back. A lot of marriages . . . don't survive the resurrection."

"And there's no way to change it."

"Not really. You'll get a prescription for Valizax. It's a hormone that stimulates the secretions of a gland associated, in some studies, with the migration. Some people claim it helps, and maybe it does, in their cases. Or maybe it's just a placebo effect. And then there's therapy."

"Therapy?"

"They'll give you the brochure when you leave. There are several support groups for migrators. Some better than others. We recommend one in particular. It's grounded in solid psychoanalytic theory, and like the drug, some people have said it improves the condition. But that's not for me to say."

I went to the support group. The good one. Once. I don't know what I was expecting. There were seven or eight people there that night, and the group counselor, who I learned wasn't resurrected, had never made the trips back and forth from his own Hell. After some coffee and uneasy socializing we went and sat in a circle. They went around, bringing each other up to date on their progress, and the counselor handed out brownie points for every little epiphany. When they got to me, they wanted to hear about my Hell.

Only they didn't call it Hell. They called it a "psychic landscape." And I quickly learned that they wanted me to consider it symbolic. The counselor wanted me to explain what my Hell *meant*.

I managed to contain my anger, but I left at the first break. Hell doesn't *mean* anything. Excuse me—*my* Hell doesn't mean anything. Maybe yours does.

But mine doesn't. That's what makes it Hell.

And it's not symbolic. It's very, very real.

6.

On the other side of the Field of Tubers, if I go straight over the crest, is the Grove of the Robot Maker. A dense patch of trees nestled at the base of a hill.

The moon is up by this time.

The robot maker is an old man. A tired old man. He putters around in the grove in a welder's helmet, but he never welds. His robots are put together with wire and tinsnips. They're mostly pathetic. Half of them barely make it up to the Battle Pavilion before collapsing. He made better ones, once, if you believe him. He's badly in need of a young apprentice.

That's where I come in.

"Boy, you're here," he says when I arrive. He hands me a pliers or a ball-peen hammer. "Let me show you what I'm working on," he says. "I'll let you help." He tries to involve me in his current project, whatever it is. Whatever heap of refuse he's currently animating.

His problem, which he describes to me at length, is that his proudest creation, Colonel Eagery, went renegade on his way up to the Battle Pavilion. Back when the robot maker was young and strong and built robots with fantastic capabilities. Colonel Eagery, he says, was his triumph, but the triumph went sour. The robot rebelled, and set up shop on the far side of the mountains, building evil counterparts to the robot maker's creations. The strong, evil robots that so routinely demolish the robot maker's own robots out on the Battle Pavilion.

I have two problems with this story.

First of all, I know Colonel Eagery, and he isn't a robot. Oh no. I know all too well that Eagery, who I also call The Happy Man, is flesh and blood.

The second is that the robot maker is too old and feeble for me to imagine that he's ever been able to build anything capable and effective at all, let alone something as capable and effective as I know Eagery to be.

Besides, Hell doesn't have a *before*. Hell is stuck in time, repeating endlessly. Hell doesn't have a past. It just *is*. The robot maker is always old and ineffectual, and he always has been.

But I never say this. My role is just as predetermined as the robot maker's. I humor him. When I'm passing through this part of Hell, I'm the robot maker's apprentice. I make a show of interest in his latest project. I help him steer it up to the Battle Pavilion. I can't say why. That's just the way things are in this corner of Hell.

This time, when I entered the grove, I found the robot maker already heading up toward the pavilion. He'd built a little robot terrier this time. It was surprisingly mobile and lively, yipping and snapping at the robot maker's heels. I fell in with them, and the robot maker put his heavy, dry hand on my shoulder. The mechanical terrier sniffed at my shoes and barked once, then ran ahead, rooting frantically in the moss.

"He's a good one, boy," said the robot maker. "I think he's got a bit of your spark in him. This one's got a fighting chance against whatever the Colonel's got cooked up."

It didn't, of course. I couldn't bring myself to look at

the poor little mechanical terrier. It was about to be killed. But I didn't say anything.

At this point in our hike through the grove the witch and the witch's horse ride by. It's another dependable part of my clockwork Hell. They turn up at about this point in my journey—the moon just up, a breeze stirring—whichever direction I choose. It's a horrible sight, but it's one I've gotten used to. Like just about everything else.

The horse is a lot more imposing freed from his stakes at the table. He's huge and sweaty and hairy, his nostrils dilated wide, his lips curled back. He's not wearing those funny glasses anymore. The witch rides him cowboy style, bareback. She bends her head down and grunts exhortations into the horse's ear. She's still beautiful, I guess. And I still love her—sort of. I feel mixed up about the witch when she rides, actually. A combination of fear and pity and shame. An odd sense that she wouldn't do it if she didn't somehow *have* to. That the horse is somehow doing it to her.

But mostly I'm just afraid. As they rode through the grove now, I stood frozen in place with fear, just like the first time.

The robot maker did what he always does: covered my eyes with his bony hand and muttered, "Terrible, terrible! Not in front of the boy!"

I peered through his fingertips, compelled to watch.

And then they were gone, snorting away into the night, and we were alone in the grove again. The terrier yipped after them angrily. The robot maker shook his head, gripped my shoulder, and we walked on.

The pavilion sits on a plateau at the edge of the woods. The base is covered with trees, invisible until you're there. The battle area, up on top, is like a ruined Greek temple. The shattered remains of the original roof are piled around the edges. The pavilion itself is littered with the glowing, radioactive shambles of the robot maker's wrecked creations. The pavilion is so infused with radiation that normal physics don't apply there; some of the ancient robots still flicker back into flame when the wind picks up, and sometimes one of the wrecks goes into an accelerated decline and withers into ashes, as though years of entropy have finally caught up with it. The carcasses tell the story of the robot maker's decline; his recent robots are less ambitious and formidable, and their husks are correspondingly more pathetic. Many of the newer ones simply failed on their way to the pavilion; their ruined bodies litter the pathway up the hill.

But not the terrier. He bounded up the hill ahead of us, reached the crest, and disappeared over the top. The robot maker and I hurried after him, not wanting him to lose his match before we even saw what he was fighting.

His opponent was a wolfman robot. As from an old horror movie, his face was more human than dog. It was a perfect example of how the robot maker's creations were so badly overmatched: what chance does a house pet have against a wolfman? It was often like this, a question of several degrees of sophistication.

Standing on two feet, the wolfman towered over the terrier. He spoke too, taunting the little dog, who could only yip and growl in response.

"Here, boy," cackled the wolfman. "Come on, pup. Come to daddy. Here we go." He gestured beckoningly. The terrier barked and reared back. "Come on, boy. Jeez." He looked to us for sympathy as we approached. "Lookit this. Here boy, I'm not gonna hurt you. I'm not gonna hurt you. I'm just gonna wring your fucking neck. Come on. COME HERE YOU GODDAMN LITTLE PIECE OF SHIT!"

The wolfman lunged, scrambling down and seizing the terrier by the neck, and took a bite on the forearm for his trouble. I heard metal grate on metal. "Ow! Goddammit. That does it." He throttled the little robot, which squealed until its voice was gone. "This is gonna hurt me more than it hurts you," said the wolfman, even as he tossed the broken scrap-metal carcass aside. The robot maker and I just stood, staring in stupid wonder.

"Ahem," said the wolfman, picking himself up. "Boy. Where was I? Oh, well. Some other fucking time." He turned his back and walked away, clearing his throat, picking imaginary pieces of lint from his body, tightening an imaginary tie like Rodney Dangerfield.

As soon as the wolfman was over the edge of the pavilion and out of sight, the robot maker ran to his ruined terrier and threw his skeletal body over it in sorrow, as though he could shield it from some further indignity. I turned away. I hated the robot maker's weeping. I didn't want to have to comfort him again. The sight of it, frankly, made me sick. It was one of Hell's worst moments. Besides, hanging around the pavilion weeping over his failures was how the robot maker had soaked up so much radiation, and gotten so old. If I stuck around I might get like him.

I snuck away.

7.

A few months after my brush with the support group I met another migrator in a bar.

I'd come back from Hell that afternoon, at work. I reinhabitated my body while I was sitting behind the mike, reading out a public service announcement. For once I kept my cool; didn't tell anyone at the station, didn't call Maureen at home. I stopped at the bar on my way home, just to get a few minutes for myself before I let Maureen and Peter know I was back.

I got talking to the guy at my right. I don't remember how, but it came out that he was a migrator, too. Just back, like me. We started out boozily jocular, then got quiet as we compared notes, not wanting to draw attention to ourselves, not wanting to trigger anyone's prejudices.

He told me about his Hell, which was pretty crazy. The setting was urban, not rural. He started out on darkened city streets, chased by Chinamen driving garbage trucks and shooting at him with pistols. There was a nuclear war; the animals mutated, grew intelligent and vicious. It went on from there.

I told him about mine, and then I told him about the support group and what I'd thought of it.

"Shit, yes," he said. "I went through that bullshit. Don't let them try to tell you what you're going through. They don't know shit. They can't know what we go through. They aren't *there*, man."

I asked him how much of his time he spent in Hell.

"Sheeeit. I'm not back here one day for every ten I spend *there*. I work in a bottling plant, man. Quality control. I look at bottles all day, then I go out drinking with a bunch of other guys from the plant. Least that's what they tell me. When I come back I don't even *know* those guys. Buncha strangers. When I come back"—he raised his glass—"I go out drinking alone."

I asked him about his wife. He finished his drink and ordered another one before he said anything.

"She got sick of waiting around, I guess," he said. "I don't blame her. Least she got me brought back. I owe her *that*."

We traded phone numbers. He wasn't exactly the kind of guy I'd hang around with under ordinary circumstances, but as it was we had a lot in common.

I called a few times. His answering machine message was like this: "Sorry, I don't seem to be *home* right now. Leave a message at the tone and I'll call you as soon as I'm *back*."

Maureen told me he called me a few times, too. Always while I was away.

8.

When I leave the robot maker at the pavilion, I usually continue north, to the shrunken homes in the Garden of Razor Blades. The garden begins on the far side of the pavilion. A thicket of trees, at the entrance, only the trees are leafed with razor blades. The moonlight is reflected off a thousand tiny mirrors; it's quite pretty, really. The forest floor is layered with fallen razor blades. They never rust, because it never rains in Hell.

The trees quickly give way to a delicately organized garden laced with paths, and the bushes and flowers, like the trees before them, are covered with razor blades. The paths wend around to a clearing, and in the middle of the clearing are the shrunken homes. They're built into a huge dirt mound, like a desert mesa inhabited by Indians, or a gigantic African anthill. Hundreds of tiny doorways and windows are painstakingly carved out of the mound. Found objects are woven into the structure; shirt buttons, safety pins, eyeglass frames, and nail clippers. But no razor blades.

The shrunken humans are just visible as I approach. Tiny figures in little cloth costumes, busily weaving or cooking or playing little ball games on the roofs and patios of the homes. I never get any closer than that before the storm hits.

It's another part of Hell's program. The witch storm rises behind the trees just as I enter the clearing. The witch storm is a tiny, self-contained hurricane, on a scale, I suppose, to match the shrunken homes. A black whirlwind about three times my size. It's a rainless hurricane, an entity of wind and dust that roils into action without warning and sends the shrunken humans scurrying for cover inside the mound.

With good reason. The storm tears razor blades from the treetops and off the surface of the paths and sends them into a whirling barrage against the sides of the shrunken homes. By the time the storm finishes, what was once a detailed, intricate miniature civilization is reduced to an undifferentiated heap of dust and dirt.

There's nothing I can do to stop it. I tried at first. Planted myself between the shrunken homes and the witch storm and tried to fend it off. What I got for my trouble was a rash of tiny razor cuts on my arms and face. By the time the storm retreated I'd barely protected a square foot of the mound from the assault.

The storm is associated with the witch. Don't ask me why. There are times, though, when I think I see a hint of her figure in its whirling form.

If I forget the mound and run for cover I can usually avoid feeling the brunt of it. Running away, I might take a few quick cuts across the shoulders or the backs of my legs, but that's it.

This time I ran so fast I barely took a cut. I ducked underneath a bush that was already stripped clean of blades; its branches protected me. I listened as the storm ravaged the mound, then faded away. A smell of ozone was in the air.

When I looked up again, I was looking into the face of Colonel Eagery. The Happy Man.

9.

The only thing that's not predictable in Hell, the only thing that doesn't happen according to some familiar junction of time and locale, is the appearance of The Happy Man. He's a free operator. He's his own man. He comes and goes as he pleases, etc.

He's also my ticket home.

When Colonel Eagery is done with me I go back. Back to home reality, back to Maureen and Peter and the radio station where I work. I get to live my life again. No matter where he appears, no matter which tableau he disturbs, Eagery's appearance means I get to go back.

After he's done with me.

Before I left the support group the counselor—the one who'd never even been to Hell—told me to focus on what he called the "reentry episode." He told me that the situation that triggered return was usually the key to Hell, the source of the unresolved tension. The idea, he said, was to identify the corresponding episode in your own past.

I could only laugh.

There's nothing in my life to correspond to Eagery. There couldn't be. Eagery is the heart of my Hell. He's Hell itself. If there had been anything in my life to even approximate The Happy Man, I wouldn't be here to tell you about it. I'd be a wimpering, sniveling wreck in a straightjacket somewhere. Nothing I've encountered in the real world comes close.

Not in *my* reality.

Frankly, if something in the real world corresponds to Colonel Eagery, I don't want to know about it.

10.

The Happy Man lifted me over his shoulder and carried me out of the Garden of Razor Blades, into the dark heart of the woods. When we got to a quiet moonlit grove, he set me down.

"There you go, Tom," he said, dusting himself off. He's the only one in Hell who knows my name. "Boy, what a scene. Listen, let's keep it to ourselves, what do you say? Our little secret, okay? A midnight rondee voo."

The Happy Man is always urgently conspiratorial. It's a big priority with him. I feel I should oblige him, though I'm not always sure what he's referring to. I nodded now.

"Yeah." He slapped me on the back, a little too hard. "You and me, the midnight riders, huh? Lone Ranger and Tonto. What do you mean 'we,' white man? Heh. I told you that one? It's like this . . ."

He told me a long, elaborate joke which I failed to understand. Nonetheless, I sat cross-legged in the clearing, rapt.

At the end he laughed for both of us, a loud, sloppy sound that echoed in the trees. "Oh yeah," he said, wiping a tear from his eye. "Listen, you want some candy? Chocolate or something?" He rustled in a kit bag. "Or breakfast. It's still pretty early. I bet that goddamned witch didn't feed you kids any breakfast, did she?" He took out a bowl and a spoon, then poured in milk and dry cereal from a cardboard box.

The cereal, when I looked, consisted of little puffed and sugar-coated penises, breasts, and vaginas, floating innocently in the milk.

I tried not to gag, or let him see I was having any trouble getting it down. I wanted to please Colonel Eagery, wanted to let him know I was thankful. While I ate he whistled, and unpacked the neckties from his bag.

I watched, curious. "You like these?" he said, holding them up. "Yeah. You'll get to wear them someday. Look real sharp, too. Like your dad. World-beater, that's what you feel like in a necktie." He began knotting them together to make a set of ropes, then looped them around the two nearest trees. "Here," he said, handing me one end. "Pull on this. Can you pull it loose?"

I put down the bowl of cereal and tugged on the neckties.

"Can you? Pull harder."

I shook my head.

"Yeah, they're tough all right. Don't worry about it, though. Your dad couldn't break it either. That's American craftsmanship." He nodded at the cereal. "You done with that? Yeah? C'mere."

I went.

This is my curse: I trust him. Every time. I develop skepticism about the other aspects of Hell; the witch's overdue breakfast, the robot maker's pathetic creations, but Colonel Eagery I trust every time. I am made newly innocent.

"Here," he said. "Hold this." He put one end of the rope in my right hand, and began tying the other end to my left. "Okay." He moved to the right. "What do you mean we, white man? Heh. Cowboys and Indians, Tom. Lift your leg up here—that's a boy. Okay." He grunts over the task of binding me, legs splayed between the two trees. "You an Indian, Tom? Make some noise and let's see."

I started crying.

"Oh, no, don't do that," said The Happy Man, gravely. "Show the Colonel that you're a good sport, for chrissakes. Don't be a *girl.* You'll—ruin all the fun." His earnestness took me by surprise; I felt guilty. I didn't want to ruin anyone's fun. So I managed to stop crying. "That's it, Tommy. Chin up." It wasn't easy, lying there like a low-slung hammock in the dirt, my arms stretched over my head, to put my chin up. I decided it would be enough to smile. "There you go," said Eagery. "God, you're pretty."

The last knot secured, he turned away to dig in his bag, and emerged with a giant, clownish pair of scissors. I squirmed, but couldn't get away. He inserted the blade in my pants cuff and began snipping apart the leg of the corduroys. "Heigh ho! Don't move, Tom. You wouldn't want me to clip something off here, would you?" He quickly scissored up both sides, until my pants were hanging in shreds from my outstretched legs, then snipped the remaining link, so they fell away. A few quick strokes of the scissors and he'd eliminated my jockey shorts too. "Huh." He tossed the scissors aside and ran his hands up my legs. "Boy, that's smooth. Like a baby."

When he caressed me I got hard, despite my fear.

"Okay. Okay. That feel good? Aw, look at that." He was talking to himself now. A steady patter which he kept up over the sound of my whimpering. "Look here Tom, I got one too. *Big*-size. Daddy-size." He straddled me. "Open up for the choo-choo, Tommy. Uh."

I didn't pass out this time until he flipped me over, my arms and legs twisted, my stomach and thighs pressed into the dirt. Blackness didn't come until then.

Then I crossed back over.

Another safe passage back from Hell, thanks again to The Happy Man.

11.

If anyone at the station had questions about my behavior, they kept to themselves.

I came back on mike again. "—bumper to bumper down to the Dumbarton . . ." I trailed away in the middle of the traffic report and punched in a commercial break on cart. "Anyone got something to drink?" I said into the station intercom.

"I think there's some beer in the fridge," said Andrew,

the support technician on shift, poking his head into the studio.

"Keep this going," I said, and left. He could run a string of ads, or punch in one of our prerecorded promos. It wasn't a major deviation.

The station fridge was full of rotting, half-finished lunches and pint cartons of sour milk, plus a six-pack of lousy beer. It wasn't Johnnie Walker, but it would do. I needed to wash the memory of Eagery's flesh out of my mouth.

I leaned against the wall of the lounge and quietly, methodically, downed the beer.

The programming was piped into the lounge and I listened as Andrew handled my absence. He loaded in a stupid comedy promo; the words "Rock me" from about a million old songs, spliced together into a noisy barrage. Then his voice came over the intercom. "Lenny's down here, Tom. Take off if you want."

I didn't need a second hint. In ten minutes I was trapped in the bumper to bumper myself, listening to the station on my car radio.

Maureen's car wasn't in the driveway when I pulled up. She was still at work. No reason to hurry home if she thought I was still away, I suppose. But the lights were on. Peter was home. And, as it turned out, so was Uncle Frank. I'd forgotten about the visit, but while I was away he'd set up in the guest room.

He and Peter were sitting together in front of the computer, playing Hell. They looked up when I came in, and

Peter recognized the change in the tone of my voice right away. Smart kid.

"Hey, Dad." He made a show of introducing us, so Frank would understand that there was a change. "Dad, Uncle Frank's here."

Frank and I shook hands.

I hadn't seen my father's brother for seven or eight years, and in that time he'd aged decades. He was suddenly a gray old man. It made me wonder how my father would look if he were still around.

"Tommy," Frank said. "It's been a long time." His voice was as faded and weak as everything else. I could hear him trying to work out the difference between me now and the zombie version he'd been living with for the past few days.

I didn't let him wonder for too long. I gave his hand a good squeeze, and then I put my arms around him. I needed the human contact anyway, after Hell.

"I need a drink," I said. "Frank?" I cocked my head toward the living room. Uncle Frank nodded.

The kid got the drift on his own. "I'll see you later, Dad." He turned back to his computer, made a show of being involved.

I led Frank to the couch and poured us both a drink.

Though I hadn't seen him since before I died, Uncle Frank knew all about my situation. We wrote letters, and every once in a while spoke on the phone. Frank had never married, and after my father died he and I were one another's only excuse for "family." He wasn't well off, but he'd wired Maureen some cash when I died. In his letters he'd been generous, too, sympathetic and un-superstitious. In my letters I'd unloaded a certain mea-sure of my guilt and shame at what my resurrection had done to the marriage, and he was always understanding. But I could see now that he had to make an effort, in person, not to appear uncomfortable. He'd been living with my soulless self for a few days, and his eyes told me that he needed to figure out who he was talking to now.

For my part, I was making an adjustment to the changes in Frank. In my memory he was permanently in his forties, a more garrulous and eccentric version of my father. Frank had been the charismatic oddball in the family, never without a quip, never quite out of the dog-house, but always expansive and charming. I'd often thought that my falsely genial on-radio persona was based on a pale imitation of Frank. Only now he just seemed tired and old.

"You've got a nice setup here, Tom," he said quietly.

"That's Maureen's work," I said. "She busts her ass keeping it all together."

Frank nodded. "I've seen."

"How long you staying with us?"

Now Frank snickered in a way that recalled, if only faintly, the man I remembered. "How long you have me?"

"You don't need to be back?" How Frank made his living had always been unclear. He'd been a realtor at some point, then graduated to the nebulous status of "consultant." Professional bullshitter was always my hunch.

But now he said, "I'm not going back. I think I want to set up out here for a while."

"Well, for my part you're welcome to stick around until you find a place," I said. He'd sounded uncomfortable, and I decided not to pry. "It's really up to Maureen, you understand. The burden's on her—"

"Oh, I've been helping out," he said quickly. "I've become quite a chef, actually . . ."

The way he trailed away told me I'd probably already eaten several of his meals. "I'm sure," I said. There was a pause. "Listen, Frank, let's break the ice. I don't remember shit about what happens while I'm away. Treat me like a newborn babe when I come back. One who nurses on a whiskey tumbler."

I watched him relax. He lowered his eyes and said, "I'm sorry, Tom. I haven't been around family, I mean *real* family, for so long. It's got me thinking about the past. You know . . ." He looked up sharply. "You're a grown man. Have been for a long time. But your dad and your mom and you as a little kid, me coming to visit— that's how I remember you. Always will, I think."

"I understand." I worked on my whiskey.

"Anyway—" He waved his hand dismissively. "It's good to see you finally. Good to see the three of you together, making it go."

"I'm glad it looks good." I could only be honest. "It isn't always easy."

"Oh, I didn't mean, I mean, yes. Of course. And anything, any little thing I can do to help—" He watched my eyes for reaction, looking terribly uncomfortable. "And Tom?"

I nodded.

"I already mentioned this to Maureen and Peter. Uh, you don't seem to pick up the phone when you're away, but now that you're back—"

"Yes?"

"If you do pick up the phone, if anyone calls, *I'm not here,* okay?"

"Sure, Frank."

"I just need to create a little distance right now," he said obscurely.

I wasn't sure whether to press him on the point. My chance was taken away, anyway, by Maureen's arrival. She walked in and peered at us over the top of a couple of bags of groceries, then took them on into the kitchen without saying a word. She knew I was back. The drink in my hand told her all she needed to know.

Frank got up and hurried into the kitchen behind her. I heard him insist on putting away the groceries by himself.

Then Maureen came out. I put my drink on the coffee table and stood up and we stood right next to each other, close without quite touching for a long time. Quiet, knowing that when words came, things might get too complicated again. In the background I could hear Frank putting the groceries into the fridge and the gentle, hurried tapping of Peter's fingers on his keyboard.

Maureen and I sat on the couch and kissed.

"Hey," came Frank's voice eventually. "Pete and I were talking about catching a movie or something. We could get a slice of pizza too, take the car and be back in a few hours—"

"Peter?" I said.

He appeared in the doorway, right on cue. "Yeah, Dad, there's a new Clive Barker movie—"

"Homework?"

"Didn't get any."

I gave Frank the car keys and twenty bucks for pizza or whatever. I was being tiptoed around, sure, but I didn't let myself feel patronized. The few breaks I get I earn, twice over.

They left, and Maureen and I went back to kissing on the couch. We still hadn't exchanged a word. After a while we went into the bedroom like that, affectionate, silent. We didn't get around to words until an hour or so later.

Turned out it was just as well.

12.

Maureen had closed her eyes and rolled over on her side, curled against me. But the muscles of her mouth were tight; she wasn't asleep. I put my hand in her hair and said her name. She said mine.

"How's it been?" I said.

She waited a while before answering. "I don't know, Tom. Okay, I guess."

"I wasn't gone too long this time," I said, though it didn't need saying.

She sighed. "That last one just took something out of me."

"What are you saying?"

She spoke quietly, tonelessly, into the crook of my arm. "I don't know how long you'll be around. I can't trust it anymore. I feel like if I let myself relax I'll get ripped off again."

There wasn't any answer to that, so I shut up and let the subject drop. "Peter all right?"

"Yes. Always. He's going to be on some debating thing now. I think he likes having Frank around."

"Do you?"

She didn't answer the question. "He's so different from when I first met him, Tom. When we got married. I thought he was such a buffoon. Such a loud, intrusive character." She laughed. "I was afraid we'd have a son like him. Now he's so *polite*."

"He's a guest in your house," I pointed out.

"It's not just that," she said. "He's gotten old, I guess."

"He said he's been cooking. Is he in your way? He'll go if I tell him to."

"He wants to move out here. Did he tell you that?"

"Yes," I said. And thought, *As well as something odd about the telephone.* I didn't say it. "But he's got money, I think. We'll find him a place—" I stopped. She still hadn't said whether she wanted him around, and the gap was beginning to irritate me. I was sensitive enough to her by now that I noticed what wasn't being said.

And she was smart enough to notice my irritation.

"He's fine, really," she said quickly. "He's actually quite a help, cooking . . ."

"Yes?"

"I've just gotten used to being alone, Tom. With you gone, and Peter out with his friends. I've had a lot of freedom."

The skin on my back began to crawl. I took my hand out of her hair.

"Say it," I said.

She sighed. "I'm trying to. I've been lonely, Tom. And I don't mean lonely for some odd old relative of yours to sleep in the guest room, either."

"Is it someone I know?"

"No."

I thought I could manage a couple more questions before I blew my cool. "Does Peter know?"

"No."

"Are you sure?"

"Jesus, Tom. Yes, I'm sure."

"What about Frank?"

"What about him? I didn't tell him. I can't imagine how he'd guess."

"There aren't any letters, then. Or weird phone calls. You aren't being sloppy—"

"No, Tom."

That was all I could take. In pretty much one motion I got up and put on my pants. Almost burst a blood vessel buttoning my shirt.

Then I surprised myself: I didn't hit her.

Instead I put on my shoes and went to the kitchen for a bottle, and sat down on the couch in the moonlight and drank.

It wasn't any good. I couldn't be in the house. I put on a jacket and took the bottle for a walk around the neighborhood.

13.

To the west, in my Hell, there's a place I call the Ghost Town. It's like a Western movie set, with cheap facades passing for buildings, and if anyone lives there, they're hiding. The moon lights the main street from behind a patch of trees, throwing cigarette butts and crumpled foil wrappers discarded there into high relief. Sometimes I can make out hoofprints in the dust.

In the middle of the street is a naked, crying baby.

Gusts of wind rise as I walk through the Ghost Town, and they grow stronger as I approach the baby, whipping the dust and refuse of the street into its face. The baby's crying chokes into a cough, sputters, then resumes, louder than before. The baby is cold. I can tell; I'm cold myself, there in the Ghost Town. By the time I reach down to pick up the baby, the wind tearing through my little chest, I'm seeking its warmth as much as offering my own.

If I pick up the baby it turns into The Happy Man. Instantly. Every time.

I've already said what happens when The Happy Man appears.

Needless to say, then, I avoid the Ghost Town. I steer a wide berth around it. I often avoid the west altogether. As much as I want to go back to my life, I can't bring myself to pick up the baby, knowing that I'm bringing on Colonel Eagery. I'm not capable of it. And I'm not comfortable walking through that town, feeling the rising wind and listening to the baby's cries, and not doing anything. Hell seems so contingent on my actions; maybe if I don't go in that direction there isn't a baby in the first place. I'd like to think so.

Anyway, it had been months since I'd walked through the Ghost Town.

But I walked through it that night, in my dreams. I don't know why.

14.

I woke up still dressed and clutching the bottle, on the living room couch. What woke me was the noise in the kitchen. Maureen making breakfast for Peter.

Head low, I slunk past the kitchen doorway and into the bedroom.

By the time I woke again Peter was off to school, and Maureen was out too, at work. I put myself through the shower, then called the station and said I wasn't coming in. They took it all right.

When I went back out I found Uncle Frank making coffee, enough for two. I accepted a cup and grunted my thanks.

"Can you handle some eggs?" he asked. "There's an omelet I've been meaning to try. You can be my guinea pig . . ."

I cleared my throat. "Uh, sure," I said.

He went into action while I let the coffee work on my mood. I was impressed, actually. Frank seemed to have diverted some of his eccentric passion into cookery. He knew how to use all the wedding-present stuff that Maureen and I had let gather dust. The smells charmed me halfway out of my funk.

"Here we go." He juggled it out of the pan and onto a plate, sprinkled some green stuff on top and put it in front of me. I waited for him to cut it in half, and when he didn't I said, "What about you?"

"Oh," he said. "I ate before. Please."

I put the whole thing away without any trouble. Frank sipped his coffee and watched while I ate.

"I used to cook for you when you were a little boy," he said. " 'Course then it was eggs in bacon grease, smeared with catsup—"

My throat suddenly tightened in a choking spasm. I spurted coffee and bits of egg across the table, almost into Frank's lap. He got up and slapped at my back, but by then it was over.

"Jeez," I said. "Some kind of hangover thing. I'm sorry . . ."

"Relax, Tom." He got me a glass of water. "Probably the memory of those old breakfasts . . ." He laughed.

"Yeah." *Or the thought of Maureen and her new pal in the sack.* I didn't say it, though. I suddenly felt intense shame. Frank represented my family, he stood in for my dad. I didn't want him to know the reason for my bender.

"Listen, Tom," he said. "What say we go down to the water today? That's not a long drive, is it?"

"Sounds great," I admitted. "I need to get out of the house."

An hour later we parked out by the Marina and walked down to the strip of beach. I expected Uncle Frank to tire quickly; instead I had to hurry to keep up. I felt like I was seeing him slowly come back to life, first in the kitchen, concocting the omelet, and now out here on the beach. He seemed to sense the deadness and emptiness in me and tried valiantly to carry on both ends of a chatty conversation. I heard glimpses of the old raconteur in his voice, which only made me wonder more what had sent it into hiding in the first place.

"Frank," I said, when he came to the end of a story, "what happened? What's got you on the run?"

He took a deep breath and looked out over the water. "I was hoping that wouldn't come up, Tom. I don't want to get you or Maureen into it."

"I'll decide what I want to get into," I said. "Besides, it doesn't necessarily protect us to keep us in the dark."

He turned and looked me in the eye. "That's a point. It's—it's the Mob, Tom. Only it's not so simple anymore, to just say Mob. There's a blurry territory where it crosses over into some federal agency . . . Anyway, it's enough to say that I got crossed up with some real bad guys. I screwed 'em on some property." He was looking out to sea again, and I couldn't read his expression. "I'm not sure how much they really care, or how long before they get distracted by something else. Could be they just wanted to throw a scare at me. I just know it felt like time to get out of town for a while."

"God, Frank. I'm sorry. That sounds tough."

"Ah, it's all my own goddamn fault. Anyway, I won't stay much longer at your place. I would have gone already if you weren't—you know, away. And Pete seemed—I don't know. I felt like I could be of some use. It took my mind off my own problems."

"Stay as long as you like, Frank."

He smiled grimly. "I'm not necessarily in the right, you know . . ."

"Don't bother," I said. "When you go through some of the shit I've gone through, it gives you a different perspective. Right isn't always a relevant concept. You're family."

He turned and looked at me, then. Hard. Suddenly he wasn't just my clichéd notion of "Uncle Frank" anymore; he was a complex, intelligent, and not always easy to comprehend man whom I'd known since before I could remember. Maybe it was just my emotional state, but for a moment I was terrified.

"Thanks, Tom."

"Uh, don't mention it."

We looked out over the water without saying anything.

"I'm hip to Maureen," said Frank after a while.

I probably tightened my fists in my pockets, but that was it.

"There isn't really anything to say," he went on. "Just that you've got my sympathy."

"Don't hold it against her," I said. "I make it pretty tough. My whole setup makes it pretty tough."

"Yeah."

"Have you met him?" I asked.

"Nope. Just a phone call I wasn't supposed to hear. Not her fault. My ears tend to prick up at the sound of the phone right now."

"Peter?"

"Jeez. I don't think so, Tom. Not that I know of. But he's a smart kid."

"No kidding."

We came to a high place over the water, with a concrete platform and a rusted steel railing. I leaned on it and smelled the mist. Birds wheeled overhead. I thought about the night before, and wondered what I was going to say to Maureen the next time I saw her.

After a while I guess I choked up a little. "God damn," I said. "I didn't even get to see my kid last night."

"That's not your fault," said Frank quietly.

"I always hang out with the kid, Frank. I'm never so wrapped up in my goddamned problems that I don't have time for him. I only just got back."

Frank got a cheerleader tone in his voice again. "Let's go pick him up at school," he said. "Smart guy like him can miss half a day."

"I don't know."

"C'mon. It's easy. You just show up and they turn him over. Big treat, makes him a celebrity with all his pals."

"You do this a lot?"

Frank got serious. "Uh, no," he said. He almost sounded offended, for no reason I could discern. "They'd never turn the child over to anyone but his mother or father." He turned away, the mood between us suddenly and inexplicably sour.

"Something the matter?" I said.

He closed his eyes for a minute. "Sorry, Tom. I guess I just all of a sudden got an image of my friends from back east showing up at the schoolyard. I'm just being paranoid . . ."

We exchanged a long look.

"Let's go," I said.

15.

It was a relief to learn what a pain in the ass it was to get a kid out of school halfway through the day. We had to fill out a visitor's form just to go to the office, and then we had to fill out another form to get permission to yank Peter from class, and then a secretary walked us to the classroom anyway.

It turned out it was a computer class. A bunch of the

kids there had played Peter's software Hell, which made me a visiting celebrity. I had to shake a lot of little hands to get back out. Frank was right: the visit would make Peter the most popular kid in school tomorrow.

We went out for hamburgers downtown, then we went back home. If Peter was disturbed by my drunken sprawl on the couch that morning, he did a good job of covering it up. He and Frank were full of computer talk, and I could see how well they were getting along.

Eventually we got around to the traditional post-Hell update, Peter and I huddled at the computer, punching in whatever new information I'd picked up on my trip. This time Frank sat in.

"Robot maker built a terrier," I said. "A little livelier than the usual crap . . ." Peter typed it into the proper file. "But Eagery's thing was a robot wolfman, as tall as me—me *now*, not in Hell. He could talk. He sounded like Eagery, actually." I turned to Frank. "The Happy Man's personality has a way of pervading his robots . . ."

Peter's cross-reference check flagged the wolfman entry, and he punched up the reference. "In the south, Dad, remember? You met a wolfman, a real one, in the woods. You played Monopoly with him, then he turned into Colonel Eagery."

"Yeah, yeah. Never saw him again."

"Boy," said Frank, speaking for the first time since we'd punched up Hell. "You guys are thorough. What do you think the wolfman means?"

I froze up inside.

But before I could speak, Peter turned, twisted his

mouth, and shook his head. "Hell doesn't *mean* anything," he said. "That's not the right approach." He'd heard the spiel a dozen times from me, and I guessed he'd sensed my tenderness on the issue; he was sticking up for his dad.

Then he surprised me by taking it further. "Hell is like an alternate world, like in *X-Men.* It's a real place, like here, only different. If you were going down the street and you met a wolfman, you wouldn't ask what it means. You'd run, or whatever."

Frank, who hadn't noticed my discomfort, winked at me and said, "Okay, Pete. I stand corrected."

Peter and I went back to our entry, more or less ignoring Frank. A few minutes later Maureen's car pulled up in the driveway. I tried not to let my sudden anxiety show, for the kid's sake.

"Tom."

She stood in Peter's doorway, still in her coat. When I looked up she didn't say anything more, just inclined her head in the direction of the bedroom. I gave Frank the seat beside Peter at the computer, and followed her.

"Look at you," she said when we were out of earshot.

"What?"

"When you're not drunk you're retreating into the computer. It's just as bad, you know. Computer Hell. You've found a way to be there all the time, one way or another. You don't live here anymore."

"Maureen—"

"What's worse is the way you're taking him *with* you.

Making him live in your Hell too. Making him think it's something great. When you're not here, he and his friends spend all day in front of that thing, living your Hell for you. Does it make you feel less lonely? Is that it?"

"I live here." I knew I had to keep my voice quiet and steady and fierce or she'd talk right over me, and soon we'd be shouting. I didn't want it to escalate. "Last thing I knew I lived here with *you*. Maybe that's not the way it is anymore. But I live here. Seems to me it's you who's got one foot out the door."

There was a moment of silence and then it hit me. Call me stupid, but it was the first time I felt the impact. Last night, making love, had been goodbye. The gulf between us now was enormous. Things weren't going to suddenly get better.

It would take a huge amount of very hard, very painful work to fix it, if it could be fixed at all.

"Do you ever think of the effect it has on *him?*" She was sticking to safe territory. I didn't blame her. She had a lot of it. "You and your goddamned *inner landscape—*"

She broke off, sobbing. It was as though she'd been saving those words, and their release had opened the floodgates. It also occurred to me that she was opting for tears so I wouldn't attack her, and I felt a little cheated.

Anyway, I took her in my arms. I'm not completely stupid.

"I don't want him to live like that," she said. Her fists

balled against my chest for a moment, then her body went slack, and I had to hold her up while she cried. After a minute we sat on the edge of the bed.

"I don't know, Tom. I don't know what's happening."

"Well, neither do I." I felt suddenly exhausted and hollow. "It seems like the ball's in your court—"

I could feel her tensing up against my shoulder. So I dropped it.

I smelled onions frying in butter. I listened: Frank was cooking again, and explaining the recipe to Peter.

"It's not an inner landscape," I said quietly. "It's a place where I live half my life. I get to share that with my son—"

She pulled away from me and stood up, straightened her clothes. Then she went into the living room, without looking back.

16.

I lay back on the bed, only meaning to buy some time. But I must have been depleted, morally and otherwise, and I fell asleep, and slept through dinner.

When I woke again the house was dark. Peter was in his room; I could see the glow of the night light in the hallway. Maureen was slipping into bed beside me.

When I reached for her she pushed me away.

I didn't make it into a big deal. I didn't feel particularly angry, not at the time. In a few minutes we were both asleep again.

17.

When I woke again, it was to the sun streaming in across the bed, heating me to a sweat under the covers. It was Saturday; no work for me or Maureen, no school for Peter. But Maureen was gone. I didn't feel too good, and I lay there for a while just looking at the insides of my eyelids. There wasn't any noise in the apartment, and I suspected they'd all gone somewhere to get out from under the shadow of you-know-who.

I didn't let it bug me: I took a nice slow shower and went into the kitchen and made some coffee and toast.

But I was wrong. Peter was home. He wandered into the kitchen while I was cleaning up, and said, "Hey, Dad."

This time I could see he knew something was wrong. I didn't have what it took to keep it from him, and I guess he didn't have what it took to keep it from me, either.

"Hey, Pete," I said. "Where's your mom?"

"They went out shopping," he said. "Also to look at some place for Uncle Frank to live."

I nodded. "What you doing?"

"I don't know. Just some game stuff I got from Jeremy."

"It looks like a pretty nice day out there—"

"I know, I know. I heard it already, from Mom." He looked down at his feet.

There was a minute or two of silence while I finished clearing the table.

"I guess I should offer to 'throw the old pigskin

around' or something," I said. "But the truth is I don't feel up to it right now."

The truth was my guts were churning. I couldn't focus on the kid. Seeing him left alone just made me think of Maureen and where she probably was right now. Frank was almost certainly playing the beard for her, and "shopping" by himself. If they came home with packages she'd have to unpack them to know what was in them.

"That's okay," he said seriously. "I don't think we have an old pigskin anyway."

I managed a smile.

"I'll be in my room, okay, Dad?"

"Okay, Peter."

Pretty soon I heard him tapping at his computer again. I sat and nursed the cold coffee and ran my thoughts through some pretty repetitive and unproductive loops. And then it hit me.

Just a twinge at first. But unmistakable.

I was on my way back to Hell.

I realized I'd felt inklings earlier that morning, in the shower, even in bed, and hadn't let myself notice. It was already pretty far along. I was probably an hour or so away from crossing over.

By this time I'd perfected a kind of emotional shorthand. I went through all the traditional stages in the space of a few seconds: denial, bargaining, fear, etc. But underlying them all, this time, was a dull, black rage.

I'd almost never had so short a time back. That hurt. The fact that I was crossing over while Maureen was holed up in her midday love nest hurt more. Unless she came back in the next hour, I wouldn't get in another word. I couldn't make up, couldn't plead, and I couldn't threaten, either, or issue an ultimatum. All the words I'd been rehearsing in my head flew right out the window. She would come home to find me a zombie again.

I felt my claim on her, and my claim on my own life —on Peter, the apartment, everything—slipping away. I had a sudden, desperate need to at least see Peter. I would cram two weeks' worth of unfinished business into the next hour. I got up and went into his room, my head whirling.

He turned from the computer when I appeared in his doorway. "Hey, Dad," he said. "Look at this. I had an idea about Hell."

I went and sat down beside him. I was afraid to open my mouth, afraid of what would or wouldn't come out. I wanted to put on a big show of fatherly affection but I couldn't think of a damned thing to say.

Peter pretended not to notice. "Look." He'd punched up our entry for the starting point: the breakfast table, the horse, and the witch's house. "You get up from the table," he said. "You go off through the hedge in some direction, east, west, north, south. But there's a direction you never go in. It's so obvious. I can't believe we never thought of it."

It wasn't obvious to me, and I felt irritation. "Where? What direction?"

"*The witch's house.* You want breakfast, right? Why not just go in and get some? Why not find out what she's doing in there?"

The idea terrified me instantly. Me, a little boy, barging into the house of that beautiful, unapproachable woman. But Peter didn't know about the emotional content of Hell. I'd kept that from him. "It's an idea," I conceded. "Uh, yeah. It's an idea."

"It could be the key to the whole thing, Dad. Who knows. You've got to find out."

"The purloined letter," I said. "Something so obvious, just sitting right out there in plain sight, but nobody notices . . ." I was drifting off into talking to myself again. I couldn't stay focused on Peter. I was thinking about Maureen and her friend, and my thoughts were very, very murky.

"Will you try?" said Peter. "Will you check it out?"

"I might," I snapped, suddenly angry. It was as though he were taunting me. But of course he didn't know. I hadn't said anything.

He pretended he hadn't heard the tension in my voice, and went on, bright-eyed. "It could be nothing, really. Just another stupid dead end. Or the door is locked or something . . ."

"No, no," I said, wanting to reassure him now. "It's a good idea, Pete. An inspiration . . ."

We drifted off into a mutually embarrassed silence.

"Is Uncle Frank a lot like my grandfather?" asked Peter suddenly.

"Well, no. Not really. Why?"

"I dunno. He just seems so different from you. It's hard for me to see how you might be related. I can't imagine what your dad was like."

"Different how?"

"Oh, you know, Dad. You're so serious. Uncle Frank seems like he's almost younger than you."

"Younger?"

"He's just sillier, that's all. He says weird things. I can't really explain, but it's like he's some kind of cartoon character, or somebody you'd tell me about in a story. He reminds me of somebody from Hell, like the robot maker, or—"

That's where Peter stopped, because I hit him.

Hit him hard. Knocked him out of his chair and onto the floor.

My anger had been spiraling while he spoke. I thought about Frank out covering Maureen's ass, the two of them leaving the kid alone so she could squeeze in a quick lay, and that got me thinking about all the manipulative, unpleasant things Frank had done over the years. And now the kid was falling for it, falling for the image of the wacky, irresponsible, cartoon-character uncle who picked you up at school in the middle of the day, who seemed so much more charismatic than boring old Dad.

I remembered falling for it myself, and I wondered if my father ever felt anything like the jealousy I felt now.

Peter sat on the floor, whimpering. I held my hand up to my face and looked at it, astonished. Then I walked out of the room. I couldn't face him. I couldn't think of what to say.

Besides, I was going to Hell.

I was glad. It was where I belonged.

18.

I sat at the table a long time, watching the horse quiver and twitch as the flies crawled over his lips, watching the other children giggle and whisper and play with their silverware, listening to the sound of insects in the woods beyond the hedge, smelling the smoke that trailed out of the witch's chimney, quietly seething. I don't think I ever hated my Hell as badly as I did now. Now that my other life, my real life, had become a Hell too.

Eventually I got out of my seat. But I couldn't bring myself to run for the hedge to the north, or in any direction, for that matter. I stood on the grass beside my chair, paralyzed by Peter's suggestion. After a minute or so I took a first, tentative step across the grass, toward the witch's hut. It seemed like a mile to the cobblestone steps at the door. I tried the handle; it turned easily. The room was dark. I stepped inside.

The Happy Man was turned away from me, facing the table, his pants down around his ankles, his pale, hairy buttocks squeezed together. Splayed out on the table, her bare legs in the air, was the witch. The Happy Man had one hand over her mouth, the other on her breasts.

"Oh, shit," he said when he heard me come in. He stopped thrusting and hurriedly pulled up his pants. "What are you doing in here?" He turned away, left the witch scrambling to cover herself on the table. Despite my astonishment at finding Eagery in the hut, I managed to ogle her for a moment. She was beautiful.

"Breakfast," I got out. "I wanted breakfast."

"Oh, yeah?" The Happy Man didn't sound playful. He was advancing on me fast. I tried to turn and leave, but he grabbed me and pinned me against the wall. "Breakfast is served," he said. He lifted me by my belt and took me to the stove. I could feel its heat as I dangled there. He opened the door with his free hand. Inside there was a pie baking; it smelled wonderful. The breakfast we'd always hoped for. Eagery dropped me onto the open door.

My hands and knees immediately burned. I heard myself pleading, but The Happy Man didn't pay any attention; he began pushing the door closed, wedging me into the hot oven with the pie, battering at my dangling arms and legs until I pulled them in, then slamming the door closed and leaning on it with his full weight.

I fell into the pie, and burning sugar stuck to my back. I think I screamed. Eagery kicked at the oven, jolting it off the floor, until I was silent. Eventually I died.

Died back into my own life, of course. Peter was right. He'd discovered a shortcut.

Lucky me.

19.

I came back in the apartment this time, sitting alone in the living room, watching television. That's how I spend a lot of my zombie hours, according to Maureen. It was midday, and I suspected I hadn't been away long at all. I checked my watch. Sure enough, less than twenty-four hours had passed. It was the second day of the weekend; my shortest stay in Hell ever, by several days.

I turned off the television and went into the kitchen to make myself some coffee. The house was empty. The day was pretty bright, and I suspected they'd gone out for a picnic or something up at the park. I had a few hours alone with my thoughts.

Still, it wasn't until I heard their car in the driveway that I had my big idea.

I had the tube on again. That was part of it. It had something to do with not wanting to face them, too. Not knowing what to say to Maureen, or Peter. When I heard the car pull up I felt my tongue go numb in my mouth.

By the time Maureen got her key in the door it was a fully hatched plan. I stared at the television as they came in, keeping my breath steady, trying not to meet their eyes. There was a moment of silence as Maureen checked me out and determined that I was still away, in Hell.

Then the conversation picked up again, like I wasn't even there.

"—what's he watching?"

"That horrible cop thing. Peter, for God's sake, turn it down. I don't want to listen to that. Or change the channel—" To Frank: "He won't notice. If he doesn't like it, he'll just get up and go away. But he never does. I've seen him sit through hours and hours of Peter's horror things . . ."

I would have enjoyed proving her wrong, but I didn't want to risk anything that would blow my cover. So I sat there while Peter flipped the dial, settling eventually on the news.

The lead story was a minor quake in L.A., and like all good Californians they took the bait, crowded around me on the couch for a look at the damage: a couple of tilted cars on a patch of split pavement, a grandmother face-down on her lawn, pet dog sniffing at her displaced wig. Maureen and Frank sat to my left, and Peter pushed up close to me at my right. It was our first physical contact in a long time—unless you counted the punch.

But Peter didn't sit still for very long. He squirmed in his seat until Maureen noticed.

"Mom?" he said. When he leaned forward I saw the big purple bruise I'd left on the side of his face.

"What?"

He held his nose and made a face. "I think Dad needs a shower."

20.

The quality of their disregard was terrifying. I wasn't, as I'd flattered myself by imagining, a monster in their midst, a constant reminder of a better life that had eluded them. They weren't somber or mournful at all. They *coped*. I was a combination of a big, stupid pet and an awkward, unplugged appliance too big for the closet. I was in the way. It was too soon for them to begin hoping—or dreading—that I'd come back, and in the meantime I was a hungry, smelly nuisance.

When Maureen leaned in close and suggested I go clean myself up, I knew to agree politely and follow the suggestion. I welcomed the chance to get away from them and reconnoiter, anyway.

When I emerged from my shower they were already at the table eating. I suppose I shouldn't have expected an invitation. They'd set a place for me, and I went and sat in it, and ate, quietly, and listened while they talked.

The subject of Peter's "injury" came up only once, and then just barely. I gathered that Frank and Maureen had decided to suppress any discussion, to play it down, and hope that Peter was still young enough that he would just plain forget. Find some childlike inner resource for blurring experience into fantasy.

Maybe they would confront me later, when I came back, with Peter out at a friend's house. But the subject was obviously taboo right now.

The discussion mostly centered on Frank's plans. The apartment he was looking at, and some second thoughts he seemed to be having about settling in this area. I sensed an undercurrent, between him and Maureen, of what wasn't being discussed: Frank's trouble. The phone calls he was avoiding. Yet more stuff for Peter not to hear. I wondered, though, knowing Peter's smarts, how much he was picking up anyway.

I was dying for a drink. I tried not to let it show on my face.

After the meal Frank pleaded exhaustion and went

into the guest room, and Maureen read a book on the bed. I set up in front of the television and tried not to think about what I was doing or why I was doing it. I walked through the apartment a couple of times on my way to the bathroom, and when I passed Peter's door he looked up from his computer, and I had to struggle not to meet his eye. He would have admired my ruse, and I would have liked to let him in on it, but that wasn't possible. So I stalked past his room like a zombie, and he turned back to his homework. I spent most of the evening on the couch, slogging through prime time. After Maureen tucked Peter into bed I followed her into the bedroom.

She made the phone call about five minutes after she turned off the lights.

"Philip?" she whispered.

A pause.

"Can you talk? I couldn't sleep." Pause. "No, he's right here in bed with me. Of course he can't hear. I mean it doesn't matter, even if he can. No. No. It's not that." She sighed. "I just miss you."

I guess he talked a bit.

"You do?" she said, her voice half-melted. I hadn't heard her that way in a while. "Philip. Yes, I know. But it's not that easy. You know. Yes. I wish I could."

They went on like that. Her voice was quiet enough that Peter and Frank wouldn't hear, but in the darkened bedroom it was like a stage play. I could almost make out her boyfriend's tinny replies over the phone.

Then she giggled and said, "I'm touching myself too."

Thank God it was dark. My face must have been crimson. I felt the room whirling like a centrifuge, the bed at the center. I weighed a thousand or a million pounds and I was crushed into my place there on the bed beside Maureen by the pressure of gravity. I couldn't move. I felt my blood pounding in my wrists and temples.

Why was I there? What was I trying to prove?

I knew, dimly, that I'd had some reason for the deception, that some part of me had insisted that there was something I could learn, something vital.

It couldn't have been this, though. I didn't need this.

So what was I after? What—

I sat bolt upright in the bed, dislodging the covers.

"Huh?" said Maureen. "Nothing, nothing. Listen, I have to go, I'll call you back." She hung up and turned on the light. I turned and looked at her in shock. She opened her mouth to scream, and somehow I got my hand over her mouth first. I wrestled her down against the bed, pushed her face into the pillow, twisted her arm behind her back, put my weight on her.

I could hear her yelling my name into the pillow, wetly. Her ears were bright red.

I tightened my grip on her arm. "Shhh," I said, close to her ear. "No noise. No noise." I listened at the hall, alert now, panicked. I had to convince her. "No noise."

"You're dead," she hissed when I let her up for air. "All I have to do is report you. You're dead." Her eyes were slits.

"Shhh." I let her go, forgot her. Focused on the hall.

There wasn't any light. Peter's night light was out, or his door was closed.

Impossible. Peter wouldn't permit it.

Someone was in the house. Frank's pals.

I slid into my pants, silently. I was operating with my Hell-reflexes now, and they were good. There wasn't going to be any hostage. I would make sure of that. I would have complete surprise.

I turned back to Maureen. "Call your pal," I whispered. "Keep it quiet. Have him bring in the cops, but quiet, and slow." She looked at me, stunned out of her outrage. "I'm serious. Call him. And stay in here. Whatever happens."

I didn't leave her time for questions. In my pants and bare feet I crept out into the hall and made my way to Peter's door.

Inside I heard him whimpering softly, as if through a gag.

I burst in.

Peter was spread-eagled on his bed, bound with neckties. His pajamas were in shreds around his ankles. Frank, who wasn't wearing anything at all, was kneeling on the side of the bed, as if praying over Peter's helpless body. One hand was resting lightly on Peter's stomach. In the other hand he held his own penis. His pubic hair was white. He looked up at me and his eyes widened for a moment, then fell. And then he grinned. His hands stayed where they were.

I picked up Peter's keyboard and smashed it against

Frank's white skull. He straightened up and stopped grinning, and reached back to feel his head.

"Tommy," he said, his voice soft, almost beguiling.

I drew the keyboard back like a baseball bat and hit him again. This time I drew blood. I didn't stop hitting him until he fell back against the floor, his mouth open, his eyes full of tears, his erection wilting.

Peter watched the whole thing from the bed, his mouth gagged, his eyes wide. When I dropped the keyboard and looked up, he met my eyes, for a minute. Then I looked away. I found his floppy disks for Hell, the main disk and the backup, and I tore them in half and tossed them onto the floor, beside Frank.

Peter didn't get untied until the police showed up. Maureen was hiding in her room and I, try as I might, just couldn't bring myself to *touch* him.

21.

I live alone now. The settlement went like this: I see Peter every other weekend—if I happen to be back from Hell, that is—and only in the company of his mother. And I don't go anywhere near the house.

Yes, Uncle Frank was Colonel Eagery, aka The Happy Man. He'd molested me as a boy, right in our house, while my father was away, and with my mother in the kitchen making breakfast. I remember it all now.

And yes, I killed him.

Needless to say, there wasn't any Mob on his trail. The

call he'd been dreading was the Baltimore police. He was on the run from a molestation offense.

Like I said, I live alone. It's a pretty nice place, and a lot closer to the station. There's a pretty nice bar around the corner. Different crowd every night.

Yes, I still go to Hell, but it's different now. There isn't any horse, or witch, or Happy Man. There isn't even a forest.

When I go to Hell now it's like this:

I'm back in the house with Maureen and Peter. I live with them again. But I'm unable to speak, or reach out to them: I'm a zombie. I start by sitting in front of the television, flipping channels, and then eventually I wander around the apartment, brushing past Maureen, but never able to speak to her, never able to take her hand or hold her or lead her into the bedroom. After a while I go and stand in the doorway of Peter's room. He turns and looks up at me, but I look away, afraid to meet his eye. I pretend to look the other way, and he goes back to his computer.

And that's it. I spend the rest of the time standing in his doorway, looking over his shoulder at the computer screen.

Watching him play my Hell.

VANILLA DUNK

Elwood Fossett and I were in a hotel room in Portland, after dropping a meaningless game to the Sony Trail Blazers—we'd already made the playoffs—when the lottery came on the television, the one where they gave away the Michael Jordan subroutines.

The lottery, ironically, was happening back in our home arena, the Garden, while we were on the road. It was an absurd spectacle, the place full of partisan fans rooting for their team's rookie to draw the Jordan skills, the rookies all sitting sheepishly with their families and agents, waiting. The press scurried around like wingless mosquitoes.

"Yo, Lassner, check it out," said Elwood, tapping the screen with his long black club of a finger. "We gonna get you and McFront some company."

He meant the white kid in the Gulf and Western Knicks jersey, stranded with his parents in that sea of black faces. Michael Front—"McFront" to the black players—and me were the two white players on the Knicks.

"Not too likely," I said. "He won't make the team unless he draws the Jordan."

Elwood sat back down on the end of the bed. "Nobody else we'd take?"

"Nope." There were, of course, six other sets of skills available that night—Tim Hardaway, if I remember correctly, and Karl Malone—but none with the potential impact of Jordan's. In a league where everyone played with the skills of one star or another, it took a Jordan to get people's attention. As for the little white rookie, he could have been anyone. It didn't matter who you drafted anymore. What mattered was what skills they picked up in the lottery. Which star's moves would be lifted out of the archives and plugged into the rookie's exosuit. More specifically, what mattered tonight was that the Michael Jordan skills were up for grabs. It was fifteen years since Jordan's retirement, so the required waiting period was over.

The Jordan skills were just about the last, too. The supply of old NBA stars was pretty much depleted. It was only a couple of years after Jordan retired that the exosuits took over, and basketball stopped growing, started feeding on itself instead, becoming a kind of live 3D highlight film, a chance to see all the dream teams and matchups that had never actually happened: Bird feeding passes to Earl the Pearl, Wilt Chamberlain going one on

one with Ewing, Bill Walton and Marques Johnson playing out their careers instead of being felled by injuries,
Earl Maginault and Connie Hawkins bringing their leg-
endary schoolyard games to the pros, seeing if they could
make it against the best.

Only a few of the genuine stars had retired later
than Jordan. After this they'd have to think up something new. Start playing real basketball again, maybe. Or
just go back to the beginning of the list of stars and start
over.

"Nobody for real this year?" asked Elwood. He counted on me to read the sports papers.

"I don't think so. I heard the kid for the Sixers can
play, actually. But not good enough to go without skills."
Mixed in among us sampled stars were a handful of players making it on their own, without exosuits: Willard
Daynight, Barry Porush, Tony Smerks, Marvin Franklin.
These were the guys who would have been the Magic
Johnsons, Walt Fraziers, and Charles Barkleys of our era,
and in a way they were the guys I felt sorriest for. Instead
of playing in a league full of average guys and being big
stars, the way they would have in the past, they were
forced to go up against the sampled skills of the basketball Hall of Fame every night. Younger fans probably got
mixed up and credited *their* great plays to some sampled
program, instead of realizing they were seeing the real
thing.

The lottery started with the tall black kid with the Pan
Am Nuggets drawing the David Robinson skills package.
It was a formality, a foregone conclusion, since he was

the only rookie tall enough to make use of a center's skills. The kid stepped up to the mike and thanked his management and his representation and, almost as an afterthought, his mom and dad, and everyone smiled and flashed bulbs for a minute or two. You could see that the Nuggets general manager had his mind on other things. The Pan Am team was one of the worst in the league at that point, and as a result they had another lottery spot out of the seven, a lean, well-muscled kid who could play with the Jordan skills if he drew them. If they came up with Robinson and Jordan the Nuggets could be a force in the league overnight.

Personally, I always winced when a talented seven-footer like Robinson was reincarnated into the league. Center was my position, and I already spent most games riding the bench. Sal Pharaoh, the Knicks' regular center, played with the skills of Moses Malone, one of the best ever, and a workhorse who didn't like to sit.

Elwood read me like a book. "You're sweatin', Lassner. You afraid the Nuggets gonna trade their center now they got Robinson?"

"Fuck you, Elwood." The Nuggets old center played with the skills of a guy named Wes Unseld. Not a superstar, not in this league, but better than me.

I played with Ralph Sampson's skills—sort of. Sampson was briefly a star in his time, mostly because of his height, and as centers go he was pretty passive, not all that dominant in the paint. He was too gentle, and up against the sampled skills of Abdul-Jabbar, Ewing, Walton, Olajuwon, Chamberlain, and all the other great centers we faced every night, he and I were pretty damned ineffective.

The reason I say I only sort of played with the Sampson skills is that, lacking the ability to dominate inside, when I actually got on the floor—usually in the junk minutes towards the end of a game—I leaned pretty heavily on an outside jumpshot. It's a ridiculous shot for a center, but hey, it was what I had to offer. And my dirty little secret was that Bo Lassner's own jumpshot was just a little better than Ralph Sampson's. So when I took it I switched my exosuit off. The sportswriters didn't know, and neither did Coach Van.

"Relax, fool," said Elwood. "You ain't never gonna get traded. You got skin insurance." He reached over and pinched my thigh.

"Ouch!"

They gave away the Hardaway subroutines, to a skinny little guy with the Coors Suns. His smile showed his disappointment. It was down to four rookies now, and the Jordan skills were still unclaimed. Our kid—they flashed his name, Alan Gornan, under the picture—was still in the running.

"Shit," said Elwood. "Jordan's moves are too funky for a white cat, man. They program his suit it's gonna break his hips."

"You were pretty into Michael Jordan growing up, weren't you?" I asked. Elwood grew up in a Chicago slum.

"You got that," he said. His eyes were fixed on the screen.

"He won't get it," I said. "There's three other teams." What I meant, though I didn't say it, was that there were three other black guys still in the draw. I had a funny feeling Elwood didn't want our rookie to pick up the Jordan moves. I could think of a couple of different reasons for that.

The Karl Malone skills went to the kid from the I. G. Farben 76ers. Down to three. Then they took a break for commercials. Elwood was suddenly pacing the room. I called the desk and had them bring us up a couple of beers, out of mercy.

The Nuggets' second man picked up Adrian Dantley, leaving it down to two rookies, for two teams: us and the Beatrice Jazz. I was suddenly caught up in the excitement, my contempt for the media circus put aside for the moment.

We watched the commissioner punch up the number on his terminal, look up, and sigh. His mouth hung open and the crowd fell silent, so that for a second I thought the sound on the hotel television had died.

"Jazz, second pick."

That was it. Alan Gornan, and the Knicks, had the rights to the Jordan skills. The poor kid from the Jazz, who looked like a panther, had just landed the skills of Chris Mullin, undeniably a great shooter, a top-rank star, but just as undeniably slow, flat-footed, and white. It was a silly twist, but hey—it's a silly game.

The media swarmed around Gornan and his parents. Martin Fishall, the Knicks GM, thrust himself between the rookie and the newsmen and began answering questions, a huge grin on his face. I thought to look over at Elwood. He hated Fishall. Elwood had his head tossed back, chugging his beer.

The camera closed in on a headshot of Alan Gornan. He looked pretty self-possessed. He wore a little diamond earring and his eyes already knew how to find the camera and play to it.

They shoved a microphone in his face. "Got anything you want to say, kid?"

"Yeah." He grinned, and brushed the hair out of his eyes. Charisma.

"Go ahead. You're live."

"Look out, New York," said Alan Gornan. "Clear the runway. Vanilla Dunk is due for takeoff." The line started out a little underplayed, almost shy, but by the time he had the whole thing out he had a sneer on his face that reminded me of nothing, I swear, so much as pictures I've seen of the young Elvis Presley.

"Vanilla Dunk?" I said aloud, involuntarily.

"Turn that shit off," said Elwood, and I did.

That was the last of Alan Gornan for the moment. The new players weren't eligible until next season. All bravado aside, it would take Gornan a few months of working with the Knicks' programming experts to get control of the Jordan skills. In the meantime, we were knocked out of the playoffs in the semifinal round by the Hyundai Celtics. It should have been a great series—and we should have won it, I think—but Otis Pettingale, our star guard, who carried Nate Archibald's skills, twisted his ankle in the first game and had to sit, and the series was just a bummer.

I spent that off-season mostly brooding, as I remember. Ringing my ex-wife's answering machine, watching TV, fun stuff like that, mostly. Plus practicing my jump-shot. Silly me. If I'd only been six inches shorter I could have been a big star . . . that's a joke, son.

Training camp was a media zoo. Was Otis Pettingale too old to carry the load for another season? What about the Sal Pharaoh trade rumors? And how were they going to fit Alan Gornan in, anyway? Who would sit to make room for the kid with the Jordan skills—Michael Front, who played with Kevin McHale's skills, or Elwood Fossett, who played with Maurice Lucas's? The reporters circled the camp like hungry wolves, putting everyone in a bad mood. They kept trying to bait us into second-guessing Coach Van on the makeup of the starting five, kept wanting to know what we thought of Gornan, who we'd barely even met.

And they all wanted a piece of Gornan. Martin Fishall and Coach Van kept him insulated at first, but it became clear pretty fast that he knew how to handle himself, and that he actually liked talking to the press. He had a knack for playing the bad boy, and with no effort at all he had them eating his "Vanilla Dunk" bullshit for breakfast, lunch, and dinner.

At practices he more or less behaved himself. The Jordan skills were pretty dynamic, and Gornan was smart enough to know how to work them into the style of the rest of the team. It was a little scary, actually, seeing how fast something new and different was coming into being. The Knicks' core had been solid for a couple of years— but of course the Jordan skills weren't going to sit on the bench.

Gornan was initially polite with me, which was fine. But nothing more developed, and by the third week of camp what had passed for politeness was seeming a little more like arrogance. I got the feeling it was the same way with Otis and McFront. He seemed to have won a friend in Sal Pharaoh, though, for no apparent reason. We played a lot of split-squad games, which meant I got to start at center for the B team. As such it was my job to clog up the middle and keep Gornan from driving, and I got a quick taste of what the other teams were going to be facing this year, with Pharaoh playing the muscle, setting picks, clearing the lanes for the kid's drives. It was a bruising experience, to put it mildly.

One afternoon after one of those split-squad events I found myself in the dressing room with Pharaoh and Elwood.

"You like protecting that motherfucker," said Elwood. "Why don't you let him take his licks?"

Pharaoh smirked. He and Elwood were the two intimidators on our team, and when they went head to head neither had any edge. "It's not about that, Elwood," he said.

"He thinks he's fucking Michael Jordan," said Elwood.

"As far as the team's concerned, he *is* Michael Jordan," said Pharaoh. "Just like I'm Moses Malone, and your stupid ass is Maurice Lucas."

"That white boy's gonna ruin this team, Sal."

Pharaoh shook his head. "Different team now, man. Figure it out, Elwood. Stop looking back." He wadded up his sweaty shorts and tossed them into the bottom of a locker, then headed for the showers.

"What was that shit?" Elwood snapped at me the minute Pharaoh was out of earshot. " 'Figure it out.' Is he trying to tell me I'm not making the cut?"

"Don't be stupid," I said. "You're in. McFront'll sit."

"White boys don't sit. 'Less they suck as bad as you."

"I think you're wrong. Don't you see? With Gornan they've got their token white starter. You're a better player than McFront." What I was saying, of course, was that the Maurice Lucas skills were more valuable than the Kevin McHale skills. Which was true, but it didn't take team chemistry into account.

"Two white forwards," he said. "They won't be able to fucking resist."

"Wrong. You and Pharaoh both in there to protect Gornan. All that muscle to surround the Jordan skills. That's what they won't be able to resist."

"Huh." He considered my logic. "Shit, Lassner."

"What?"

"Shit," he said. "I smell shit around here."

At the start of the season Coach Van played Gornan very conservatively, off the bench. He was a rookie, and we were a very solid team, so it was justifiable. But not for long. When he got in he was averaging more points per minute than Elwood or McFront, and they were points that counted, that won games. He was a little shaky on defense, but the offensive impact of the Jordan subroutines was astonishing, and Gornan was meshing well with Sal Pharaoh, just like in the practices. Otis Pettingale's offense at guard was fading a bit, but we had plenty of other weapons. Our other guard was Derrick Flash, who with Maurice Cheeks's skills was just coming into his own. We reeled off six wins in a row at the start of the season before taking a loss, to the Hyundai Celtics, on a night where Gornan didn't see many minutes. That was the night the chanting started, midway through the third quarter: "Vanilla Dunk! Vanilla Dunk! Vanilla Dunk . . ."

The next night he started, and scored 43 points, in a game we won easily. He was a starter after that. McFront was benched, which broke the heart of his fan club, but the sports pages agreed that Elwood belonged on the floor, and most of them thought we were the team to beat. We should have been.

The trouble started one night when we were beating —no, make that thrashing—the Disney Heat, 65 to 44 at the start of the third quarter. I was in, actually. I guess Gornan had been working overtime with the programming guys, and he hauled out a slamdunk move all of a sudden, one where he floated up over three of the Disney players, switched the ball from his right to his left hand, and flipped it in as he fell away. It was a nice move— make that an astonishing move—but it wasn't strictly necessary, given the situation.

No big deal. But a minute later he did it again. Actually

this time he soared under the basket and dropped it in backwards. As we jogged back on defense I heard Elwood muttering to himself. The Disney player tossed up a brick and I came up with the rebound, and when I looked upcourt there was Gornan again, all alone, signaling for the pass.

I ignored him—we were up more than twenty points —and fed it in slow to Otis. Otis dribbled up a few feet, let the Disney defender catch up with Gornan, and we put a different play together.

Next time the ball got into Gornan's hands he broke loose with it, and went up to dunk. The crowd there in Miami, having nothing better to do, started cheering for us to pass it to him. Elwood's mood darkened. He began trying to run the team in Otis's place, trying to set up plays that locked Gornan out of the action. I could feel the resistance—like being part of a machine where the gears suddenly start grinding.

Coach Van pulled me out of the game. From the bench I had a clearer sense of how much Gornan was milking this crowd, and of how much they were begging to be milked. He was giving them Michael Jordan, the legend they'd never seen themselves, the instant replay man, the one who stood out even in a field of stars. And the awful thing about Gornan's theatrics was that they worked, as basketball. We were up almost thirty points now. He'd reduced the Disney team to spectators.

A minute later Elwood joined me on the bench, and McFront went in. Elwood put a towel over his head and then lowered his head almost below his big knees. The bench got real quiet, which meant the noise from the crowd stood out even better.

Elwood toweled off his head and stood up suddenly, like he was putting himself back in. He turned and looked at me and over at Coach Van. Then he spat, just over the line and onto the court, and turned and walked towards the locker room.

Coach Van jerked his thumb at me, meaning I should go play therapist. Needless to say my contribution wasn't sorely needed on the court. Sometimes I wondered if they kept me around because I knew how to talk to Elwood.

I found him dressing in his street clothes, without having showered. When he looked up at me I almost turned and ran back to the bench. I held up my hands, pleading not guilty. But of course the skin on those hands was white.

"You see that shit out there," he said. It was a command that I nod, not a question. "That's poor taste, man."

"Poor taste?"

"That dunk is from the third game of the '91 finals, Lassner. That's sacrilege, hauling it out for no reason, against these Disney chumps."

"You *recognize* the dunk?"

" 'Course I recognize the dunk. You never watch any Jordan tapes, man? That dunk is a *prayer.* He can't just—"

"Whoa, Elwood. Hold on a minute. You're sampling, I'm sampling. This isn't some purist thing here, man. Get some perspective."

"Michael Jordan, Lassner. You ever see the tape of Michael crying after winning in '91?"

"At least he's on our team. Jeez, what would happen if you had to play *against* the almighty Jordan, or somebody with his skills—you'd probably fold up completely!"

"It's not just the dunks, Lassner. He won't play defense. He's always up the court cherry-picking, waiting for the easy pass. Michael was a great defensive player!"

"C'mon, Elwood. This is a showtime league and you know it. You're one of about five guys playing serious defense. *Everybody* goes for the fancy moves. That's what the sampling is all about. He's just better than most, because he's got the hot skills package. *Somebody* had to get the Jordan skills."

"It didn't have to be some little white jerk."

Once it was out it was kind of a relief. Black and white was the issue. Of course. As much as that was supposed to be a thing of the past. I'd known all along, but in some stupid way I guess I'd thought not saying anything might make it better.

"I'm a white guy with a black guy's skills," I pointed out.

He waved it aside. "Not important. It's not Jordan. You play white, anyway."

What was it about basketball that made it all seem so stark? As though it were designed as a metaphor—the white style of play so plodding and corporate and reliable, the black style so individual and expressive and so often self-destructive, so me-against-the-world. When a black guy couldn't jump they said he had "white legs," or if he was slow it was "white man's disease." Basketball was a white sport that blacks had taken over and yet the audience was still pretty much white. And that white audience adored the black players for their brilliant moves—thanks to sampling, that adoration would probably kill the sport—and yet was still thought to require the token white face, for purposes of "identification."

Solve basketball, I sometimes thought, and you'd solve everything.

"Okay," I said. "He's a jerk. But *white* shouldn't matter. Jordan wasn't a black separatist, as I remember. I mean, call me naive, but scrambling the racial stuff up was supposed to be one of the few good things about this sampling deal, right?"

"Michael's career meant something," Elwood mumbled. "Should be treated with respect."

"Look who turns out to be Mr. Historical," I said. "You have to get hip, Elwood. Basketball is postmodern now."

"What's that supposed to mean?"

"Means Michael's career might have meant something, but yours doesn't, and neither does Vanilla Dunk's —so relax."

Once Gornan started hauling out the realtime poster shots the media wouldn't let it go. He was all over the sports channels, dunking in slow-mo, grinning and pumping his fists. He made the cover of *Rolling Stone*, diamond earring flashing, spinning a basketball with one hand, groping a babe with the other. Then his agent started connecting with the endorsement people, and you couldn't turn on the tube without seeing Vanilla Dunk downing vitaburgers at McDonald's, Vanilla Dunk slurping on a Pepsi or a Fazz, Vanilla Dunk checking out the synthetic upholstery inside a new Chrysler SunFrame.

With Gornan playing the exuberant Michael Jordan game and Elwood playing angry we kept on winning. In fact we opened up a sizeable lead over the Celtics in the division, and it wasn't necessarily a good thing. Being too far ahead was almost as bad as floundering in the basement of the division. Without the tension of a tight race to bind us together as a team all the egos came rushing to the forefront. Otis was struggling with accepting his fading powers and diminished role, and we all missed the way his easy confidence had been at the heart of the team. McFront was sulking on the bench. Pharaoh was playing hard, trying to make the new team work, trying to show by force that Gornan fit in. Meanwhile Gornan's theatrics got more and more outrageous, and every slam dunk was another blow to the dam holding back Elwood's rage.

One afternoon in Oakland before a game with the IBM Warriors someone made the mistake of leaving the TV on in the visitors' clubhouse. Elwood and Otis and I were sitting playing cards when a pre-taped interview with Gornan turned up on the sports channel.

The interviewer seemed to be trying to work around to the subject of race. "How'd you choose your nickname, Dunk?" he asked. "Why Vanilla, in particular? What point are you trying to make?"

Gornan shrugged. "Hey, don't get heavy," he said. "They call me Vanilla 'cause I'm completely smooth and completely sweet. It's simple."

"Why not something else, then?" said the interviewer. "Chocolate, say."

Gornan laughed, and for a minute I thought he was going to grant the man his point. Instead he realigned his sneer and said: "Chocolate don't go down smooth."

"What are you saying, Dunk?"

"Nothing, man. Just that I'm not chocolate. That's why I'm like a breath of fresh air—I go down smooth. People are ready for that, ready to lighten up. Chocolate's sweet, but it's always got that bitter edge, y'know?"

And then, God help me, he turned to the camera and gave it a big wink.

I got up and shut the TV off, but it was too late. Elwood had already slammed his cards down on the table and stalked out. Otis looked sick. I prayed that Gornan wasn't in the locker room. I went through and found Elwood out on the edge of the floor, watching the Warriors take their warmups.

At game time we managed to get out on the floor without any explosions. But from the opening tipoff I knew it was going to be a bad night. When the ball got into Elwood's hands he drove like a steamroller up the middle and went up for a vicious dunk. Then he stole an inbound pass and did it again, only this time he fouled his man on the drive. Everyone on the floor looked nervous, even the Warriors—even, for once, Gornan, who was usually oblivious.

The Warrior hit his free throws and the game resumed. The pattern came clear soon enough: Elwood was calling for every pass, and when he got it he was going up for the dunk, every time. He was trying to play Gornan's game, but he was too big and strong, too angry to pull it off. He was stuffing a lot of shots but he'd accumulated four fouls before the second quarter. When Coach Van finally pulled him, he had twice as many points as Gornan or anyone else, but the Warriors were ahead.

He sat until halftime, and with McFront in we got the game tied. During the break Coach Van called Elwood into an office and closed the door. Meanwhile Gornan was off in his usual corner of the locker room smoking a cigarette, but he had a hollow, haunted expression on him, one I'd never seen before.

Elwood was back in for the start of the third quarter, and whatever Coach Van had said to him in his office hadn't worked: he picked up right where he'd left off, breaking for insane inside moves at every opportunity, going up for ill-fated dunks and making some of them, smearing a lot of guys with his sweat. The Oakland crowd, which had been abuzz with expectations of seeing the Vanilla Dunk Revue, fell to a low, ugly murmur. When Elwood got called for another foul I was almost relieved; that made five, and with six he'd foul out of the game, and it would be over.

But he wasn't quite done. On the next play he pulled

down a rebound and dribbled the length of the court, flattening a Warrior on his way up. I waited for the ref's whistle, but no whistle came. The Warrior center braced himself between Elwood and the net. Elwood ran straight at him, tossed off a perfunctory head fake, and then went up with a spinning move, his bulk barely clearing a tremendous head-on collision with the jumping center. He jammed the ball down with both hands and hit the glass so hard it shattered.

Suddenly the arena was dead silent, as Elwood and the Warrior center fell in a tangle amid a rain of Plexiglas fragments. When the two men got up unhurt the roar started. The referees called the game a Warrior victory by forfeit, and Elwood took them on singlehandedly; we had to drag him off the floor.

When we got him into the clubhouse we found Gornan already showered and in his street clothes, giving his version of events to the press.

I looked up the details on Maurice Lucas's career once. I was working on a theory that the basketball skills you sampled contained an element of the previous player's personality, some kind of style or attitude that was intrinsic to the way they played, something that could be imparted, gradually, to the later player, along with the actual basketball skills.

Well, bingo, as far as Maurice Lucas and Elwood Fossett were concerned. Lucas, it turned out, spent a considerable part of his career feeling misunderstood and underpaid. Specifically underpaid in comparison to the white players on his team. As a result he spent a lot of time playing *angry*. I mean apart from the forcefulness that came with him (and Elwood) being so big and strong; his game was specifically fueled by rage.

Another result of the conflicts in his career was that he was widely understood to have dogged it, to have played intentionally poorly, as a kind of protest, during some of the key years of his career. Which got me thinking: the skills that Elwood inherited might also contain an element of this struggle that Lucas had waged against himself, to suppress his skills, to not give the best of what he had to the company men he hated.

Elwood wouldn't have known, either. Maurice Lucas's career was before his time. Elwood's interest in basketball history went back no further than Michael Jordan's rookie year.

McFront started in Elwood's place the next night, and Elwood went back to the lockers, got dressed, and walked out. Gornan had a great two quarters, undeniable as basketball, unsurpassable as spectacle, and in the locker room at the half he was more exuberant than usual, clowning with Pharaoh and McFront, turning the charm he'd previously saved for the media on his teammates. It was a fun scene, but it made me a little sick to see Elwood being drummed out so easily, even if he'd opened the door to it himself, with his walkout.

On the bench during the second half I scooted up next to Coach Van.

"You're letting this team fall apart," I said.

"Come on, Lassner."

"What?"

"You're not gonna start this in the middle of a game." He sounded tired of the conversation before it had even started. "Nobody's letting the team fall apart. This could be a championship team."

"This could have *been* a championship team. Now it's a championship Vanilla Dunk and his Dunkettes."

He made a face.

"What does ownership say?" I asked.

"What do you think? Fishall wants Gornan starting every game. The fans want it too. As long as we're winning I'm gonna have a tough time arguing for anything else."

"Yeah."

"I want Elwood out there too, Bo, but if he doesn't even suit up—"

"I know, I know."

"Look, I can't make everybody like Gornan. *I* don't particularly like him. But if you get Elwood back in here, he'll see playing time. The backboard—that's no big deal. Just more headlines, is the way Fishall sees it. But this walkout business—"

He didn't finish his sentence. Something happened out on the floor, something that, as it turned out, would change everything. There was a crash, and a loud sigh, and the crowd fell to silence. It was so quiet you could make out the squeak of the team doctor's sneakers as he crossed the floor, rushing towards the fallen player.

I got up and peered over the top of the cluster of players, but couldn't see anything. So I counted heads. It was a Knick on the floor, and height—or rather, lack of it—told me it was Sal Pharaoh.

In a minute they had him on his feet, and the crowd started buzzing again, which made things feel more normal. Pharaoh walked with his head bowed, while the doctor peeled the exosuit away from his damaged wrist. They hurried him off towards the trainer's room and a couple of kids with towels rushed over and wiped the sweat off the floor where he'd fallen.

Coach Van slapped me on the ass. "Wake up, Lassner. Get in there."

I stumbled out onto the floor and we restarted the game. We'd built up a good lead, and even without Pharaoh or Elwood available we cruised to victory—mostly on the strength of Gornan's play, I have to admit. He was the only one on the floor who didn't seem a little stunned by Pharaoh's going down. I did my best to fill the role of Gornan's protector, though I must admit I felt a renegade urge to do what Elwood would have wanted, and leave him out there naked.

At the start of the fourth quarter, before Coach Van pulled the starters out, it hit me that with me, McFront, and Vanilla Dunk our entire frontcourt was white—the first time the Knicks had more whites than blacks on the floor since I joined the team.

Sal Pharaoh had broken his right wrist in the fall, and he'd be out for at least six weeks, probably more—I learned that from the television in our hotel room that night. Elwood burst in half an hour later, and he learned it from me.

What it meant, of course, was that I was the starting center for the time being. It also meant good things for Elwood, if he behaved himself. With Pharaoh out he was our only enforcer, so he'd probably get the nod over McFront. With me in instead of Pharaoh we also lost a lot on defense and rebounding, and Elwood was a better defender and rebounder than McFront.

On the other hand, Pharaoh had served as a buffer between Gornan and Elwood—also between Gornan and the rest of the league, all those teams frustrated by being beaten by a white hotdog who was getting more endorsements in his rookie year than they'd see for their whole careers. I wasn't going to be able to serve that role. I wasn't strong enough, or black enough. That role fell to Elwood. The two of them had to play together or the team was in trouble.

Two nights later, in L.A., against the Time Warner Lakers, I saw that the team was in trouble.

The Lakers were a team that would have tested us with Pharaoh on the floor. It was bad timing that we hit them on the first night without him, and the first night since Elwood's walkout. We should have had a patsy, a fall guy, to give us confidence, to give Elwood and Gornan a chance to have some fun together. No such luck.

In the first quarter Gornan was playing his usual game, to the delight of the crowd. He was scoring a lot of the time but we weren't coming up with any rebounds, and our defense had nothing, and very quickly the

Lakers were up by ten points. I got all passive, started leaning on my jumpshot, and left the inside open, waiting for Elwood to take over. But Elwood was invisible. He was playing man-to-man defense so stubbornly that he had nothing left for the fast break. He was putting on a clinic, demonstrating what Gornan was doing wrong, but Gornan wasn't paying any attention, and the crowd didn't have the faintest idea what was going on.

At halftime the Lakers were fifteen points up, and in the second half things really started breaking down. Gornan tried to compensate the only way he knew how, by diving for ridiculous steals, hogging the ball even more, putting on an air show. He got fouled so hard I actually started to get a little worried about him, but each time he jumped back up with a grin. I tried to play a little post-up but the Lakers' center, who had Artis Gilmore's skills, was making me look stupid. Our guards were working the margins, trying to get us into the game from the perimeter, but the Lakers were picking up every rebound, so missed shots from the outside were very costly.

Elwood lost his patience, started falling off the defense and trying to mount a show of his own. As usual he strung together some impressive slams, and for a minute the momentum seemed ours, but another minute later he racked up two fouls in a row and the Lakers beefed up their score at the free throw line. There isn't any way to defend against free throws—not that anyone was playing defense.

Gornan responded as only he could, by taking up increasingly improbable moves. They had two or three guys on him every time he touched the ball, and he was turning it over a lot. He was airborne, but a lot of balls were being stripped away on the way up.

By the fourth quarter I was exhausted, and humiliated. Coach Van called a time out and I jogged reflexively towards the bench, but he wasn't taking me out. He subbed McFront in for Elwood and sent in another rookie for Gornan. We lost the game by 23 points, our worst margin of the season so far.

We lost in a similar fashion the next night, and at the end Coach Van called me and Elwood and Gornan into his office. I assumed the idea was to mediate between the two of them, and that I was there more or less as Elwood's official interpreter.

"What's happening, guys?" said Coach Van.

Gornan jumped right in. "We need a center who can play, Coach."

"What?" I blurted.

"Sorry, man," said Gornan. "But let's face facts."

"I was starting for this team before you—"

"Whoa," said Coach Van. "Relax, Bo. Alan, that wasn't exactly what I had in mind. Seems to me the team is suffering from what I'd call a feud."

"Feud?" Gornan played completely dumb. Elwood just sulked in his chair.

"I don't care about the personal stuff," said Coach Van. "It's a matter of how you play. You have to play like you like each other. You have to be able to pretend on the court. You guys don't seem to be managing it."

"Hey, me and Bo get along fine," said Gornan. "Far as

I know. But he's just not as strong as Pharaoh under the net. If me and Elwood's games are hurting, that's the reason why."

"This is ridiculous," I said. Gornan's strategy began to dawn on me. He was going to pretend he hadn't even noticed Elwood's hostility. It was instinctively brilliant, and vicious. He'd avoid the appearance of a black-white conflict by cutting me down instead.

I looked over at Elwood, but he wasn't offering me any help.

"Look," said Gornan. "Me and Elwood are playing the same as when the team was winning. Lassner here is the difference."

"Are you gonna take this?" I said to Elwood. "He's saying that the way you've been playing in the last few games is your normal game. Can't you see what a veiled insult that is? You can play a hell of a lot better—"

"You getting down on my game, Lassner?" growled Elwood. "You a fine one to fucking talk, man."

"No, no, I mean, I'm just trying to say, look at what *he's* saying—"

"Enough, Bo. Be quiet for a minute. Maybe I've misunderstood the situation—"

"Coach," I protested, "Gornan is twisting this—"

"Enough! I don't know the details, I don't want to know the details. What matters is the chemistry sucks right now. All three of you are playing below your capabilities. That's my opinion, and I've told ownership as much, and I'll tell the press the same when we get home. That's all for now."

94

End of meeting.

We lost the last two games of the road trip and flew back to New York. On the plane I slept and dreamed of missed shots. The cabbie who took me back to my Brooklyn apartment asked me how I felt about the trade.

"What trade?" I asked, and the cabbie just said, "I'm sorry."

The Disney Heat were a mediocre team with one big star: Gerald Flynnan, their center. He played with the skills of Hakeem Olajuwon, and he carried their team to the lower rounds of the playoffs each year, but no further. The rest of the team was talented but young, disorganized, and possibly stupid.

Knicks management had offered me, Elwood, and a first round lottery pick to the Heat in exchange for Flynnan, and the Disney team had taken the bait. The Knicks picked up a dominant center to replace the injured Pharaoh, and to fill his shoes in protecting Vanilla Dunk. And they'd gotten rid of the tension in their frontcourt by unloading Elwood; McFront and Dunk would start.

What the Heat got was a mid-season mess: an angry, talented star and a tall white guy with a jumpshot. The lottery spot wouldn't help the team until next year. Elwood and I were flown down and in the Disney uniforms before we knew what hit us, and the coach tossed us into a game before we'd even had a chance to introduce ourselves to the other players.

The result was an ugly loss, but then the players there seemed pretty used to that.

The crowd too. The Disney fans were a jaded, abusive bunch, mostly concerned with heckling Coach Wilder for not playing local favorite Earlham "Early" Natt, a talented eccentric who carried the skills of Marvin Barnes. At the start of the game they cheered Elwood and greeted me with shouts of "Where's Gerald?" but by halftime they were drinking beer and shouting for Early Natt, a request which Coach Wilder ignored except in the final, hopeless moments of each game. Natt looked pretty dynamic when he got in, which explained the crowd's affection. He also paid zero attention to defense or team play, which explained the coach's resistance.

The same pattern held in the two losses that followed. That brought us to the all-star break. Elwood and I were 0–3 with our new team, and nobody was particularly happy. I couldn't figure Elwood—he was playing quiet, walking quiet, and, I suspected, mixing a little thinking in with his brooding. For my part I was just trying to keep my head above water—to my embarrassment, I was too out-of-shape not to be exhausted by starting every night. Plus management and media caught on that I was the communicative one of the new pair, which meant I was answering questions for me and Elwood both.

The all-star break gave us most of a week before we played again, and Elwood surprised me by suggesting we get out of town. He'd located a beach hotel on Key West with a nearby high-school gym we could rent. I agreed. Without having to say so, we were both avoiding paying any attention to the all-star game, which was sure to be yet another installment of the Vanilla Dunk show.

Elwood shocked me again by getting up first that morning, to rouse me out of bed. He called up a breakfast on room service; I swear in all our years rooming together I'd never seen him pick up a phone before.

At the gym he said, "Okay, Lassner. I'm gonna teach your tall white ass how to play a trapping defense."

"What?"

"You heard."

"What is this punishment for, Elwood? What did I do? Just tell me."

"Here—" He threw me the ball.

And proceeded to do exactly what he'd promised.

The next day word had got around—possibly with Elwood's help, I never found out—that a couple of pros were working out in the local gym. Six guys showed up: confident, tall kids out to impress, all lean and strong from boating on the island, a couple of them with real talent. Elwood worked them into the clinic he was giving me, and they and he spent the next four days busting my ass.

I went back to Miami exhausted, and Elwood still wouldn't tell me what he was getting at.

It quickly became clear, however, that he'd been looking at the schedule. The first team we played after the break was the Knicks. That afternoon in practice, while the rest of the team was drilling, he took Coach Wilder aside.

"Let me call the plays tonight," he said, as if it were the most natural thing in the world.

"What?"

"Let me call the plays." He actually smiled.

"We're playing the Knicks."

"Exactly."

"What are you saying, Elwood?"

"You traded for me, man. Give me a night to run the show. One night. If you don't like the results we go back to your way tomorrow. Nobody will ever know."

I walked over to show my support—for what, I didn't exactly know. "Give him a half, at least," I said.

"He did this in New York?" asked Coach Wilder. "Called plays?"

"Yes," I lied.

Elwood pulled Early Natt off the bench as we took the floor at the start of the game, saying to him only, "Go crazy."

I got Elwood aside. "Okay," I said. "I've waited long enough. What's the deal here, Elwood?"

"We're gonna defend these mothers," he said. "That's the deal. Our guards can play a zone defense if they hang back. You and me are boxing out Dunk, taking the rebounds, stripping the ball. Don't hold anything back."

"What's Early doing?"

"Cherry-picking. Outdunking the Dunk."

"I never saw Marvin Barnes play," I said, "but I didn't

think he could hang with Michael Jordan. Early is stupid, Elwood."

"We're not playing against Michael Jordan," said Elwood. "We're playing against Vanilla Dunk. Jordan had an integrated game. The best there ever was. Dunk's just a show. I've played a little one-on-one with Early. He can put on a show if he doesn't have to think about defense or passing, and if the coach isn't breathing down his neck. That's our job, Lassner. Keep Early from having to think about anything. He'll put on a show. Trust me."

Gerald Flynnan, the Knicks' new center, beat me on the tip-off, so the Knicks came up with the ball. I followed Elwood's lead—after the week of drills, it was second nature. We charged the ball, my hands up wide and high to block the pass, Elwood's hands low for the steal off the dribble. Our guards scurried behind us on the zone defense, picking up the slack.

Otis Pettingale beat us on a headfake and went up. Score: Gulf and Western 2, Disney 0.

One of our guards fed it in to me, and Elwood hissed, "Up to Early!" I did what I was told. Early Natt was halfway up the court. He twisted through three Knicks, not looking back to see if he had any support, and scored. Tie game.

The second time up the court the ball was in Vanilla Dunk's hands, and Elwood seemed to go into another time signature. He was all over him. Dunk dribbled back and circled and came up again. I put up my hands and cut off a pass opportunity. Dunk hesitated, and Elwood stripped the ball away. A flip pass upcourt into Early's hands and we were ahead.

The crowd went wild. Not because they had any idea what me and Elwood were up to, but because Early was in the game, showing off, doing the only thing he knew how to do: score. The Knicks brought the ball back to us, and this time Elwood took it away from McFront, tipping it into my waiting hands. Not waiting to be told this time, I tossed it to Early. Score.

The strategy was working, at least for the moment. No team in the league played this kind of defense, and it had the Knicks confused. High on the novelty of it, and the crowd's response, we roared to a fifteen-point lead by halftime. Elwood ran back to bench and spread his hands in a mute appeal to Coach Elder.

"This one's yours," said the coach.

In the second half the Knicks adjusted somewhat, and I got tired and had to sit for a few minutes. Flynnan bulled his way through Elwood for six straight points, and Otis added a couple of outside shots, and they nearly tied it. But Vanilla Dunk looked all flummoxed, and he never got into the game. A few minutes later we opened up the lead again and we ended up winning by five points.

I took Elwood aside in the locker room. The media all wanted Early Natt anyway. "When I was sitting in the third period I checked my suit," I said. "It wasn't working."

Elwood just smiled, and made a little pair of imaginary scissors with his fingers.

"You fucked with my suit?"

"I just noticed you play better without it, man. You think I didn't see you were turning it off?"

"That's just for my jumpshot!"

"I saw you in practice in Key West, white boy. You play better without it. Notice I ain't saying you play *good*. Just better."

"Fuck you, Elwood."

It was a nice night, but it was just a night. A fluke loss by the almighty Knicks—it happens sometimes. The Vanilla Dunk Revue went back to cakewalking its way to a championship, while we struggled on, treading water in the middle of our division, barely clinging to our playoff hopes. Surprisingly, Elwood didn't seem that interested in applying the defensive techniques we'd developed together against any of the other teams. Oh, we trapped here and there, but Elwood didn't ever take command the way he had. He seemed to go back into a trance, like he'd done when we were first traded. We won our share of games, but nobody was particularly impressed. As for Early Natt, he saw more minutes, but they only seemed to give him more opportunities to blow it, and soon enough he was in the doghouse. Elwood had abandoned him. I guess Elwood liked that one-dimensional game a little better on a hapless black man than he liked it on an arrogant white one, but not so much that he wanted to encourage Early to make it a regular habit.

Elwood and I were shooting alone in the gym when

I asked, "Why don't we go back to that trapping game?"

He didn't even turn around, just sank a shot as he answered. "Element of surprise the only thing makes it work, Bo. Teams'd see through that shit if we hauled it out two nights in a row."

"Some great teams won with defense, back—"

"Shut up, Bo. You don't know what you're talkin' about."

"What have we got to lose?"

"Shut up."

Elwood's playing got more and more distracted, and we went on a losing streak, but I didn't catch on until two weeks before the end of the season, when the Knicks came to town again. I waited for Elwood to rouse us again, to make a big demonstration, and instead he played in what was becoming his usual trance. He almost seemed to be taking a masochistic thrill in letting Vanilla Dunk run wild.

The next day I glanced at the papers, and I realized that, for once, Elwood was watching the standings.

We had to lose three games in the standings to drop out of a regular playoff spot, and into the wild card spot. The wild card team played the team with the conference's best record in the first round of the playoffs, in a quick best-of-five series, a sort of warm-up for the real playoffs.

The Knicks, thanks to their win over us the night before, were now the team with the best record, by one game over the Pistons.

In other words, the victory over the Knicks earlier in the season wasn't the main point; that was just Elwood finding out if he could do it.

Elwood and Coach Wilder yelled at each other for a straight half hour in the visiting coach's office in the bowels of the Garden. In the meantime I was left to play diplomat with the press and the rest of the team. I'd never been in the visitors' locker rooms of the Garden before, and it frankly got me a little depressed. I'd never dared mention it to Elwood, but I *missed* the Knicks.

When they came out it was Coach Wilder who looked beaten. Elwood didn't say anything to me, but his eyes said he'd won his point. When we got out on the floor he flipped the practice ball to Early Natt, then crooked a finger and beckoned Early over to him.

"Remember when I told you to go crazy?" he said.

Early just nodded, smiling defensively. He looked a little intimidated by the roar of the Garden crowd.

"We gonna do that again. Remember how?"

Early nodded.

"Just stay uptown, look for the pass. Stay open, that's all." Elwood turned to me, but didn't say anything, just stretched his arms up in the air. I mirrored them with my own—albeit six inches higher.

Our moment was swallowed in a roar, as the Knicks came out of the lockers and were greeted by the crowd in the Garden. I looked out and then back down at the Heat uniform on my chest. I felt about as small as a seven-foot guy can feel, at that moment.

This time I somehow beat Flynnan on the tip-off, flipping the ball to one of our guards. We went up the court and scored, Elwood sinking a jumper from midway out. The Knicks inbounded and I realized I was frozen, that I wasn't following Elwood into the trap defense. The Knicks got the ball to Vanilla Dunk. Dunk flew upcourt, Elwood dogging his steps, and broke loose for a fabulous mid-air hook shot. I cursed myself.

Elwood grabbed the ball and hurled it upcourt to Early who ran into a crowd and had the ball stripped away. Defense again. This time I rushed the ball—it was in Otis's hands—and forced a weak pass to Flynnan, who was too far out for his shot. I jumped on Flynnan, my hands in his face, and heard a whistle. I'd fouled him.

Flynnan went to the line and hit both shots. 4–2, Knicks.

Elwood rushed the ball to Early again, passing into a thicket of Knicks, and Early was immediately fouled. Early went to the line and missed one.

The Knicks came up and Flynnan rolled over me for an easy layup. God, he's a big motherfucker, I wanted to whisper to Elwood, but Elwood wasn't meeting my eye.

Elwood went up, got caught in traffic, and bailed out to one of our guards, who threw up a brick from outside. Flynnan and I fought for the rebound, and Flynnan won. He dumped it out to Vanilla Dunk, who immediately had Elwood all over him. I rushed up from behind and stabbed at the ball.

Dunk twisted out from between us, head-faked, made

a move. The move didn't come off. He and Elwood tangled up and fell together. A whistle. The ref signaled: offensive foul, Knicks. Number double zero, Alan Gornan. Vanilla Dunk.

Dunk got up screaming. Elwood shook himself out and turned his back. The ref rushed up between them while a kid wiped the sweat off the floor.

Then Dunk yelled one word too many.

"What?" Elwood turned fast and got in his face, real close, without touching. The ref squirted out of the way.

"I said nigger," repeated Dunk.

They both drew back a fist. I grabbed Elwood from behind, so he couldn't get his shot off. Don't ask me why I grabbed Elwood instead of Dunk.

Vanilla Dunk's punch was off-line. It slammed into Elwood's shoulder. That was his only shot. The other Knicks were all over him.

The refs threw them both out of the game, and soon, all too soon, it was restarted. With Elwood gone it was too much a matter of me against Flynnan, and it was Flynnan's night. I couldn't hang with him. For help on offense all I had was Early, who seemed completely cowed by the Garden and baffled with Elwood gone. I tried to dump it off to him, but he'd lost sight of the basket, kept trying dumb passes instead. Whereas Flynnan had McFront, who'd found his midrange shot, and was pouring in pull-up jumpers.

They blew us out. An hour later I was sitting on the edge of my hotel bed, watching it on television. Early

Natt and one of our guards were there with me, but the room was silent except for the tube. Elwood had disappeared, so we didn't have to be ashamed to watch the sportscast.

It was Vanilla Dunk all the way. He'd run straight to the press, as usual, and the tape of his interview was replayed every fifteen minutes. The commissioner had already decided: both players were available to their teams for the rest of the series. Elwood would be fined five thousand. Dunk, who'd thrown a punch, would pay fifteen thou. I'd saved Elwood ten grand by grabbing him. And probably saved Dunk a broken jaw.

They barely even mentioned the fact that we'd lost. I guess the New York press considered that pretty much a foregone conclusion.

I flipped to MTV just in time to catch Vanilla Dunk's new video: "(Dunkin') In Yo Face."

Elwood showed up just in time for the second game. I never did find out where he spent that night. For a minute I was afraid he was stoned on something—I'd seen him stoned, and gotten stoned with him, but never before a game—because he looked too happy, too loose. I even wondered for a second if he somehow thought we'd won last night.

There wasn't time to confer. He flipped a thumbs-up signal to Coach Wilder, and called Early over to him. The coach just shook his head. A minute later the refs started the game.

I put my head down and vowed to get physical with

Flynnan. I wanted rebounds, I wanted blocked shots, I wanted steals. I wanted Elwood not to hate me, primarily. He still wasn't meeting my eye.

Otis missed a shot and Elwood came down with the rebound, and passed it to Early with nearly the same motion. Early ducked underneath Flynnan and jumped up to the height of the basket. Slam.

The Knicks came upcourt and put the ball in Dunk's hands. Elwood and I swarmed him. He faked a move, pivoted, then faked a pass, which shook Elwood for half a second. Half a second was all Dunk needed: he went up.

But I got my hand around the ball, and stuffed his shot backwards, out of his hands. It bounced upcourt, to Early, who was alone.

Slam.

The Knicks came back up, and McFront hit from outside. We took it back up and this time Elwood faked to Early and twisted inside himself for a pretty backwards layup. 6–2, Visitors.

Otis brought it up for the Knicks, and flipped it to Flynnan, inside. I went up and matched his jump, forced him to dump it off or be stuffed. He looked for help, didn't find any, and Elwood took the ball away from him. Early was waiting upcourt, like a puppy dog. 8–2.

So it went for the first half. We kept Dunk frustrated with our hectoring defense, and I took my game straight to Flynnan, however bruising. McFront's hand wasn't as hot as the night before. Elwood was hyperkinetic on defense.

And on offense, we were making Early look like the star the fans back in Florida had always hoped he would be. All he had was a handful of one-on-one moves, but if you kept him from having to think about anything but the basket, he was sensational.

We ended the half with a 22-point lead. The Knicks nibbled away in the second half, Otis shining like the Otis of old for a few minutes, but it was our night. We dug in on defense and finished fourteen points up. The crowd drained out of the Garden in silence. We were taking the series back to Florida tied at a game apiece. There were two games on our homecourt, then back to New York.

Unless somebody won two in a row.

For the third game the Knicks just looked tired. They weren't adjusting to our defensive pressure. Vanilla Dunk was wearing his cynical sneer, but you could see it drove him crazy not to be able to cut loose. The Miami crowd gave Flynnan, their ex-hero, a hard time, and he responded by getting sheepish—for the first time I felt I could actually push him around a little.

This one was Early's game. He played to the crowd, and the slams just kept getting showier. Elwood poured in a few himself, but Early was the star that night. We led all the way, and the game was over by the third quarter. Both teams pulled their regulars and started thinking about the next game.

Elwood was glowing on the bench. We all were. We

had a chance to take it from them. They had to beat us tomorrow to even stay alive. This was supposed to be their year of destiny, the Vanilla Dunk Victory Tour, and we had them down 2–1. The wild card team.

Flynnan woke up. Dunk was still moribund, but Flynnan woke up; I knew because he started punishing me. I was taking down some rebounds, but I was paying in flesh. I looked for help, but who was going to help me? That's the horror of the center: there's just two of you seven-foot monsters out there, and you're enemies. If the other guy's a little bigger and meaner, who's going to tell him to leave you alone? Some shrimpy 6'5" guard? The Tokyo army? The ref? Your mother?

This one wasn't a game. It was a trench battle. Elwood and I were working together, stripping balls away, bottling up the middle, but there was no communication between us. Just sweat and grunts. We had to keep our eyes peeled or we'd be flattened. McFront and Dunk were both fighting to open the lanes, throwing elbows, double-faking to make sure we got our faces in the way. Where were the whistles? I'm sure the Knicks were asking the same question at their end. The refs were letting us duke it out.

It was Knicks 34, Heat 30 late in the second quarter: a defensive struggle. We'd forced the Knicks into our game, and they were playing it. Every time Early touched the ball he was mobbed. He'd dump it back out and our guards would chuck it up from the outside and hope for the best. Most of our points belonged to Elwood, who was scoring by grabbing rebounds and muscling back up for the layup.

We were holding on until two minutes before the half, when Dunk broke loose for a couple in a row, and we went to the lockers down eight points.

Elwood stood to one side, a wild look in his eyes. He wasn't playing coach anymore; he was too far inside himself. He and Dunk had been in each other's faces every minute of the first half, and I could feel the hate burning off Elwood's skin, like gasoline vapor. I could almost imagine that Elwood would rather lose this one and take it back to New York, just to maximize his crazed masochistic war with Dunk, just to push it to the very edge.

I personally had a strong preference for ending it here.

Coach Wilder, seeing that Elwood wasn't receiving, looked over at me. I shrugged. The rest of the team milled nervously, waiting for someone to break the silence.

"Okay boys," said Coach Wilder courageously. "Let this get away and it's just another tied series going back to New York. That's handing it to them."

No one spoke. Elwood's foot was tapping out accompaniment to some internal rhythm.

"You're only eight points back," said the coach. "Just keep tying them up on defense. They'll turn it over when they get tired."

With his voice trailing away, he sounded like he didn't believe himself. I felt like patting him on the head and sending him to the showers. The fact was it was Elwood's team now, and Elwood didn't give halftime pep talks. We would all have to feed off his energy on the floor; it would happen there or it wouldn't happen at all.

We drifted apart, and what seemed like seconds later we were back on the court. The ball was ours; Elwood hit from midway out and we fell back on defense. We stuck to our one plan, of course: I caged Vanilla Dunk with my long arms, and Elwood harassed the ball from underneath. This time the gamble worked, and we forced a bad pass, which one of our guards picked up. He found Early and Early found the net. We'd closed the gap to four points.

And that's where it stayed. Everyone gritted their teeth and went back to the trenches; even Vanilla Dunk and Early were playing defense. Both sides would have fouled out if the refs hadn't been squelching the whistle. We forced turnovers, then turned it over ourselves, rolled our eyes, and fell back for defense again. Elwood was a maniac on rebounds, but he'd pass it up to Early and Early would disappear in a cloud of Knick uniforms. Otis stripped the ball from him with two seconds left in the third quarter and chucked up an improbable three-point shot from midcourt which only hit net, putting them up seven points as the buzzer for the fourth sounded.

At the start of the fourth Elwood began trying to do it all, to outrebound everybody at *both* ends of the court, to steal the ball, pass it to Early, then run up and set a pick for Early and rebound Early's shot if he missed. I watched in amazement, near total exhaustion myself just from our frantic play on the defensive end. In frustration with the Knicks' defensive adjustments he started going up himself, with his usual too-powerful stuff moves, scoring some points but committing fouls the refs couldn't ignore. Still, he bulled us to three points back, then doubled over with a leg cramp.

Coach Wilder called a time out. Elwood limped back to the bench.

"Okay, Elwood, you got us close. Now you better sit."

"Uh-uh," said Elwood. "I'm stayin' in. Listen, Early—"

Early leaned in, his eyes wide.

"You gotta figure out one new trick, 'cause they're bumping you off, man."

"What?" said Early in his high, frightened voice.

"Pass off when you go up now. Don't shoot. Find the big man here." Elwood jerked his thumb at me. "He's big and white, you can't miss him, man. Just throw it up to him every time you get a clean line."

"Elwood," I began to complain, "I'm not like you. I can't go back and forth. I won't make it back on defense if I'm up fighting with Flynnan under their basket."

"Don't go up under their basket," he said. "Shoot from wherever you are when you get the ball, man."

"What?"

"I seen your jumpshot, Lassner. Just shoot."

The time out was over. Elwood hobbled out, massaging his own thigh, and we took the ball up. We fed it in to Early and he drew three men. He spun out and five hands went up between him and the basket.

He didn't try and shoot over the hands. Instead he

turned and lobbed a clumsy pass high in the air to me, halfway back to our end of the court.

"Shoot!" hissed Elwood.

I tossed it up, not even noticing which side of the three-point line I was on. It went in.

I panted a thank-you prayer and zeroed in on the ball, which was in Flynnan's hands. I threw myself in his path and forced him to give it up, miraculously avoiding destruction in the process. Elwood followed the ball out to Vanilla Dunk, who pumped, pivoted, pumped, head-faked, shrugged, anything to try to get out of Elwood's cage. He lifted the ball up and I batted it out of bounds.

Elwood stole the inbound pass and scored on a solo drive for a layup.

The Knicks brought it up and Otis, looking frustrated with Dunk, shot from outside. He missed. Elwood directed the ball to Early, who drove to the basket and was surrounded there. He threw it out to me where I stood at the top of the key. "Shoot!" said Elwood again. The ball floated up out of my hands, and hit.

Tie game, four minutes left.

Elwood got too excited and fouled McFront on the next possession. McFront, ever-solid, hit both from the line, putting the Knicks up two. Elwood brought the ball up to midcourt then passed it directly to me, and nodded.

Swish. My jumpshot was on. Practice, I guess.

We traded turnovers again, and then the Knicks called time-out with just over two minutes left. Their season was getting very, very small. We only went halfway to the bench and then just hovered there, waiting for the

Knicks to come back out. There wasn't anything to say. We were too pumped up to huddle and trade homilies. Too much in the zone.

The Knicks brought it up and Flynnan staked out prime real estate under the net. I sighed and went in to try and box him out. He got the ball and I went up with him, tipped the shot away. Elwood took it and charged upcourt, slamming it home at the other end.

Since he was all the way up there anyway he decided to steal the inbound pass and do it again, and we suddenly had a four-point lead.

But Elwood was tired, and at the wrong end of the floor. They sent Vanilla Dunk up. I tried to stop him alone; we both jumped. I landed what seemed like a couple of years before he did. His jam was a poster-shot, I heard later. I sure didn't see it.

We came up again and sent Early in to try and answer. He got caught in traffic and bailed it out to me, and I shot from where I stood all alone, in three-point territory.

That made four in a row for me, and a five-point lead for the team.

They answered with a quick basket. So quick that I glanced at the clock; we were in a position to run the clock out. I brought it up slow, dribbling with my big body curled protectively around the ball.

"Nobody foul!" I heard Coach Wilder yell from the sidelines. Thanks, Coach. I passed it to Elwood. He passed it to one of our guards, who passed it back to me. Flynnan lunged for the ball, and I passed it away again. It got passed around the circuit, everybody touching it except Early, who wouldn't have known what to do with it. He only existed in two dimensions: up and down. Time was beyond him.

The ball came back to me with a two seconds on the shot clock. What the hell, I thought, and chucked it up. Swish.

We'd won. Five points up with 16 seconds. No way for them to come back. The Knicks milked it, of course, using two time-outs, scoring once, but two commercials later we got official confirmation. When the final buzzer sounded, we had a nice healthy three-point edge.

The locker room was mayhem. All the Disney executive people I'd managed never to meet wanted to shake my hand. The media swarmed, media-like. Some beer company exec gave Early Natt an award for series MVP and they stuck a mike in his face and Early just grinned and made this sort of bubbling sound with his lips, ignoring the questions. Another bunch of TV people isolated me and Elwood by our lockers, and I readied myself to do the talking once again.

"Well, Elwood, care to break your media silence for once?"

Elwood paused, then grinned. "Sure, asshole, let's break some silence. What you wanna know?"

The reporter clung to his pasted-on smile. "Uh, you were a real leader out there, Elwood. Some would say the MVP belongs to you. You took an unconventional mix of talents and made them work together—"

Elwood stuck his big finger against the reporter's chest. "You wanna know who the star of this team is?"

"Uh—"

"This dude here, man. He's taught himself to play without sampling, man, 'cause the skills they gave him sucked, and he didn't even tell anybody. Me, Early, Vanilla Fucking Dunk, all them other dudes are playing with exosuits, but not my man Lassner, man. He's a defensive star. He can hang with the exosuits, man, and that's a rare thing." He laughed. "He's also got this funny jumpshot ain't too bad. Big white elbows stickin' out all over the place, but it ain't too bad. No suit for that either."

They turned to me. I nodded and shrugged and looked back to Elwood.

"How does it feel beating Michael Jordan?" The question was directed at either one of us, but Elwood picked it up again.

"Didn't beat Michael Jordan," he said angrily. "Beat Vanilla Dunk. If that was Jordan we wouldn't have beat him."

"What's going to become of your feud?"

Elwood's face went through a quick series of expressions; angry, then sarcastic, then sealed-up, like he wasn't going to talk anymore. Then he went past that, smiling at himself for a minute before answering the question.

What came out was a strangely heartfelt jumble of sports clichés. I don't mean to be insulting when I say that I don't think I ever saw Elwood speak from a deeper place within himself than at that moment. I really do think he was the last modernist in a sport gone completely postmodern.

"Ain't no feud. Alan Gornan is a rookie, man, and you got to give him time to put it together. I was honored to play alongside the man in New York and I'm honored to face him now. I hope we meet again—after the Heat wins this championship, that is. I'm sure he'll grow into the suit. Ain't no feud. I plan to beat the man every time I can, but when he beats me it ain't gonna be Michael Jordan then, neither, man. It's gonna be Gornan, or Dunk or whatever he wants to call his ass, and when he does I'll shake the dude's hand. Here, you oughta ask the big white dufus some questions now."

That should be the end of the story, but it isn't. Elwood and I were in a bar two hours later when the sports channel switched to a live broadcast of Vanilla Dunk's press conference, his last with the big Knicks logo on the wall behind him.

His agent spoke first. "Mr. Gornan has reached an agreement with United Artists Tokyo, regarding his motion picture and recording career—"

"What about the Knicks?"

"UA Tokyo has purchased Mr. Gornan's contract from Gulf and Western. This is a binding, five-year agreement which guarantees Mr. Gornan eight million a year before box-office—"

"I wanted to wait till the end of the season to make this announcement," said Dunk. "Didn't think it would come this quick, but hey—" he paused to sneer "—that's the way it goes. Look out America, we're gonna make some movies!"

"Dunk—what about basketball?"

He smirked. "That's a little rough for me, y'know? Gotta stay pretty." He rubbed his face exaggeratedly. "You'll see plenty of action on the screen, anyway. Might even dunk a few." He winked.

Elwood and I sat watching, silently transfixed. The implications sank in gradually. The Jordan skills were gone; league rules stated that they were retired with the player. The occasion that Elwood had so slowly and painfully risen to had vanished, been whisked away, in an instant.

"Tell us about the films," said a reporter.

"Ahh, we're still working out my character. Called Vanilla Dunk, of course. Gonna do some fightin', some rappin', some other stuff. Not like anything you've ever seen before, so you'll just have to wait."

"The contract includes album and video production," added the agent. "You'll be seeing Vanilla Dunk on the charts as well as on the screen."

"Your whole sports career is over, then? No championships?"

He snorted. "This is bigger than a sports career, my friend. *I'm* bigger. Besides, sports is just entertainment. I'm still in the *entertainment* business."

"Your decision anything to do with Elwood Fossett?"

He cocked his head. "Who?"

I turned away from the television. I started to speak,

but stopped when I saw Elwood's expression, which was completely hollow.

And that *is* the end of the story.

I'd like to say we went on to win the championship, but life doesn't work that way. The Hyundai Celtics beat us in the next round of the playoffs. They were completely ready for our trapping defense, and we were lucky to win one game. Elwood faded in and out, tantalizingly brilliant and then godawful in the space of five minutes. The Celtics went on to lose to the Coors Suns in the final.

I myself did win a ring, later, after I was traded to the Lakers. That led indirectly to a fancy Hollywood party where I got to drunkenly tell Alan Gornan what I thought of him. I garbled my lines, but it was still pretty satisfying.

Elwood I mostly lost touch with after my trade. We partied whenever the Lakers went to Miami, and when the Heat came to L.A. I had him over for dinner with my second wife—an awkward scene, but we played it a few times.

When I think about what happened with him and Vanilla Dunk, I always come around to the same question. Assuming that it's right to view the whole episode as a personal battle between the two of them—who won? Sometimes I drive myself crazy with it. I mean, who came out on top, really?

Other times I conclude that there's something really pretty fundamentally stupid about the question.

LIGHT AND THE SUFFERER

My brother showed me the gun. I'd never seen one up close before. He kept it in a knapsack under his bed at the Y. He held it out and I looked at the black metal.

"You want me to hold it?" I said.

"What, at the place?"

"No, I mean now. I mean, do you want me to touch it or something. Now. I mean like, get comfortable with it." He stared.

"Don't look at me like I'm crazy. What do you want me to do with the gun?"

"Nothing. I'm just showing it to you, like 'Look, I got it.' Like, 'Here's the gun.' "

My brother was two years younger than me. I was just back from dropping out of my junior year of college, at

Santa Cruz, and was living, quite unhappily, at my parents' tiny new house in Plainview, Long Island.

Our parents, Jimmy and Marilla, had kicked Don out for the final time while I was away at school. They hadn't heard from him for almost a year. I went and hung out at Washington Square and found him within a few hours.

"Okay," I said. "Right. Nice gun."

"Don't get freaked."

"I'm not freaked, Don." I paused.

"Then let's go, right?"

"Let's go, Don," I said, and I swear I almost added: *This is good, we're brothers, we still do things together.* I almost said: *See, Don.*

Our parents named my brother Donovan because all their friends had already named their kids Dylan, I guess. It wasn't important to Don. His only chance of ever hearing Donovan was if MC Death sampled "Season of the Witch" or "Hurdy Gurdy Man" in a rap.

Myself being a bit older, I knew those songs in their original versions, not from the radio, of course, but from the days when our parents still played their records.

I followed my brother downstairs. It was night. We walked the short distance to Washington Square Park but stopped half a block away. I stopped.

"What?" said Don.

"Nothing. Should we call the airport? Find out—"

"Like you said, there's always gonna be a plane, Paul."

We went into the park, through the evening throngs, the chessplayers and skatebladers, and I stood on the pathway waiting, shrugging off offers of nickel bags, while Don found his two friends, the ones who were supposed to kill him for stealing drugs.

"—gotta *talk* to you."

"Randall sick of yo shit, Light."

"Can we go up to your apartment, Kaz? Please?"

Don walked them towards me. A fat black man with a gigantic knitted hat: Kaz. Another black man, smaller in every way, with a little beard, and wearing a weirdly glossy, puffed-out gold coat: Drey.

Nobody my brother knew had a regular name. And they all called him "Light," for his being white, I suppose.

"The fuck is this?" said Drey, looking at me.

"Paul," Don mumbled.

"Looks like yo fuckin' brother, man."

"All us white dudes look like brothers to you, nigger."

Drey grinned, then tightened his mouth, as though remembering that he was supposed to be angry at Don.

We walked out of the park, east on Third Street. All the way Kaz mumbled at Don: "Can't believe you, man; you fuckin' come around here; you took Randall; can't believe you, man; fuck you think you doin'; look at you stupid face; you think you talk you way out of this; I should be doin' you; fuckin' crackhead; can't believe you man." Et cetera.

And Don just kept saying, every thirty seconds or so: "Shut up, Kaz, man." Or: "Gimme a minute, man."

We went into a door beside a storefront on First Avenue, and up a flight of stairs. Don and I ahead of Kaz and Drey, through the dark.

Kaz stepped around and let us in, and I looked down and saw Don take the gun out of his coat. Don wanted to pull it coming in; he'd said he knew that Kaz kept guns in the house. But not on his person. That was crucial.

We all got inside and Kaz closed the door, and Don turned around. "You're dead," said the fat black man the minute he saw the gun.

The place was just about empty: crumbling walls, a bed. And a cheap safe, nailed instead of bolted to the floor, price tag still showing. A safe house, literally. Crash and stash, as Don would say.

Don waved the gun between Kaz and Drey. "You're dead," said Kaz again. Drey said: "Shit."

"Shut up. Paul, take their shit. Clean Drey up, then Kaz. Find the keys on Kaz."

I stepped up to play my part. Keys on Kaz. I put my hand on Drey, who hissed: "Motherfucker." It turned out the weird shiny gold coat was on inside out; the gold was the *lining* of a rabbit-fur fake leopard. Strange. I ran my hands through the fur, searching out Drey's pockets.

I found a wad, singles on the outside, which I pocketed. Then an Exacto knife, which I tossed on the floor behind me, at Don's feet. He kicked it to the wall.

When I turned to Kaz he slapped my hands away, a strangely girlish move.

"You a chump, Light," he said, ignoring me. "Randall shoulda killed your ass already. He gonna now."

"We're all Randall's chumps, Kaz, man. Now I'm taking and you can tell Randall what you want."

"I ain't no chump, man, Light. You the chump. Randall

tried to treat you right. You fuckin' smokehead. You could be playing with the cash like me, like Randall says. 'Staid you *usin'*." He hurled the word like it was the only real insult he knew.

It was true. Don had used the drugs he was supposed to deal for Randall.

"Playing with the cash now, Kaz."

I reached for Kaz's pockets again, and again he slapped me away. "You dead, brother."

Don stepped up and clapped Kaz's temple with the side of the gun.

"Ain't no cash, Light, man," Kaz whimpered. He looked down. "Ain't sold it yet, you stupid fuck."

"Open the safe."

"What did you mean 'You dead, *brother*,'?" I asked. "Don told you I'm not his brother. Or are you just using that as an expression?"

Kaz just shook his head and got out the key to the safe. Drey said: "Fuckin' idiot."

Inside the safe was all bottles. Crack. Nothing else. Two big plastic bags full of ten- and five-dollar bottles. I'd never seen that much in one place. Don had, of course; specifically, when Kaz and Randall brought him up here to entrust him with a load of bottles to sell.

That time there had also been a large supply of cash, which was what we were here supposedly to steal.

"Fuck you expected?" said Drey.

"You dead," said Kaz.

Don didn't hesitate. He took the two bags of bottles and quickly felt behind them, but there was nothing else in the safe. He slammed the door shut and pushed the gun up at Kaz's face again. "Your roll, Kaz."

"You a fuckin' chump." Kaz got out his money, another fat wad with ones on the outside. Don took it and stuffed it in his pocket. Then he shook the two bags of bottles into the two big side pockets of his parka, tossing the plastic bags aside when they were empty.

"Fuck you gonna do?" said Drey. "Sell the shit? Randall gun you down."

"Gimme the keys," said Don to Kaz. "Sit down. Both of you."

"Shit."

Don waved the gun some more, and Kaz and Drey sat down on the floor. Don pushed me back out into the hallway ahead of him, then shut the door and locked it from the outside with Kaz's key.

That was when we saw the Sufferer. It was sitting on the landing of the stairway above us, looking down. On its haunches in the dark it looked just like a giant panther, eyes shining.

I assumed it was waiting for someone else. I'd only seen the aliens twice before, each time trailing after somebody in trouble. That was what they liked to do.

Don didn't even glance at it. I guess leading his lifestyle, he passed them pretty often. He put the gun in his belt and ran downstairs, and I followed him. The Sufferer padded down after us.

Don hailed a cab on First Avenue. "La Guardia," he said, leaning in the window.

"Manhattan only," said the cabbie. Don pulled out

Kaz's money and began peeling off ones. I looked behind us, thinking of Kaz and Drey and the unlocated guns in the apartment. Had Don really locked them in? Even if he had, they could shoot us from the front windows, or off the fire escape, while we haggled with the cabbie.

I saw the Sufferer push out of the door and settle on the sidewalk to watch us.

"Fifteen dollars before the fare," said Don. "C'mon."

The driver popped the locks, and Don and I scooted into the back, Don's coat-load of bottles clinking against the door.

"La Guardia," said Don again.

"Take the Manhattan Bridge," I said. "Canal Street."

"He knows where the Manhattan Bridge is, Paul."

"He said Manhattan only."

"You picking somebody up?" said the driver.

"Domestic departures," I said.

"What airline?"

"Uh, Pan Am."

"There is no more Pan Am," said the driver.

"Wow. Okay, uh, Delta?"

"Does it matter?" said Don.

"He has to take us *somewhere*," I explained patiently. Sometimes it seemed like Don and I grew up in separate universes. "The airport is big. Delta should have a lot of flights to California. We can start there, anyway."

The cab went down first to Canal and entered the funnel of traffic leading onto the bridge. I always mention the Manhattan Bridge because a lot of people just reflexively take the Brooklyn, though it isn't really faster or more convenient. People prefer the Brooklyn Bridge, I guess because it's prettier, but I like the way you can be driving alongside a *subway train* on the Manhattan Bridge.

So I looked out the window, and what I saw was the Sufferer, running alongside the cab, keeping time even when the traffic smoothed out and we accelerated across the empty middle of the bridge. It loped along right beside us, almost under my window. Our cabbie was going faster than the other cars, and when we passed one the Sufferer would drop back, trailing us, until the space beside my door was clear again.

Don was in his own world, leafing through the roll he'd stolen and counting the bottles in his pockets by feel. I didn't draw his attention to the Sufferer. The cabbie hadn't noticed either.

"You can't take the gun on the plane," I said to Don, quietly.

"Big news," said Don sarcastically.

"It's okay," I said, responding to his annoyance as some kind of plea for reassurance, as I always had. "We won't need it in Cali."

"Yeah," he said dreamily.

"We're really going," I said. "Things'll be different there." I felt it slipping away, the hold my proposal had had on him an hour ago.

"What," he snorted. "Nobody has guns in California?"

"You're going to live different, there." I looked up to see if the cabbie was listening. "So why don't you leave the gun here in the cab, okay, Don? Just push it under the seat. Because it's crazy going into the airport with it. Crazy enough just carrying all the drugs."

"I'll put it in a locker. Just in case."

"What? In case of what?"

We pulled off onto the BQE and headed for the airport. I checked the window. There was the Sufferer, rushing along with us, leaping potholes.

"What?" said Don, noticing.

"One of those aliens."

"The one from Kaz's?"

I shrugged—a lie, since I knew. "How much money did you get from Kaz?" I said, trying to change the subject.

"Four hundred. Chump change from a chump. Fuck is it doing out there?" He leaned over me to look out the window.

"Hey," said the cabbie. "You got a Sufferer."

"Just drive," said Don.

"I don't want trouble. Why's it following you?"

"It's not following anyone," I said. "Anyway, they don't cause trouble. They *prevent* it. They keep people out of trouble."

"Right. So if they follow you, you must be trouble."

Don took the gun out of his belt, but kept it below the level of the Plexiglas barrier above the seat. I tried to scowl at him, but he ignored me.

"You don't like it, why don't you try to kill it with the car?" he said to the driver in a low, insinuating voice.

"You're crazy."

"Right. So just take us to the airport and shut up." He looked at me. "How much you get?"

"Two hundred and fifty dollars. Sidekick change from a sidekick." The joke was out before I thought to wonder: but who's the sidekick *here?* It was possibly a very important question.

Don snorted. "Barely afford the tickets." He put the gun back into his belt.

The Sufferer accompanied us through the maze of exits and into the roundabout of the airport. We pulled up in front of Delta. Don paid the cabfare and rolled off twenty extra, then paused, and rolled off another twenty. "Pull up there and wait ten minutes," he said.

"Don, we're getting on a plane. Besides, even if we weren't, it isn't hard to catch a cab at the *airport.*"

"Just in case. Me and this dude got an understanding. Right, man?" He cocked his head at the driver.

The cabbie shrugged, then smiled. "Sure. I'll wait."

I sighed. Don was always turning passersby into accomplices. Even when it didn't mean anything. It was a kind of compulsive seduction, like *Women Who Love Too Much.*

"You're getting me worried, Don. We're flying out of here, right?"

"Relax. We're at the airport, right? Just wait a minute." He put his mouth at the driver's little money window. "Pull up over there, man. We'll walk back, we don't have bags or anything. Just get out of the light, okay?"

We pulled past the terminal entrance, into a dead zone

of baggage carts. The Sufferer trotted alongside, on the pedestrian ramp, weaving around the businessmen and tourists leaking out of the terminal.

Don rolled his window down a couple of inches, then got out a glass pipe and shook out the contents of a five-dollar vial into the bowl.

"Donnie."

"Hey, not in the cab!"

"Minute, man." He flicked his lighter and the little rocks flared blue and pink and disappeared. So practiced, so fast.

The Sufferer leaned close in to my window and watched. When Don noticed he said: "Open your door and whack that fuckin' thing in the face."

"Don't smoke that crap in my cab," said the driver.

"Okay, okay," said Don, palming the pipe away. He pointed a finger at the cabbie. "You'll wait, right?"

"I'll wait, but don't do that in my cab."

"Let's go, Don."

"Okay."

I opened my door and the Sufferer stepped aside to let us pass. We got out onto the walkway. Don stopped and shook his head, straightened his parka, which was burdened with the loaded pockets, and pushed the gun out of sight under his sweatshirt. We walked up to the entrance. The doors were operated by electric eye, and they slid open for us, then stayed open as the Sufferer followed.

Don and I both instinctively hurried into a mass of people, but no crowd could have been big enough to keep it from being obvious who the alien was with. A baggage guy stood and watched, his eyes going from the Sufferer to us and back again. He could as easily have been airport security—maybe he was.

"We've got a problem here, Don," I said.

"Yeah." He made a mugging face, but didn't meet my eye.

"Let's—here, you've gotta find a place for the gun, anyway." I steered him out of the flow near the ticket agents, to a relatively empty stretch of terminal: newspaper vending machines, hotel phones, and a shoeshine booth. I didn't see any lockers, though.

The Sufferer sat and cocked its head at us, waiting.

"What do your friends do when this happens?"

"What?" said Don sarcastically. "You mean when some big black animal from space follows them to the airport after an armed robbery?"

"When these things—when one of these things shows up, Don. I mean, it must happen to people you know."

"One dude, Rolando. Thing started trailing him. Rolando fell in love, like him and the thing fucking eloped. Last I saw Rolando. Just that one dude, though."

As people passed us they'd stare first at the Sufferer, then follow its gaze to us.

"Ironic," I said. "It wants to help you, right? At least, I assume so. But it doesn't know that you're planning to go to California to dry out. It probably doesn't even understand how airports work, how it's fucking this up for you. How important it is for you to leave the city."

I was babbling. I couldn't help myself. I wanted to hear

him say *Yes, I mean to get on a plane and change my life in California, Paul. You had a good idea.* Instead of his grunting, distracted assent. It didn't help that his big last farewell heist had netted pockets full of crack instead of cash.

And I didn't for the life of me know what to do with the Sufferer.

"It doesn't want to help me," Don said.

"Yeah, well, in this case, anyway, it isn't. We're already gonna fit a bad profile, buying tickets at the last minute with cash. If there's a Sufferer trailing around they'll search us for sure."

"They let it on the plane?"

"I don't think so. I mean, how could they? So all we have to do is dump the drugs *and* the gun, then they can search us all they want, doesn't matter, we're gone."

"Uh-uh."

"What?"

"I'm on parole, Paul. Breaking parole to go. I can't get checked out."

"What? You never told me you were in prison!"

"Shut up, Paul. *Sentenced* to parole, one year. Nothing, man."

"For what?"

"*Nothing,* man. Now shut up. What, you think I wasn't breaking the *law?*"

"Okay, okay, but listen, we just have to get on a plane. We have to try. So stash the stuff—"

"Nah. This is no good. I got an idea." He headed back to the terminal exits.

"Don!"

The Sufferer and I followed him out. He jogged back to the cab, hands protectively over the flaps of his coat pockets. We got back in and Don said: "Get us out of here."

"Back."

"Yeah, that direction. But get off the fuckin' freeway."

"Have to be on the freeway—"

"Yeah, yeah, I mean as soon as you can."

I actually thought we'd lost the Sufferer when we exited into a blasted neighborhood of boarded-up and gutted storefronts, but by the time we'd driven, at Don's request, back under the freeway and into a dark, empty cobblestone lot, the alien came loping up behind us.

The freeway roared above us, but the nearby streets were vacant. The people in the cars might as well have been in flying saucers, whistling past stragglers in the desert.

Don gave the cabbie another ten and said: "Get lost for fifteen minutes. Leave us here and circle around, find yourself a cup of coffee or something." The cabbie and I exchanged a look that said *Coffee? Here?* but Don was already out of the cab.

I got out and the cab rumbled away over the cobblestones and around a corner. The Sufferer didn't glance at it, just sat like an obedient dog and watched us.

Don ignored it, or pretended to, and walked over and took a seat on the fender of a wrecked truck. It was getting cold. I thought, stupidly, about the meal we would have been eating, about the movie we would have been watching, on the plane.

Don took out the pipe again and loaded it with a rock of crack. The wind bent the blue column of flame from his lighter one way, then Don sucked it the other, into the pipe. The Sufferer hurried up like a hunting cat to where Don sat. I stepped back.

Don curled his shoulder protectively around the pipe and glared back at the alien. "Fuck *you* want?"

The Sufferer nudged at his elbow with its hand-like paw.

"Leave me the fuck alone."

"Don, what are you doing? It can't help it. What are you trying to do, bait it?"

Don ignored me. He flicked his lighter again, tried to get a hit. The Sufferer jogged his elbow. Don kicked at it. The alien danced back easily out of the way, like a boxer, then stepped back in, trying to square its face with Don's, trying to look him in the eye.

Don kicked out again, brushing the Sufferer back, then pocketed the pipe and drew out his gun.

The alien cocked his head.

"Hey, Don—"

Don fired the gun straight into the Sufferer's chest, and the alien jumped back and fell onto the cobblestones, then got back on its feet and walked in a little circle, shaking its head, blinking its eyes.

Don said: "Ow, fuck, I think I sprained my arm."

"How? What happened?"

"The gun, man. It bucked back on me. Shit."

"You can't kill it, Don. Everybody knows that. The shots'll just bring the police."

Don looked at me. His expression was dazed and cynical at the same time. "I just wanted to give it a piece of my fuckin' mind, okay, Paul?"

"Okay, Don. Now what about going back to the airport?"

"Nah. We gotta lose this thing."

The Sufferer circled back around to where Don sat still holding the gun, kneading his injured forearm with his free hand. The alien sat up like a perky cat and tapped at Don's jacket pocket, rattling the load of bottles.

"I guess it just wants to see you get clean, Don. If you get rid of the bottles it'll leave us alone and we can fly to California."

"You believe that shit, Paul? Where'd you read that, *Newsweek?*"

"What?"

"That this thing is like some kind of vice cop? That it wants me to kick?"

"Isn't that the idea?" The stuff I'd read about them wasn't clear on much except that they followed users around, actually.

"Yeah? Watch this." Don clicked the safety on the gun and handed it to me, then got out his pipe and loaded it. He braised the rock with flame from the lighter, but this time when he got it glowing he turned it around and offered it to the Sufferer. The alien grasped the pipe in its dexterous paw and stuck the end in its mouth and toked.

"I think I read about that," I said, lying. "It's like an empathy thing. They want to earn your trust."

Don just smirked at me, then snatched his pipe away from the Sufferer, who didn't protest.

"I'm cold," I said. "You think that cab is coming back?"

"Fuck yes," said Don. "You kidding? We're a fucking gold mine." He shook out another rock.

The Sufferer and I both watched. Suddenly I wanted some. I'd done a lot of uncooked coke with some of my Upper West Side friends the last year of high school, but I'd only smoked rock twice before, with Don each time.

"Give me a hit, Don," I said.

He loaded the pipe and handed it and the lighter to me, ungrudgingly.

I drew in a hit, and felt the crazy rush of the crack hit me. Like snorting a line of coke while plummeting over the summit of a roller coaster.

The Sufferer opened its weird, toothless black mouth and leaned towards me, obviously wanting another hit.

"Maybe the idea is to help run through your stash," I said. "Help use up your stuff, keep you from O.D.ing. Because their bodies can take it, like the bullets. Doesn't hurt them."

"Maybe they're just fucking crackheads, Paul."

The cab's reappearance startled me, the sound of its approach masked by the rush of cars overhead. And of course, I was thinking of cops.

Don took his gun back, jammed it in his waistband, and we got into the back. Don held the door open for the Sufferer. "Might as well get it off the freeway," he said. "Gonna be with us next place we go either way." The Sufferer didn't hesitate to clamber in over our feet and settle down on the floor of the back, pretty much filling the space.

"Okay, but we need a plan, Donnie." I heard myself beginning to whine.

"Where to?" said the cabbie.

"Back to Manhattan," said Don. "East, uh, 83rd and, uh, Park." He turned to me. "Chick I know."

"You can't go back to the city."

"Manhattan is a big place, Paul. Far as Randall and Kaz is concerned, 83rd Street might as well be California."

"Don't talk to me about California. Like you know something about California."

"Paul, man, I didn't say shit about California. I'm just saying we can hide out uptown, figure some shit out, okay? Take care of the Crackhead from Space here, right?"

"Uptown. New York is a world to you, you don't know anything but uptown or downtown or Brooklyn. California's a whole other place, Donnie, you can't imagine. It'll be *different*. The things you're dealing with here, they don't have to be—you don't have to have these *issues*, Donnie. Randall, uptown, whatever."

"Okay, Paul. But I just wanna take care of two things, okay, and then we'll go, let's just get rid of the Creature and just move this stuff to some people I know, okay? Get cash for this product, then we'll go."

The Sufferer shifted, stepping on my foot, and looked up at us.

"Okay." I was defeated, by the two of them. It was like they were in collusion now. "Just don't talk about California like it's *Mars,* for God's sake. We're going there, you'll see how it is, and then you can tell me what you think. It'll blow your mind, Donnie, to see how different it can be."

"Yeah," he said, far away.

We were silent into Manhattan. At 83rd Street and Park Avenue Don paid the cab fare, and we got out. The three of us. The street was full of cars, mainly cabs, actually—nobody up here owned a car—but the sidewalk was dead, except for doormen. In a way Don was right about New York. This was another place. The thought of him selling crack on Park Avenue gave me a quick laugh.

Don led us into a brightly lit foyer. "Annette Sweeney," he told the doorman.

The doorman eyed the Sufferer. "Is she expecting visitors?"

"Tell her it's Light."

We went up to the ninth floor and found Annette Sweeney's door. Annette Sweeney lived well—I knew that before we even got inside.

She opened the door before we could knock. "You can't just always come up here, Light."

"Annette, chill out. I got some stuff for you. If it's not a good time—"

Annette baited easily. Don's hook gave me an idea what they had in common. "No, Light, I'm just saying why don't you call? Why don't you *ever* call me? What do you have?"

"Just some stuff." He stepped in. "This my brother."

"Hi." She was staring at the Sufferer. "Light, look."

"I know. Forget it."

I stepped in, and so did the Sufferer. Like it owned the place.

"What do you mean? When did this happen?"

"Shut up, forget it. It's a temporary thing."

"What did you do?"

Don went past her, left the rest of us in the doorway, and flopped on her couch. The apartment was big and spare, the architectural detail as lush as the outside of the building, the furniture modern, all aluminum and glass.

"I haven't seen you for weeks, Annette. What did I do? I did a lot of shit, you want to know it all? I come here and you ask me questions?"

Annette fazed easily. She tilted her head so that her hair fell, then brushed it away and pursed her lips and said: "*Sorry*, Light." I saw a rich girl who thought that when she hung out with my brother she was slumming. And I saw my brother twisting her incredible need around his fingers, and hated them both for a second.

Then she turned to me and smiled weakly and said: "Hi. I'm Annette . . . I didn't know Light had a brother," and I felt immediately guilty for judging. It didn't hurt that she was beautiful, really striking, with black hair and big black eyes.

I took her hand. The Sufferer pushed past us, brushing my hip, and leapt onto the couch beside Don. "Yeah, well, he does," I said. "I'm Paul."

"It's funny, 'cause my brother is staying with me right now. That's why I was so weird about Light just dropping by."

"You got a brother?" said Don, distractedly. He'd pulled all the little bottles out of his pockets and piled them on her rug. The Sufferer just sat upright on the couch and watched him.

"Yeah. He's out right now, but he might come back."

"That's cool," said Don. "We'll party."

"Um, Douglas might not really wanna . . . *Jesus*, Light."

"What?"

"Well, just—your new friend. And all that stuff."

"I guess the two kind of go together," I said.

"Very funny," said Don. "He's harmless, he's our—what, *mascot*. Like Tony the Tiger. Smoke rock—it's grrrreat!"

"Doesn't it freak you out?"

"Nah." Don chucked the Sufferer on the chin. "You can't believe all that shit you hear. It just wants to hang. That's all they want. Came from space to party with me. You should of seen it following the cab, though—it was like a video game."

Annette shook her head, grinning.

"Hey, Paul, come here for a minute," said Don, jumping up, nodding his head at the door to the bedroom.

"What?"

"Nothing. Lemme talk to you for a minute though."

We left Annette and the drugs and the Sufferer in the living room, and sat on the edge of the bed. "Don't talk about this California thing," Don said in a low voice. "Don't let Annette hear about us leaving because she'll fucking flip out if she hears I'm going away and I don't need that, okay?"

"Okay," I said, then: "Don?"

"What?"

"Maybe we should call Jimmy and Marilla. Let them know you're okay."

"They kicked me out. They don't care."

"Just because they couldn't let you live there anymore doesn't mean they don't worry about you. Just to let them know you're still *alive*—"

"Okay, but later, okay?" He had a distracted expression, one I was beginning to recognize: *I want a hit.*

"Okay."

Don tapped me on the back and we went back out. The Sufferer had the pipe, but Annette looked like she'd had possession of it recently enough. The room was filled with that sour ozone smell.

She didn't ask what we'd been talking about in private. Didn't even seem to wonder. In general, her self-esteem around my brother seemed kind of low.

"Here," said Don, plucking the pipe away from the alien. I knelt down on the carpet with them and accepted the offer. Between Don and Annette and the Sufferer it was seriously questionable whether any of the drugs would get sold—which was fine with me. Whether or not using up Don's supply was part of the alien's strategy— assuming the alien had a strategy—didn't matter. It could be my strategy.

Annette got up and found her cigarettes and brought one back lit, adding to the haze. Then she brushed her hair back and, seemingly emboldened by the cocaine and nicotine, began talking. "Really, though, Light, you should look out, with this thing hanging around you. I heard about how there are people who'll beat you up just because you've got one of these things following you around. It's a reactionary thing, like AIDS-bashing, you know, blaming the victim. Also won't the police, like, search you or something, hassle you, if they see it?"

"The police know me. They already hassle me. I don't mean shit to the police. Tony the Tiger doesn't change that."

"It's just weird, Light."

"Of course it's weird," said Don. "That's why we love it, right, Paul? It's from another dimension, it's fucking weird, it's science fiction." The Sufferer cocked its head at Don as if it was considering his words. Don raised his fists like a boxer. The Sufferer opened its mouth at him, a black O, and its ears, or what I was mistaking for its ears, wrinkled forward. Now that I could see it up close, it really didn't look so much like a cat. The face was really more human, like the sphinx with a toothless oc-topus mouth.

Don waved his hands in its face and said: "Dee-nee dee-nee, dee-nee dee-nee"—Twilight Zone Theme.

"Well, when's it going to leave you alone?" She took another rock of crack and stuffed it into the end of an unlit cigarette.

"I'm gonna lose it," he said.

"That's supposed to be pretty hard, Light. I mean, it's like an *obsession* for them."

"Would you stop quoting the, whatever, the Geraldo Rivera version, or wherever you got that crap? I said I'm gonna lose it. You can help. We can trap it in your bedroom and I'll cut out."

"I think it can hear you, Don," I said.

"That's so fucking stupid, man. It's from another planet."

Of course we all turned to look at it now. It stared back and then pawed at the pile of bottles on the carpet.

"Hey, cut it out," said Don. He reached out to push it away, then winced. "Fuck."

"What?"

"You think you could rub my arm? I sprained it or something." He reached under his sweatshirt and freed himself of the gun, dropping it with a clatter on a little table beside the couch.

"Uh, sure, Light," Annette said absently, goggling at the gun. She put her cigarette in her mouth and scooted up beside Don and took his arm in her lap. The Sufferer went on rattling the bottles.

"What about at the airport?" Don said. "You didn't think it could understand us then."

"I'm wrong, it was just a feeling."

"Why'd you have to say that? You creeped me the fuck out."

"Airport?" said Annette.

"Uh, that's where we had to go to get the stuff," I said, gesturing at the rug, taking up the burden of covering Don's slip out of guilt, out of habit.

"You scored at the *airport?*"

Don shrugged at her, and said: "Sure."

Annette lit the loaded cigarette. The rock hissed as it hit the flame. "What are you doing with all this?"

"Well, I really gotta sell some," said Don. "I was wondering if you wanted to call some of your friends. I don't wanna go downtown now."

"I don't know, Light." She looked at the Sufferer, who was still rattling at the vials. "Won't it narc on us?"

"Don't be stupid."

"Even if it doesn't, that's what everybody'll think if they see it here."

"Just set it up, okay? We can arrange something so they don't have to meet Tony the Tiger." He lit a rock and toked.

"Well, anyway, my brother is coming back tonight so I don't think you can deal out of my house, Light."

"What does that have to do with it? It's *your* house, right?"

"Well, I don't know. He's my *older* brother."

"Paul is my older fucking brother," Don said. "So what?"

Maybe Annette's older brother knows how to take care of his sibling, I thought. Like I obviously don't.

There was a sound of a key fumbling in a lock. "Speak of the devil," said Annette.

Douglas turned out to be quite a bit older than Annette, or at least the way he dressed and held himself made it seem that way. He came up to where we all were sprawled on the couch and the carpet and said, to me: "Are you Light?"

"No," said Don, "that's me."

Douglas's eyes played over the scene: the gun, the vials, the alien sitting like a giant snake-skinned cougar on the carpet.

He reached down and picked up the gun.

"Ann, why don't you go lock yourself in the bedroom," he said.

"*Doug*-las," she whined.

"Do it."

"Don't be a chump," said Don. "This is her place."

"Shut up. I know all about you. We're going to have a little talk. *Go*, Ann."

"I told you," Annette said to Don as she got up from the couch. "Uh, nice to meet you, Paul. Sorry."

As she slouched her way to the bedroom, the Sufferer jumped up and followed her. Douglas took a step back, startled. I watched the gun. Douglas handled it badly, but I was pretty sure the safety was still in place.

The Sufferer was suddenly, inexplicably agitated. It ran ahead of her into the bedroom, looked out the far window at the lights of the building across 83rd Street, and back at us.

"What's it doing?" said Doug angrily.

Don shrugged. Annette stood waiting at the doorway.

"Get it out of there," said Doug, gesturing with the gun.

"Hey, that's not my responsibility," said Don. "You're the dude who's taking charge."

The Sufferer wrinkled its ears forward and stared glumly at Don. Don glowered at Douglas.

"Here," I said. I went in and pushed at the Sufferer. Its flesh was like a dense black pudding, and it felt like it weighed about a thousand pounds. I tried to prod it towards the door, but it wouldn't budge. Annette came into the bedroom and tried to help me push, to no avail.

Don, his movements exaggerated and slow, put a rock of coke into the glass pipe and flicked his lighter enticingly. The Sufferer trotted forward, like it had read the script, and Annette and I almost fell on our faces.

Douglas didn't find it funny. "Get back out here," he said to me, and when I obliged he reached over and slammed the door shut with Annette inside. "Sit down," he told me, and I did it.

The Sufferer, of course, paid him no mind. It went past us all, into the kitchen.

"What's on your mind?" said Don drawlingly, lighting the pipe.

"I want you and your monster out of Annette's life, *Light*," said Douglas. "She's told me plenty about you."

"Why not? I'm her boyfriend."

"You're not her boyfriend," snarled Douglas. "You're her dealer. Only you're not even around enough to do a good job of that." From the kitchen came a crash of breaking glass. Douglas looked in, then turned back to Don. "You get Annette hooked and then she's gotta go out and find her own because you smoked up your whole shipment. You pathetic piece of human garbage."

"Fuck told you that shit?"

"What, is it a shock to find out that you're known, you sleazeball?"

Another crash from the kitchen, and then a sound like chimes: the Sufferer wading through the glass or ceramic it had broken.

"What's your—monster-thing doing?" said Douglas. I got the feeling that his castigating Don was the fulfillment of a long-standing fantasy, only the Sufferer wasn't part of the scenario.

"I told you, it's not my thing, I don't tell it what to do, man."

"Is that why you're trying to unload all this stuff on my sister—the monster won't let you use it anymore?"

Don just smirked. "The monster's 'using it' with me. I don't tell it what to do and it don't tell me what to do."

"It's following you because you're dead, you loser. You're smoking your life away—it's like your death angel."

"That's not right," I said. "It's nothing like that. It's an empathy thing, it's responding to the *life* in Don—"

"Yeah, right. The life. You people are walking corpses.

And I'll finish you off myself if you don't leave my sister alone."

"You wanna kill me, huh?" said Don.

"I will if I have to. Before you destroy my sister's life like you destroyed your own. Before one of those death creatures comes prowling around for her."

"You don't know what you're talking about," I said. "You never met a Sufferer before, you have no idea how they operate."

"You never met me before, either," said Don.

"I heard all I need to know from your sleazebag pusher friends," said Douglas.

"What?" said Don, suddenly attentive.

"When you disappeared, Annette started buying from this black dude who called around for you. Real pimpy type of guy. I had to call the cops on him. I *should* call the cops on you."

"Who—Annette!" Don jumped up.

"Randall," said Douglas. "Randall whose shipment you singlehandedly smoked up. I'm surprised you're not dead by now."

Annette looked out of the bedroom. "You gave him my number, Light, remember? He called here looking for you about, I don't know, four or five days ago—"

"Let's get the fuck out of here," said Don. "Give me my gun." He knelt down and began scooping the vials back into his parka.

"Take your crap with you," said Douglas. "Go get nice and high on it. But I think I'd better keep the gun."

"*Fuck* you, man—"

"No, fuck *you.*" Douglas clicked the safety off. I was surprised he knew how. Then he put his foot on Don's shoulder and shoved him back on his ass on the carpet. "No more bullshit, Light. You leave Annette alone, no calls, no late-night visits, got it? And I'm keeping the gun. You're lucky I don't call the cops."

"Call the cops, see if I give a damn, man. You don't have a fucking clue." Don stood up. He came up to Douglas's shoulder, but he was crowding the gun, and Douglas took a step back. I thought about trying to step in and realized my whole body was trembling.

The Sufferer came out of the kitchen, pumping forward on its massive black legs, and rushed up to where Douglas stood. It opened its strange black mouth and emitted a sound, something between a howl and a moan. Actually, it sounded like a man bellowing as he fell down a bottomless well, complete with echoes and Doppler effects.

At the same time chunks of broken glass fell out of its mouth at Douglas's feet, and on his shoes.

Douglas pointed the gun and fired, at almost the exact same spot on the alien's big bulldog chest. The noise, in the quiet apartment, was deafening. Douglas dropped the weapon and grabbed his hand, wincing.

Don immediately picked it up.

"Go," he said to me, and nodded at the door. Then he bent back down to collect the last of his vials, sweeping up the empties along with them.

Douglas stood holding his hand, watching the Sufferer. The creature had rolled back on its haunches at the impact of the gunshot, and now it was shaking its head vigorously, and spitting out more shards of glass.

Don pushed the gun back into his belt and hustled me towards the door, and then turned and slapped Douglas ever so lightly on the cheek. Like he wanted to wake him up, not hurt him. "You mess up your hand?" he said.

Douglas didn't say anything.

"Maybe your sister can rub it for you. See ya."

We ran to the elevator, the Sufferer leaping after us.

Out on the street Don said: "Hell was it doing?"

"It got you your gun back," I said.

"Yeah, but what was it doing, eating the dishes?" He knelt down and looked in the Sufferer's mouth. "Jesus." He reached in and pulled out a chunk of glass that was lodged there. The Sufferer snorted and shook its head.

"It's like the one soft spot, the whatchacallit, Achilles tendon," Don said. "I wonder if I could kill it by shooting it in the mouth?"

"*Donnie!* That's not cool. It saved you up there. Besides, you can't kill them, I read it—"

"Okay, shut up." He tossed the glass out into the street, under a parked car.

"Now what?" I said, and then quickly made my nomination: "The airport? Or Port Authority, catch a Greyhound upstate?"

Don didn't say anything.

"Upstate, New York State, isn't breaking parole, right? You can do anything you want, doesn't matter if the Sufferer's following you. I bet they've never seen one of these guys up there, huh?"

"I gotta sell the shit," said Don. "The triangle on 72nd and Broadway. I can move it there. C'mon, we can walk across." He started towards Central Park.

We ran after him, me and the Sufferer. "Don, wait. Why can't we just go? What are you stalling for?"

"Damn, Paul, you can't just show up with this idea and *rush* me out of town. Maybe I don't *want* to go to California. Maybe at least you ought to let me clear up my damn business before we go, okay?"

"What? *What?*" As if the robbery hadn't happened, or as if it weren't connected to the plan, a plan he'd already agreed to.

"Relax, okay. Damn. We'll go. Just let me unload the stuff, okay?"

We walked to the edge of the park on the empty streets, the three of us. In silence, until Don said, without turning: "It's been a while since we were in touch."

"What? Yeah, I guess. What do you mean?"

"That's all, just it's been a while. We didn't, like, keep up on each other's lives or anything."

"Yeah," I said, chilled.

Central Park at night made me think of high school, of smoking pot with my Upper West Side friends. White people's drugs, drugs for the kids who stay in school, go to college. While back in Brooklyn, Don was finding the other kind, the drugs for the black kids, the ones who wouldn't go to college even if they bluffed it through high school.

Now my West Side friends were all off at college, in various parts of the country, and I was back in town to sell drugs at 72nd and Broadway, under their parents' windows.

The Sufferer seemed to like the park. Several times it roamed wide of us, disappearing briefly in the trees. When we crossed Central Park West, though, it was back close at our heels.

We set up at the benches on the triangle, along with some sleeping winos. There was a black kid, too, who kept crossing the street to the subway and ducking inside, then crossing back to the triangle. He and the Sufferer exchanged a long look, then the kid went back to his pacing routine, and the Sufferer jumped over the bench, into the little plot of land the pavement and benches encircled. I hoped it would stay there, more or less out of sight from the street.

"This is dead, Don."

"Relax. It's where you come, up here. It's the only place to score."

"It's Tuesday night."

"Junkies don't know weekends, man."

"We're gonna get arrested. This is just like a target, like sitting in the middle of a target."

"Shut up. You're being a chump. Forget the cops."

A chump. The unkindest cut. I shut up. Don got out his pipe and smoked away another rock of the product. I had a hit too. The Sufferer didn't seem as interested.

And we waited.

The traffic on Broadway was all cabs, and—surprise! —two of them pulled over and transacted business with Don. One was slumming West Side yuppies on their way to a club, men overdressed, women waiting in the back of the cab, relieved laughter when the males returned safely. The other was two blacks in the front seat, the cabbie and a pal, with the cab still available. I ached to push Don in the back and take off, but I stayed shut up.

Another customer walked up, from the park side. He caught up with the kid, who shook his head, nodded at us, and made his jog across the street to the subway station again while the street was clear. Don made the sale and the guy headed back the way he'd come.

I was just noticing that this time the kid hadn't come back to the triangle when the truck pulled up. A van, really, like a UPS delivery truck but covered with layers of graffiti and minor dents, and missing doors on both sides. It pulled around the triangle the wrong way, bringing down a plague of honking from cabs.

Don said: "Oh shit."

"What?"

"That's Randall's truck." But he didn't move, or reach for the gun.

The driver kicked the emergency brake down and turned to us holding a toy-like machine gun. I figured it wasn't a toy. "Is that Randall?" I said.

"Nah. Shut up now."

The man in the passenger seat came around the front. Well dressed, unarmed. "Light," he said.

"Yo, Randall."

"Get in the back. This your man?" He raised his chin at me. His voice had a slight Caribbean lilt.

Don shrugged.

"You took my safe house tonight, my man?" Randall asked me. He was clean and pretty, like some young, unbeaten boxer. But he had a boiled-looking finger-thick scar running all along the right underside of his jaw, and where it would have crossed his ear the lobe was missing.

"That's me," I said, dorkily.

"Come along." He made it sound jolly. He opened the back. Inside were Kaz and Drey, sitting on tires, looking miserable.

I tried to catch Don's eye, but he just trudged forward and stepped up into the back. I went after him.

I glanced over my shoulder, but didn't spot the Sufferer. Randall climbed in behind us, slammed the two doors shut, and went up to the front. There wasn't any divider, just a big open metal box with two bucket seats in front of the window, and a steering wheel on a post to the floor. The driver handed Randall the little machine gun and took off across Broadway, down 72nd Street.

Don and I leaned against the back. I looked out the back window and just caught sight of the pay phone on the far side of the subway entrance.

We rattled to the end of 72nd, under the West Side Highway and parked out on the stretch of nothing before the water. It's always amazing to get to the edge of Manhattan and see how much stuff there is between the city—you know, the city that you think of, the city people use—and the real edge of the island. You think of it as being like a raft of skyscrapers, buildings to the edge, and instead there's the edge of the island. Boathouses, concrete and weeds, places that nobody cares about.

Unfortunately, at the moment.

The driver serving as gunman again, Randall opened the back and steered us out into a dark, empty garage, a sort of cinderblock shell full of rusted iron drums and piles of rotting linoleum tile. The floor was littered with glass and twisted, rusty cable. A seagull squawked out of our path, flapping but not taking off, then refolded its wings and wobbled outside once we were safely past. Kaz and Drey both looked back dubiously, acting more like fellow captives than Randall's henchmen, but Randall kept nodding us forward, until the moonlight from the garage entrance petered out and we all stood in darkness.

"You messin' up, Light," said Randall.

"Here's your stuff," said Don, scooping in his parka pockets. He sounded afraid. I wondered where the Sufferer was.

"That's good. Give it to Drey. You make a little green out there?"

"Yeah."

"You smoke up a little, there, too?"

Before Don could squeak "Yeah" again Randall stepped forward and smacked him, viciously hard, across the mouth. Don's foot slipped and skidded through the broken glass, but he kept from falling.

"Relax, relax," said Randall suddenly, as though some

protest had been raised. "We ain't killing you tonight, Light. But we gotta talk about this funny stuff, you chumps playing with my money. You think you takin' Kaz but it's all my money, right?"

"Yeah."

"It's like it's all a game, like *Monopoly* money, you and Kaz can just fuckin' *play* with it."

"Kaz didn't do anything wrong," said Don.

"Kaz a sucker get taken by a chump like you." He raised his hand and Kaz flinched. Leaving his hand in the air, he turned to me. "Who's your man here?"

"Paul."

"He your brother?"

"Nah."

Randall looked at Kaz and Drey. "This the dude?"

Kaz nodded.

Randall stared at me, but he was still talking to Don. "You tell him Randall got some easy money, some play money, just laying around? You tell him I'm a fuckin' chump?"

"Randall, we didn't even take your money. Just some dope, man. We only took money off Kaz and Drey."

"My dope *is* money, stupid. My dope is *product*. Not for you to fuckin' smoke. Why you so stupid, crackhead?"

At that moment a shadow slipped in through the moonlit garage entrance, then almost disappeared into the darkness. The Sufferer. I felt relieved, like it was the cavalry. But when it came into the circle it stepped up beside Randall, and then I saw that it wasn't the same.

It was bigger than ours, its eyes were longer, slits instead of ovals, and the strangely human nose was pushed to one side. A scarred Sufferer, for Randall.

"Here's my thing," said Randall. "I heard you got a thing, yourself. You been seen around *town* together."

"Uh, yeah. So what?"

"So what? That the only reason I came up here to talk to you myself, you think I bother with a fuckin' chump like you? Only reason my man didn't do you in a drive-by on Broadway."

"What, you like them? You can have mine."

"Naw, why you have to get fresh, Light?" He leaned over and slapped Don again, but lightly. It was the same slap Don had used on Douglas, exactly the same. Don was a reflexive mimic. "You disappoint me."

Don didn't speak.

"What does it want?" said Randall.

"I don't know."

Randall made a face. "I can't get rid of the sucker. It wants me to stop—stop livin' the life?"

"I said I don't know."

"Because I'm not a *user*, Light, I'm not like you. What's it trying to say to me?" Randall lurched forward and Don flinched. Intimidation, I sensed, was a way of life for Randall. It even leaked into interactions where he wanted to propagate trust. He couldn't help it.

"Nothing," said Don.

Randall turned and paced in a tight, impatient circle. "I wanna know, Light. Why this thing in my life, what the *meaning* is. Tell me."

It occurred to me that Randall thought Don knew because he was *white*.

"Nothing."

"Must want something, everybody wants something, Light. It stop you from using?"

"It doesn't give a shit, Randall. It smokes rock. It's a party animal, man."

"Gonna turn me in? Working for the Narcotics?"

"Sure, I don't know. This is fuckin' stupid, Randall."

Randall wheeled. "What you sayin'? It's gathering *evidence*, man? Tell me what you know!"

Kaz and Drey shifted nervously. The gun man cleared his throat.

"Nothing, Randall, man. It can't fuckin' talk, it's from another *planet*, man. Can't turn you in. Relax. It's really got you rattled, man."

"So tell me what it wants."

"Nothing. It's just . . . trying to, you know, get along." Don sighed. "Really, Randall. Everybody wants it to be *about* something, or up *to* something, but it's just, like . . . *attracted*. All the explanations are bullshit."

"That's not right," I blurted. "It's like a guardian angel. It's drawn to you because it senses something—"

I hesitated, and saw that I had everyone's undivided attention.

"—because it feels this sense that you're, uh, *important*, your life is important, and so it's drawn to you." I was going in circles. "It's not *judging* you, it's not moralistic. That's why it doesn't try to stop you, try to change your behavior, why it'll even share the pipe. Drugs aren't the point, it's not some simplistic thing like they make it out to be, it's more subtle than that. It wants to be around you and protect you because—your life is important. And it's afraid that you don't—care enough. So it's trying to do that, to *care*—"

I wanted to convince them, somehow, because I wanted to convince myself.

While I was talking, Don's Sufferer had crept in, like some kind of affirmation of my words. It padded past Don and Randall, stopping a foot or so away from Randall's Sufferer. I stopped talking. The two aliens stared at each other, and the distance between them suddenly seemed very small.

I thought of the aliens' incredible strength. I wished Don's was bigger than Randall's, instead of the reverse.

"Guardian angel," mused Randall. "That your guardian angel, Light?" The sneer in his voice made me sorry I'd spoken at all.

"Yeah," said Don. "It'll always be with you now, Randall. Gonna live your life with you, see everything you do."

"Fuck you trying to say?"

"Nothing. Just that you gotta live right, now, Randall. You're being watched." Don wasn't saying it because it meant anything to him. He was just yanking Randall's chain.

"Huh." Randall thought this over. "Light, you don't know shit about shit. You don't know what I do, how I live."

"Maybe not, Randall."

"I gotta get my money back, Light. Drey, take the money off Light."

Don handed it over, preemptively. I thought of the gun.

"I gotta put a hurt on you, Light, like you put on me. How'm I gonna do that?"

"I dunno."

"What you got that I can take? You ain't got nothing."

The Sufferers suddenly both stood, and I braced for some kind of violence between them. Instead they turned and walked out of the garage together, into the frame of moonlight, and then disappeared around the corner, heading towards the water. To settle their differences?

With them gone I felt naked, doomed.

"Kaz," said Randall, "you gotta do my hurtin' for me, my man. For what Light did to you."

"Naw, Randall," whined Kaz. "Naw, man."

"Hit him."

"Naw. He still got a gun, Randall, anyway. You didn't take it off him."

"So take it off him." Randall pointed at me. "You go, chump. You got lucky. Don't fuck with me no more. Don't go around with this dude Light, he's bad news. Go."

"What?" I said.

"Get lost. I ain't gonna fuck with you. You didn't know what you was doing."

"We'll go together," I said. "He's, uh, my brother."

"Go." Randall pointed, and the driver raised the gun at me.

"Go ahead, Paul," said Don.

"No, I'm his brother," I said, getting hysterical. "No."

Randall shoved me towards the door, and the driver followed. I took a few steps.

"Take him, Kaz," commanded Randall, done with me. "Take his gun."

"Naw, don't make me, Randall."

"Do it!"

"I'm his *brother*—"

The driver kicked me, and aimed the gun at my stomach. Inside, Kaz was advancing sheepishly on Don.

I ran, into the glare of moonlight.

Where was the Sufferer? I ran towards the water. Behind me, the clatter of voices: Don, Randall, Kaz. I ran, gasping.

When I found the Sufferers I thought they were killing each other. They were half hidden behind a pile of shredded, stinking tires, in a puddle of stagnant water streaked with oil rainbows. They lay entwined, limbs twisted together, both moaning like echoing wells, their bodies twitching, paws treading air, ears wrinkled back.

Fucking. Making love—the moment it hit me was the moment I heard the shot.

I turned in time to see the four shadows sprinting for the truck. Kaz's voice: "You made me, you made me, you shouldn't of fuckin' made me—"

They'd driven off before I got back to Don.

He was lying on the floor scrabbling in the glass with a hand already sticky with blood. In the dark the blood looked black, and watching it seep out of his stomach was like watching his white sweatshirt disappear into the gloom. It was happening fast.

"Fuck, Paul," he said, when he saw me.

"I'm going to get help," I said.

"Wait, don't leave me—"

"I'll be back—"

I ran out, back under the freeway, and found a woman walking her dog in the park. "For God's sake, my brother got shot, down in the old garage down there, please can you call an ambulance, please—" I fumbled it out between gasps, repeated everything, pointing, and when she agreed I turned and ran back, clutching a knot in my side; a cramp from running, but it felt like a sympathetic wound.

Moving too fast, I slid in his blood, and my knees buckled at seeing how little of the white of the sweatshirt was left. I sat down, in blood and glass, and held his hand.

His gun lay to one side, and I felt suddenly sure that he'd been shot with his own gun, Kaz trying to take it from him. The gun we could have left behind so many times in so many different places.

"I can't see you, man," said Don.

"Your eyes?" My voice was trembling, on the verge of sobs.

"No, stupid, I mean move around here, don't sit behind me."

I shifted. "An ambulance is coming, okay, Donnie? So just hang on. Guess you'll have to talk to the police or something, huh?"

An hour ago I was still picturing Don in California.

Now the dream of seeing him in a hospital bed seemed maybe too much to dare hope for.

"You're so stupid about the cops, Paul." His voice was husky, and as he went on, it got rougher and softer. "I don't care about the cops. When they arrested me before I told the guy 'Thank you, you saved me.' 'Cause I was a skeleton, I weighed about ninety pounds, and I knew I would dry out, get healthy in jail. That's all jail is, man, guys gettin' fed, getting healthy again, doing pushups, so they can go out and do it again. Shit, if they'd given me time instead of parole I might be off rock now."

I started weeping.

"C'mon, Paul, relax."

"We could be on a plane right now," I said. "We were right there, we were at the airport. The Sufferer, the Sufferer ruined everything."

"Nah, man, I didn't want to go. Tony the Tiger didn't blow it."

"Why? Why couldn't we just go?"

"I was all freaked out. I mean, it sounds great, right? Start over, cut out, leave all the shit behind. But I wasn't ready. I was just going along, I didn't want to disappoint you."

"What do you mean?"

"If California is my big second chance, Paul, I don't wanna go fuck it up with my pockets full of rock. I wanted it to be like you said, but I wasn't ready, I was afraid. If I went and I was still all fucked up there—I didn't want to disappoint you, Paul. At least if we didn't go I hadn't fucked up *California*. It was still there, like this beautiful picture you were painting, you know—"

His voice was trailing off, and I could barely hear him for my own sobbing.

"It was sort of hard for me to think about California or whatever, anything else, with all that rock in my coat, Paul. When we took Kaz for rock instead of cash . . . I had to get rid of it, and if I had to get rid of it, why not get high, you know? You don't know . . . you don't know how much I . . . like to get *high,* Paul. You haven't been *around* me that much. We haven't been in touch. I'm not just, like, the little kid you knew. I been . . . *doing* stuff—"

"My fault, the whole thing about robbing Kaz. You did that because of my stupid idea, to get cash for the tickets."

"Yeah, yeah, let's blame it all on you and the monster. Whatever. But the California thing . . . wasn't stupid. It was a good idea, so relax now, okay?"

"Okay."

"Shut up now and stop making me talk so much, right?"

"Okay."

"We'll go . . . we'll still go to California."

I didn't say anything, and Don closed his eyes, and we were quiet. The pace of blood leaking through his shirt slowed down. Time seemed to slow with it.

"I'm gonna pass out now," he said.

"Okay," I managed.

"I'm just . . . passing out, right, I'm not *dying.*"

He couldn't see his sweatshirt. "Right," I said.

He was dead for almost five minutes before I finally heard sirens, and they weren't even close yet.

I made a quick calculation about talking to a long series of people about what happened, starting with the ambulance people and the police and ending with our parents, versus getting the hell out of there. It wasn't a hard call.

I took Don's pipe and lighter and put them in my pocket and ran, south under the highway, and circled around a couple of blocks back to Broadway.

I hopped the turnstile and took the IRT downtown, to the Village, then walked across West 3rd Street to Washington Square Park, where life went on as usual, all night every night, every night for the last thirty years, probably. I sat on the same bench I'd been on at noon, waiting for Don to turn up, finding him after so long. Now I had to share it with a guy who was sleeping, but his smell and my stare kept anyone else away.

I wondered if I was waiting for Kaz. I couldn't think of what I would do or say if he showed, so I guessed I wasn't.

I started feeling sleepy about the same time the sky began to lighten up. The deadest hour in the park, when the night is officially over. A few businessmen walked across, and joggers. It was their park now, for a few short hours.

I got off my bench and managed to find someone dealing. There's always someone dealing. If I'd said to him: "You seen Kaz?" or "You seen Light?" he probably would have said: "Naw, man. But he be around later. What you want him for?"

Instead I just scored a five-dollar vial and went back to my bench.

I put it into Don's pipe and flickered the lighter over it and drew a hit, and at that moment the Sufferer walked up. It sat down in front of me and cocked its head.

I tried to ignore it, which worked for about five seconds. Then, riding the rush from the crack, I jumped on it and started beating its face with my fists. "You didn't do anything!" I screamed. The Sufferer just twisted slowly away from my blows, squinting its big eyes, shifting its feet to accommodate my assault. "You didn't help him at all! You didn't change anything!"

A crowd began to gather around us. "You were fucking, you were fucking when they killed him!" My voice cracked with rage, and I tasted my snot and tears as they ran down my face. I beat at it, my fists aching, then tried to reach for its mouth, its "Achilles tendon," but it just butted me away with its cheek. "You didn't help him at all!"

A couple of Rastafarians came forward out of the crowd and plucked me away. "Easy there, little man, come on. It didn't hurt you now, you just hurting yourself. Easy up."

I squirmed out of their grasp and fell to the pavement in front of the Sufferer. The alien opened its mouth and moaned silently at me, then took a step away from me. The crowd ducked quickly out of its way, though it hadn't made a sudden or violent movement yet.

Sickened, trembling, I crawled off the pavement, into the grassy section behind the benches.

Soon enough the little knot of attention that had gathered around us was dissolved back into the park. The Sufferer wandered away too.

When the trembling passed I got up and staggered out of the park, half blind with hunger and exhaustion. The Village swirled around me, oblivious. I thought about Don weighing ninety pounds, reaching the end of his run, thanking the cops for taking him off the street, for noticing him at all.

I don't know how long I walked before I passed out on the bench on Sixth Avenue, in front of the basketball courts, but when I woke again, the sun was low. People were going home from work. I was freezing. The Sufferer was staring at me, its face inches from mine.

I reached out, weak, wanting to hit it or twist its ears and to take its warmth at the same time.

It pulled away, and turned and trotted down Sixth. "You fucker," I said. "It would have been better if you'd never come at all."

I could have been talking to myself. Maybe I was.

I watched the Sufferer turn the corner, and I never saw it again after that.

The Brooklyn Bridge has a walkway. The Manhattan used to, but doesn't anymore. I crossed the bridge under an orange sky. I walked through downtown Brooklyn to Flatbush Avenue, and took the Long Island Railroad to Plainview, to tell Jimmy and Marilla that I knew what had happened to Don, to Donovan, to Light.

FOREVER, SAID THE DUCK

Pearl O'Hennies was in the corner talking to Notable Johnson. "Can you believe her gall, calling everyone up like this."

"But my dear, that's exactly what *he* did," said Notable. "They're the only two really here. We're all samples."

They were talking about their hosts, who were in another of the blank, featureless rooms.

"What is it, a contest?"

"A contest, you mean to see who had more *lovers?* I think they're above that. They've known each other all these years—"

"Why don't they just call each other up, then? Why all this?"

"Well they could be with each other, of course. In the real world, instead of a dull, poorly furnished virtual space like this one. But then *we* wouldn't all be here. It is about us, you see. Even if they won't talk to anyone but each other."

"I heard they've got games planned, for later."

"What, Spin the Bottle?"

Cambert Moid stepped over to where they stood. "Have you ever seen anything like it?" he asked.

"Hello, Cambert," said Pearl crisply.

"Hello, Pearl. I suppose I should say, long time no see. But"—he mimicked a Southern accent—"I don't rightly know if that's true. I suppose our real selves could have warmed up to each other by now. Besides, this is hardly 'see,' now is it?"

"You talk too much, Cambert," said Pearl.

"I'll let you two catch up," mumbled Notable Johnson, and he slipped away. He was en route to the monitors where guests were punching up drink simulations when he ran into Caitlice Frisman.

"Caitlice!"

"Oh, Johnny." She put her arms around him. "Nice, nice, nice. But what, excuse me, what the *hell* are you doing here?" She leaned in close. "You sleep with that remorseless pussycat?"

"I take it you refer to our host."

"Yours, not mine," she corrected.

He nodded his shameful assent to her question.

"Well, a party like this is what you get, what you deserve, for a glitch like that—but enough. You're in charge of your own regrets. Just tell me when it happened."

"You're humiliating me, Cait," he said affectionately.

"Two years—how should I count it?—two years after us, after you and I—"

"Then you know how we've been, and you must tell me. Because I—this copy here is from right after we broke—you weren't even *talking* to me, Johnny. But you're from later, and so you know how we've been, out there, in our real selves."

"Oh, fine, Cait. Nothing could keep us from—coffee every Monday."

"Ah."

They both fell to a moment of sadness. Then Caitlice said flippantly, "So am I magnificently fat now?"

"Oh, no, you look terrific. But that reminds me, Cait, listen: Gavin Urnst is here, a very early sample, and last I knew he was in the hospital, quite sick—"

"We mustn't tell him here," she said quickly. "Ruin his time, when he can't do anything. Any more than you would tell me if I *was* fat. Do you think he—"

"Died? I can't know. Anyone, I mean, you or I—"

"Shh."

They were quiet again for a minute.

"Cait, if this thing goes long, let's find each other. I mean, it could get unbearable. I've heard they're hoping we'll all pair—"

"Shhh. Say no more. It's a date. Save the last dance for me. And now I must mingle, darling."

Notable nodded. Caitlice turned and attached herself immediately to a group containing Millard Heron, O.K. Tinkers, and Wendy Airhole.

"This is such an indignity," Wendy said. "I was only

with him as a favor, just stayed long enough to qualify for the copying. I wanted him to have me to *access*, but not for this fucking party. I remember thinking that I shouldn't, just out of pity for my poor copy—that is, me, now, *here*. God."

"Hmmm," said Millard Heron. "He told *me* it was the other way. That he only slept with you—"

"Oh Millard, what do you know?" Wendy breathed out in a weary rush. "The things women have to tell men just to keep them from imploding with insecurity, just to keep their dicks hard long enough to be *entertaining*—and then to think they go around repeating it to each *other*—"

"Hey, we're at a party," said Caitlice, singingly. "Make the best of it, there's no harm done here. You, the real you, doesn't care about this, doesn't object, won't recall it. You and I, the real you and I, might be having *our very own version of this same party right now*—"

"I would never," said O.K. Tinkers. He shuddered. "Oh, I would never want to see them all, all in the same place—"

The four laughed, resentment suddenly abolished.

"This *could* be a sort of nightmare for them," Wendy speculated merrily. "If we somehow joined forces—"

Caitlice took her by the elbow, tsk-tsking. "Excuse us, boys. Come for a drink simulation, Wendy."

"You think I should lighten up, Cait, don't you?"

"I think you could be having fun." Caitlice steered her away from O.K. and Millard.

"My kind of fun is darker than yours, Cait. Doesn't the,

the *smugness* of it just creep you out? But I'll have a drink if you like. It'll just get me bitchier. They made a mistake calling this particular lady out of storage."

"Stop vamping," said Caitlice, delighted. "I know your act too well."

"I'm just warming up. I'm going straight to the source tonight, Cait. And you're right, I should have a drink."

"Straight to the source?"

"They *think* they're here together," Wendy said, lowering her voice.

"Who?" But Caitlice knew.

"Our hosts, the 'real' ones. But I'm going to get between them. Take him 'home' at the end of the party."

At the console they each tapped up a drink's worth of process distortion.

"Here, stand still, let me check something." Caitlice reached over and dug in Wendy's pocket, and pulled out a green ticket.

"What's that?" said Wendy.

"All the guests at this party have a ticket in their pockets, green or red. A little extra our hosts wrote into tonight's program. Red means you're his guest, green *hers*."

Wendy didn't speak, but her smile fell.

"I guess anyone they both had copies of, they had to choose whose version to bring," said Caitlice, "because they wouldn't want *two* of people, you know—"

"That was a one-time thing, a kink. I should be here with *him*, it was me and him that really had any kind of—"

177

"Don't be defensive." Cait turned out her pocket to reveal a ticket: green.

"You, we both—" Wendy giggled.

"I always liked her better."

"Well, I'll be."

"It's interesting, isn't it, the way we all pride ourselves on going both ways, but it's the mixed matches that go public while the same-same stuff stays under the table. It still makes us blush."

Wendy put her hands on her hips, instantly convinced. "I *know*. Really. What closeted wimps we are. God, doesn't that burn you up?"

"No, dear, it burns *you* up, like everything else. I just said it was interesting."

"Oh!" Wendy put her wrist to her forehead, exaggeratedly. "You are just so superior. Hey, are you a plant?"

"What?"

"You're with *them*, aren't you?" Wendy poked Caitlice between her breasts. "You're real, you're with them, a plant, to facilitate the party."

"No, no, no. I'm a sample, like you."

"*Cait*—"

"On my honor."

Wendy pursed her lips. "Well, okay. Let's go then."

Arman Danzig stepped up from behind them, his cigarette in a long holder. "Go where, ladies? Is there somewhere to go?"

"We have to get to *them*, Cait," said Wendy, ignoring him. "The real ones. Where the action is."

Caitlice shook her head, and trembled slightly. "I want

to be at the party. There are people to meet, people I haven't seen in a long time." She grabbed Arman's elbow, though she didn't like him. "Lovely, funny people in a ridiculous situation. I don't need—"

"This *is* interesting," said Arman.

"People *not* here is the situation," said Wendy. "Including you. People not meeting, a total and complete lack of anything actually happening. The only way to be real is to affect *them* somehow—"

"No. You. I don't need to do that. That's for you." Caitlice lightened suddenly, smiled, having convinced herself. "But I'll sneak up and watch, later. I'd like to see you do it."

"Think of it," Wendy continued, inspired. "The only way to even know any of this happened would be to make such a splash, such a big dent in their evening that they're so shaken they have to come and *talk* to you about it, I mean the *real* you. 'Wendy listen I can't get *her* to talk to me anymore because of what your copy and I did at the party'—he'd have to confess all about this sick little party—'and I want you to go talk to her about it,' and then I'd say, 'Look dear my ticket was green I was never your guest at all.' That would be something."

"Yes, and if you did a good enough job you could have them *both* coming to you afterwards with confidences, pleading their individual cases," mused Arman.

"Have we met?" said Wendy.

"I'm sorry," said Caitlice. "Arman Danzig, Wendy Airhole."

"And what color is *your* ticket?" said Wendy.

Arman's lip twitched around the holder. "I believe that's a personal question, Ms. Airhole."

"I'll show you mine—"

"What if I said I hadn't bothered to wonder the color of yours?" said Arman. "Or check the color of mine."

They were enchanted with one another.

"Look at what you've let slip," said Wendy. "You've suggested you'd have to check to know—that they've both got copies of you. But can there really be that many of us?"

She turned to Caitlice, but Caitlice had tiptoed off.

"Don't look now," Arman stage-whispered, "but it's our quarry." He jabbed backwards over his shoulder with the holder. Their hosts were passing through the room.

"They're mobbed," said Wendy. "It's disgusting."

"Sycophants all. Harmless. Just—traffic. A hedge we must clamber over."

Wendy liked him better and better. "Then let's."

Arman nodded and stepped sideways into the little crowd. "Oh, hello," he said to Darth Gatsby, who stood on the fringe.

"Hello, Arman," said Darth miserably.

"Are you having a wonderful time?" Arman asked, openly staring past Darth, at the hosts.

"Yes, of course," Darth moaned.

Arman noted with approval that Wendy was inserting herself on the other side of the group, working her way into a conversation with Fran Krapp and Hella Winkie.

Arman nudged past Darth to where Candy Bale stood listening to her host expound.

"—wrinkles in the program," he was saying. Candy wavered towards him, rapt. "There are side rooms in this space, for instance. You just have to find them. So if you start to notice that people you saw earlier aren't around—"

"Like a game of sardines!" Candy blurted.

"Right," he said.

Arman reached down and fondled Candy's realistic buttock as he pushed between the two of them. She gave an exaggerated gasp and opened her mouth at Arman.

"Sardines indeed," he sneered at her. "Or guppies." He twitched his cigarette and performed a slight bow. "I'm sorry. Do go on with what you were saying."

"Hello, Arman," said their host.

"Hello. But please. Don't let me interrupt. I am—we're both, obviously, hanging on your words. What other 'wrinkles' are built into tonight's program?"

"Well, I can't go into it all, but you'll find a few things revealing themselves over time anyway. But here, this is one trick nobody's picked up on. If I stick my tongue in someone's mouth"—at this he took Candy by the waist and put his mouth close to hers—"my drink or drug load is transferred." He kissed her, and Arman watched as her eyes closed, then opened again, wide.

She staggered backwards as he released her.

"I'd had two drinks," their host explained.

"But I'd already *had* two," said Candy.

"That makes four, then, doesn't it?"

"Oh," said Candy. "—Hic—."

"I see," said Arman. "Could she return it, now? By putting her tongue in your mouth?"

"I shouldn't tell you everything. But the second kiss of any kind doubles the load, and distributes it evenly. We'd then each be carrying four drinks, for instance."

"So you share the intoxication of anyone you seriously take up with," mused Arman. "No hope of sloughing yours off unless you kiss and run." He stood on tiptoe and made an insinuating face at Wendy, who had worked into a group with her hostess.

"Here, Arman," giggled Candy, lurching at him, mouth open. Putting his cigarette holder back in his mouth, Arman stepped deftly to one side and took her by the arm instead.

"Look," he said, lifting her chin with a finger. He pointed at Darth Gatsby, who'd been squeezed out of their group and was standing looking wan. "Go. Fetch."

Candy exploded towards Darth, and away from Arman.

"But now you're sober," Arman said to his host. "That can't be any fun."

"True enough. Join me?"

They moved towards the console together, and away from the crowd that ringed Wendy and her hostess. Arman caught a sly smile from Wendy as he turned away: they'd separated the hosts.

"So tell me," said Arman, "what *do* you have planned for tonight? Is it true you want us all to pair up?"

"It's a party. People can do what they want."

"While you and she pull the strings, you mean."

"Every party includes random factors, determined by the hosts. But the *outcomes* are unknown—"

"Ah. But is *your* outcome unknown?"

"I don't see why not—"

"Then let's take that tramp Candy and find one of your little sardine rooms, yes?"

Arman caught his host's nervous glance back over his shoulder.

"What?" said Arman. "Can't be separated from your 'real world' buddy? This isn't summer camp. Come on." He prodded gently at his host's elbow.

"I might just—"

"It's a *party*," Arman said menacingly. "Don't be all impossibly coupled. It's too early for that. I *know* you, I know what you're capable of—"

"Yes, and I know what *you're* capable of, Arman." Sighing, his host reached into his pocket and brought out a little pearl-handled revolver.

"What," Arman scoffed. "The coward's way out? Am I disinvited?"

"No, no. I would never do that. A guest at my party stays as long as he likes. Spends the night, ideally. You know that. You're not disinvited. But you are dosed with MDMA and on the other side of the party—"

—and when his host pulled the trigger, Arman found himself to be exactly that. He was several rooms away, wedged behind a conversation between Pearl O'Hennies and Omidan Rosengreen, and burdened with an irritatingly benign and rosy worldview.

"Feh," he muttered, and grabbed Pearl O'Hennies from behind. He twisted her around and planted his tongue in her mouth, then pulled away, wiping his lips, and stalked off angrily into the crowd.

"Seems you have an admirer," said Omidan.

"Goodness," said Pearl, still astonished, her mouth wide.

"Or was that that drink thing?"

"Something—not just a drink, I'm not sure—"

"Well he certainly had quite an effect on you, one way or another. People are behaving strangely at this affair, but I suppose some of us haven't 'gotten out' in quite a while."

"You, uh, get called up very much?" asked Pearl in a small voice. She struggled to flatten out her perceptual processing. It seemed to her that as a program she ought to be able to prevail over this influence. Then she noticed that Omidan was talking, answering a question which presumably she, Pearl, had asked, though she couldn't now recall what it was.

"Oh, Omidan," she interrupted, "don't you feel sorry for them, resorting to this, wanting to spend time with *us?*"

Omidan, eyebrows arching, said, "That's an interesting way to look at it," then paused, and looked at Pearl intently. "What *are* you on?"

"I don't know," said Pearl. She pursed her lips, wide-eyed, then began giggling. "Maybe I should kiss you," she said. "You can tell me what you think."

A figure materialized in the corner behind them:

Wendy Airhole. She blinked at them in astonishment for a moment, then scowled.

"Where did you come from?" asked Omidan.

"I was exiled to the margin," said Wendy sourly.

"For what reason?"

"Why is anyone ever exiled to the margin? For threatening the center."

"You should adopt the outlook that a party, by definition, has no center," said Omidan. "We certainly don't feel on the margin ourselves here. Something quite extraordinary has just befallen Pearl."

"You're the second person to lecture me about my attitude here tonight," said Wendy philosophically. "What happened to Pearl?"

"Arman Danzig kissed her, not at all in a friendly way. Now she's tripping or something, she's got processing trouble."

"For instance," said Pearl, giggling, "you just turned into Dizzy Duck, I think, or is it Douglas? With the hat? This is just getting stronger and stronger."

"It's Douglas Duck, with the hat," said Omidan, "and I see it too. Wendy just blinked away, as fast as she came, and now here's Douglas Duck, with feathers and a bright orange beak."

"It's still me," said Douglas Duck in Wendy's voice, angrily.

"This is new," said Omidan, not hearing. "There wasn't anyone fictional here before. There isn't any way that either one of them could have—*slept* with Douglas Duck, is there?"

"I don't know. I wish I could think—look how pretty that duck's hat is, Omidan. Can I touch your hat, duck?"

"It's me," said Wendy again, louder. "I'm just in a Douglas Duck body."

"Oh, how nice. I never saw a real cartoon before. Can I touch you?"

"Maybe she doesn't want to be touched," said Omidan. "She probably needs to get used to her new body."

"We're all real cartoons, here," said Douglas Duck, annoyed. "In a manner of speaking."

"But not with such—bright, glowing colors," said Pearl.

"Am I the only one?" Douglas Duck hopped up, trying to see over their heads into the crowd.

"No," said Omidan. "Look, there's an Arnold Schwarzenegger. I wonder if everybody will change eventually? There's a Bumpy the Cat, talking to the alien monster from that movie, whatsitcalled. And Alfau the Alligator! Oh, I love that show. I wonder who got to be Alfau the Alligator—"

"This is the last straw," said Douglas Duck. "Their respect for us is nil."

"It would seem so," said Omidan.

"They love us," said Pearl. "They want us to be happy."

"I thought they wanted us to pair off," groused Douglas Duck.

"Do you have genitals?" asked Omidan politely.

Douglas's white gloved hands pulled at the elastic waistband of his pants. "Sort of."

Notable Johnson and someone who'd changed into Deconstructor Dawg came up to them. "Hello, Pearl," said Notable. "Have you seen Caitlice?"

"Notable! Uh, no, not for a while, but—"

"I'm having trouble spotting her," he fretted. "She must have taken on one of these characterizations."

"Yes, it makes it hard," said Omidan.

"You look unhappy," said Pearl. She threw her arms around Notable's neck and thrust her lips against his. "Mmmph."

Deconstructor Dawg introduced himself to Douglas Duck. "O.K. Tinkers," he said.

"Hello, O.K.," said Douglas. "It's me, Wendy."

"Wendy! I heard about your plan, to get between them—"

"Let's not talk about it."

By the time Notable Johnson located Caitlice Frisman, who was hidden in the body of a Philip Guston self-portrait complete with one eye, one booted foot, facial stubble, and an enormous, gnarled cigar, he himself was incarnated as the health-food vampire, Count Granola.

They reclined together in near-total darkness on a large couch in a small side room.

"Oh, Cait," said the Count. "I was afraid I wouldn't find you, when everybody was suddenly creeping off—"

"Nonsense," she said, tousling his slick hair with her clubby, clownlike fingers. "I promised we'd be together. It's just that—you know how I feel about parties."

"Yes," he said, a little sadly.

"When Darth Gatsby gave Fran Krapp all his drinks—"

"Cait," he interrupted, "you and I could never have stayed together. I mean, for real, out there."

"Of course not, silly," she said. "That's why this is so nice. Such a treat."

In another side room, on a mattress on the floor, Douglas Duck and Albert Einstein lay on either side of Candy Bale, each idly caressing her body as she lay unconscious. Candy was one of a handful of guests whose form had remained constant throughout the party. Douglas Duck had taken off his hat and pants, and Albert Einstein wore only a shirt, and was smoking a cigarette in a holder.

"Well, Arman," said the duck, "they really had their way with us, didn't they?"

"Yes, darling." Albert Einstein drew on his cigarette. "Everyone had their way with everyone. Everyone always does."

"I—for all the, for everything—it really *was* a party, wasn't it?"

"Yes, darling."

The duck cocked his head and opened his bill as if to speak, then suddenly stopped.

"What?" said Albert.

"I wish it could go on forever," said the duck.

FIVE FUCKS

1.

"I feel different from other people. Really different. Yet whenever I have a conversation with a new person it turns into a discussion of things we have in common. Work, places, feelings. Whatever. It's the way people talk, I know, I share the blame, I do it too. But I want to stop and shout no, it's not like that, it's not the same for me. I feel different."

"I understand what you mean."

"That's not the right response."

"I mean what the fuck are you talking about."

"Right." Laughter.

She lit a cigarette while E. went on.

"The notion is like a linguistic virus. It makes any conversation go all pallid and reassuring. 'Oh, I know, it's like that for me too.' But the virus isn't content just to eat conversations, it wants to destroy lives. It wants you to fall in love."

"There are worse things."

"Not for me."

"Famine, war, floods."

"Those never happened to me. Love did. Love is the worst thing that ever happened to me."

"That's fatuous."

"What's the worst thing that ever happened to you?"

She was silent for a full minute.

"But there, *that's* the first fatuous thing I've said. Asking you to consider *my* situation by consulting *your* experience. You see? The virus is loose again. I don't want you to agree that our lives are the same. They aren't. I just want you to listen to what I say seriously, to believe me."

"I believe you."

"Don't say it in that tone of voice. All breathy."

"Fuck you." She laughed again.

"Do you want another drink?"

"In a minute." She slurped at what was left in her glass, then said, "You know what's funny?"

"What?"

"Other people do feel the way you do, that they're apart from everyone else. It's the same as the way every time you fall in love it feels like something new, even though you do the exact same things over again. Feeling unique is what we all have in common, it's the thing that's always the same."

"No, I'm different. And falling in love is different for me each time, different things happen. Bad things."

"But you're still the same as you were before the first time. You just feel different."

"No, I've changed. I'm much worse."

"You're not bad."

"You should have seen me before. Do you want another drink?"

The laminated place mat on the table between them showed pictures of exotic drinks. "This one," she said. "A zombie." It was purple.

"You don't want that."

"Yes I do. I love zombies."

"No you don't. You've never had one. Anyway, this place makes a terrible zombie." He ordered two more margaritas.

"You're such an expert."

"Only on zombies."

"On zombies and love is bad."

"You're making fun of me. I thought you promised to take me seriously, believe me."

"I was lying. People always lie when they flirt."

"We're not flirting."

"Then what are we doing?"

"We're just drinking, drinking and talking. And I'm trying to warn you."

"And you're staring."

"You're beautiful. Oh God."

"That reminds me of one. What's the worst thing about being an atheist?"

"I give up."

"No one to talk to when you come."

2.

Morning light seeped through the macrame curtain and freckled the rug. Motes seemed to boil from its surface. For a moment she thought the rug was somehow on the ceiling, then his cat ran across it, yowling at her. The cat looked starved. She was lying on her stomach in his loft bed, head over the side. He was gone. She lay tangled in the humid sheets, feeling her own body.

Lover—she thought.

She could barely remember.

She found her clothes, then went and rinsed her face in the kitchen sink. A film of shaved hairs lined the porcelain bowl. She swirled it out with hot water, watched as the slow drain gulped it away. The drain sighed.

The table was covered with unopened mail. On the back of an envelope was a note: *I don't want to see you again. Sorry. The door locks.* She read it twice, considering each word, working it out like another language. The cat crept into the kitchen. She dropped the envelope.

She put her hand down and the cat rubbed against it. Why was it so thin? It didn't look old. The fact of the note was still sinking in. She remembered the night only in flashes, visceral strobe. With her fingers she combed the tangles out of her hair. She stood up and the cat dashed away. She went out into the hall, undecided, but the weighted door latched behind her.

Fuck him.

The problem was of course that she wanted to.

It was raining. She treated herself to a cab on Eighth Avenue. In the backseat she closed her eyes. The potholes felt like mines, and the cab squeaked like rusty bedsprings. It was Sunday. Coffee, corn muffin, newspaper; she'd insulate herself with them, make a buffer between the night and the new day.

But there was something wrong with the doorman at her building.

"You're back!" he said.

She was led incredulous to her apartment full of dead houseplants and unopened mail, her answering machine full of calls from friends, clients, the police. There was a layer of dust on the answering machine. Her address book and laptop disks were gone; clues, the doorman explained.

"Clues to what?"

"Clues to your case. To what happened to you. Everyone was worried."

"Well, there's nothing to worry about. I'm fine."

"Everyone had theories. The whole building."

"I understand."

"The man in charge is a good man, Miss Rush. The building feels a great confidence in him."

"Good."

"I'm supposed to call him if something happens, like someone trying to get into your place, or you coming back. Do you want me to call?"

"Let me call."

The card he handed her was bent and worn from traveling in his pocket. CORNELL PUPKISS, MISSING PERSONS. And a phone number. She reached out her hand; there was dust on the telephone too. "Please go," she said.

"Is there anything you need?"

"No." She thought of E.'s cat, for some reason.

"You can't tell me at least what happened?"

"No."

She remembered E.'s hands and mouth on her—a week ago? An hour?

Cornell Pupkiss was tall and drab and stolid, like a man built on the model of a tower of suitcases. He wore a hat and a trench coat, and shoes which were filigreed with a thousand tiny scratches, as though they'd been beset by phonograph needles. He seemed to absorb and deaden light.

On the telephone he had insisted on seeing her. He'd handed her the disks and the address book at the door. Now he stood just inside the door and smiled gently at her.

"I wanted to see you in the flesh," he said. "I've come to know you from photographs and people's descriptions. When I come to know a person in that manner I like to see them in the flesh if I can. It makes me feel I've completed my job, a rare enough illusion in my line."

There was nothing bright or animated in the way he spoke. His voice was like furniture with the varnish carefully sanded off. "But I haven't really completed my job until I understand what happened," he went on. "Whether a crime was committed. Whether you're in some sort of trouble with which I can help."

She shook her head.

"Where were you?" he said.

"I was with a man."

"I see. For almost two weeks?"

"Yes."

She was still holding the address book. He raised his large hand in its direction, without uncurling a finger to point. "We called every man you know."

"This—this was someone I just met. Are these questions necessary, Mr. Pupkiss?"

"If the time was spent voluntarily, no." His lips tensed, his whole expression deepened, like gravy jelling. "I'm sorry, Miss Rush."

Pupkiss in his solidity touched her somehow. Reassured her. If he went away, she saw now, she'd be alone with the questions. She wanted him to stay a little longer and voice the questions for her.

But now he was gently sarcastic. "You're answerable to no one, of course. I only suggest that in the future you might spare the concern of your neighbors, and the effort of my department—a single phone call would be sufficient."

"I didn't realize how much time had passed," she said. He couldn't know how truthful that was.

"I've heard it can be like that," he said, surprisingly bitter. "But it's not criminal to neglect the feelings of others; just adolescent."

You don't understand, she nearly cried out. But she saw that he would view it as one or the other, a menace or self-indulgence. If she convinced him of her distress, he'd want to protect her.

She couldn't let harm come to E. She wanted to comprehend what had happened, but Pupkiss was too blunt to be her investigatory tool.

Reflecting in this way, she said, "The things that happen to people don't always fit into such easy categories as that."

"I agree," he said, surprising her again. "But in my job it's best to keep from bogging down in ontology. Missing Persons is an extremely large and various category. Many people are lost in relatively simple ways, and those are generally the ones I can help. Good day, Miss Rush."

"Good day." She didn't object as he moved to the door. Suddenly she was eager to be free of this ponderous man, his leaden integrity. She wanted to be left alone to remember the night before, to think of the one who'd devoured her and left her reeling. That was what mattered.

E. had somehow caused two weeks to pass in one feverish night, but Pupkiss threatened to make the following morning feel like two weeks.

He shut the door behind him so carefully that there was only a little huff of displaced air and a tiny click as the bolt engaged.

"It's me," she said into the intercom.

There was only static. She pressed the button again. "Let me come up."

He didn't answer, but the buzzer at the door sounded. She went into the hall and upstairs to his door.

"It's open," he said.

E. was seated at the table, holding a drink. The cat was curled up on the pile of envelopes. The apartment was dark. Still, she saw what she hadn't before: he lived terribly, in rooms that were wrecked and provisional. The plaster was cracked everywhere. Cigarette stubs were bunched in the baseboard corners where, having still smoldered, they'd tanned the linoleum. The place smelled sour, in a way that made her think of the sourness she'd washed from her body in her own bath an hour before.

He tilted his head up, but didn't meet her gaze. "Why are you here?"

"I wanted to see you."

"You shouldn't."

His voice was ragged, his expression had a crushed quality. His hand on the glass was tensed like a claw. But even diminished and bitter he seemed to her effervescent, made of light.

"We—something happened when we made love," she said. The words came tenderly. "We lost time."

"I warned you. Now leave."

"My life," she said, uncertain what she meant.

"Yes, it's yours," he shot back. "Take it and go."

"If I gave you two weeks, it seems the least you can do is look me in the eye," she said.

He did it, but his mouth trembled as though he were guilty or afraid. His face was beautiful to her.

"I want to know you," she said.

"I can't let that happen," he said. "You see why." He tipped his glass back and emptied it, grimacing.

"This is what always happens to you?"

"I can't answer your questions."

"If that happens, I don't care." She moved to him and put her hands in his hair.

He reached up and held them there.

3.

A woman has come into my life. I hardly know how to speak of it.

I was in the station, enduring the hectoring of Dell Armickle, the commander of the Vice Squad. He is insufferable, a toad from Hell. He follows the donut cart through the offices each afternoon, pinching the buttocks of the Jamaican woman who peddles the donuts and that concentrated urine others call coffee. This day he stopped at my desk to gibe at the headlines in my morning paper. "Union Boss Stung In Fat Farm Sex Ring—ha! Made you look, didn't I?"

"What?"

"Pupkiss, you're only pretending to be thick. How much you got hidden away in that Swedish bank account by now?"

"Sorry?" His gambits were incomprehensible.

"Whatsis?" he said, poking at my donut, ignoring his own blather better than I could ever hope to. "Cinnamon?"

"Whole wheat," I said.

Then she appeared. She somehow floated in without causing any fuss, and stood at the head of my desk. She was pale and hollow-eyed and beautiful, like Renée Falconetti in Dreyer's *Jeanne d'Arc*.

"Officer Pupkiss," she said. Is it only in the light of what followed that I recall her speaking my name as though she knew me? At least she spoke it with certainty, not questioning whether she'd found her goal.

I'd never seen her before, though I can only prove it by tautology: I knew at that moment I was seeing a face I would never forget.

Armickle bugged his eyes and nostrils at me, imitating both clown and beast. "Speak to the lady, Cornell," he said, managing to impart to the syllables of my given name a childish ribaldry.

"I'm Pupkiss," I said awkwardly.

"I'd like to talk to you," she said. She looked only at me, as though Armickle didn't exist.

"I can take a hint," said Armickle. "Have fun, you two." He hurried after the donut cart.

"You work in Missing Persons," she said.

"No," I said. "Petty Violations."

"Before, you used to work in Missing Persons—"

"Never. They're a floor above us. I'll walk you to the elevator if you'd like."

"No." She shook her head curtly, impatiently. "Forget it. I want to talk to you. What are Petty Violations?"

"It's an umbrella term. But I'd sooner address your concerns than try your patience with my job description."

"Yes. Could we go somewhere?"

I led her to a booth in the coffee shop downstairs. I ordered a donut, to replace the one I'd left behind on my desk. She drank coffee, holding the cup with both hands to warm them. I found myself wanting to feed her, build her a nest.

"Cops really do like donuts," she said, smiling weakly.

"Or toruses," I said.

"Sorry? You mean the astrological symbol?"

"No, the geometric shape. A torus. A donut is in the shape of one. Like a life preserver, or a tire, or certain space stations. It's a little joke of mine: cops don't like donuts, they like toruses."

She looked at me oddly. I cursed myself for bringing it up. "Shouldn't the plural be *tori?*" she said.

I winced. "I'm sure you're right. Never mind. I don't mean to take up your time with my little japes."

"I've got plenty of time," she said, poignant again.

"Nevertheless. You wished to speak to me."

"You knew me once," she said.

I did my best to appear sympathetic, but I was baffled.

"Something happened to the world. Everything changed. Everyone that I know has disappeared."

"As an evocation of subjective truth—" I began.

"No. I'm talking about something real. I used to have friends."

"I've had few, myself."

"Listen to me. All the people I know have disappeared. My family, my friends, everyone I used to work with. They've all been replaced by strangers who don't know me. I have nowhere to go. I've been awake for two days looking for my life. I'm exhausted. You're the only person that looks the same as before, and has the same name. The Missing Persons man, ironically."

"I'm not the Missing Persons man," I said.

"Cornell Pupkiss. I could never forget a name like that."

"It's been a burden."

"You don't remember coming to my apartment? You said you'd been looking for me. I was gone for two weeks."

I struggled against temptation. I could extend my time in her company by playing along, indulging the misunderstanding. In other words, by betraying what I knew to be the truth: that I had nothing at all to do with her unusual situation.

"No," I said. "I don't remember."

Her expression hardened. "Why should you?" she said bitterly.

"Your question's rhetorical," I said. "Permit me a

rhetorical reply. That I don't know you from some earlier encounter we can both regret. However, I know you now. And I'd be pleased to have you consider me an ally."

"Thank you."

"How did you find me?"

"I called the station and asked if you still worked there."

"And there's no one else from your previous life?"

"No one—except him."

Ah.

"Tell me," I said.

She'd met the man she called E. in a bar, how long ago she couldn't explain. She described him as irresistible. I formed an impression of a skunk, a rat. She said he worked no deliberate charm on her, on the contrary seemed panicked when the mood between them grew intimate and full of promise. I envisioned a scoundrel with an act, a crafted diffidence that allured, a backpedaling attack.

He'd taken her home, of course.

"And?" I said.

"We fucked," she said. "It was good, I think. But I have trouble remembering."

The words stung. The one in particular. I tried not to be a child, swallowed my discomfort away. "You were drunk," I suggested.

"No. I mean, *yes*, but it was more than that. We weren't clumsy like drunks. We went into some kind of trance."

"He drugged you."

"No."

"How do you know?"

"What happened—it wasn't something he wanted."

"And what did happen?"

"Two weeks disappeared from my life overnight. When I got home I found I'd been considered missing. My friends and family had been searching for me. You'd been called in."

"I thought your friends and family had vanished themselves. That no one knew you."

"No. That was the *second* time."

"Second time?"

"The second time we fucked." Then she seemed to remember something, and dug in her pocket. "Here." She handed me a scuffed business card: CORNELL PUPKISS, MISSING PERSONS.

"I can't believe you live this way. It's like a prison." She referred to the seamless rows of book spines that faced her in each of my few rooms, including the bedroom where we now stood. "Is it all criminology?"

"I'm not a policeman in some cellular sense," I said, and then realized the pun. "I mean, not intrinsically. They're novels, first editions."

"Let me guess; mysteries."

"I detest mysteries. I would never bring one into my home."

"Well, you have, in me."

I blushed, I think, from head to toe. "That's different,"

I stammered. "Human lives exist to be experienced, or possibly endured, but not solved. They resemble any other novel more than they do mysteries. Westerns, even. It's that lie the mystery tells that I detest."

"Your reading is an antidote to the simplifications of your profession, then."

"I suppose. Let me show you where the clean towels are kept."

I handed her fresh towels and linen, and took for myself a set of sheets to cover the living room sofa.

She saw that I was preparing the sofa and said, "The bed's big enough."

I didn't turn, but I felt the blood rush to the back of my neck as though specifically to meet her gaze. "It's four in the afternoon," I said. "I won't be going to bed for hours. Besides, I snore."

"Whatever," she said. "Looks uncomfortable, though. What's Barbara Pym? She sounds like a mystery writer, one of those stuffy English ones."

The moment passed, the blush faded from my scalp. I wondered later, though, whether this had been some crucial missed opportunity. A chance at the deeper intervention that was called for.

"Read it," I said, relieved at the change of subject. "Just be careful of the dust jacket."

"I may learn something, huh?" She took the book and climbed in between the covers.

"I hope you'll be entertained."

"And she doesn't snore, I guess. That was a joke, Mr. Pupkiss."

"So recorded. Sleep well. I have to return to the station. I'll lock the door."

"Back to Little Offenses?"

"Petty Violations."

"Oh, right." I could hear her voice fading. As I stood and watched, she fell soundly asleep. I took the Pym from her hands and replaced it on the shelf.

I wasn't going to the station. Using the information she'd given me, I went to find the tavern E. supposedly frequented.

I found him there, asleep in a booth, head resting on his folded arms. He looked terrible, his hair a thatch, drool leaking into his sweater arm, his eyes swollen like a fevered child's, just the picture of raffish haplessness a woman would find magnetic. Unmistakably the seedy vermin I'd projected and the idol of Miss Rush's nightmare.

I went to the bar and ordered an Irish coffee, and considered. Briefly indulging a fantasy of personal power, I rebuked myself for coming here and making him real, when he had only before been an absurd story, a neurotic symptom. Then I took out the card she'd given me and laid it on the bar top. Cornell Pupkiss, Missing Persons. No, I myself was the symptom. It is seldom as easy in practice as in principle to acknowledge one's own bystander status in incomprehensible matters.

I took my coffee to his booth and sat across from him. He roused and looked up at me.

"Rise and shine, buddy boy," I said, a little stiffly. I've never thrilled to the role of Bad Cop.

"What's the matter?"

"Your unshaven chin is scratching the table surface."

"Sorry." He rubbed his eyes.

"Got nowhere to go?"

"What are you, the house dick?"

"I'm in the employ of any taxpayer," I said. "The bartender happens to be one."

"He's never complained to me."

"Things change."

"You can say that again."

We stared at each other. I supposed he was nearly my age, though he was more boyishly pretty than I'd been even as an actual boy. I hated him for that, but I pitied him for the part I saw that was precociously old and bitter.

I thought of Miss Rush asleep in my bed. She'd been worn and disarrayed by their two encounters, but she didn't yet look this way. I wanted to keep her from it.

"Let me give you some advice," I said, as gruffly as I could manage. "Solve your problems."

"I hadn't thought of that."

"Don't get stuck in a rut." I was aware of the lameness of my words only as they emerged, too late to stop.

"Don't worry, I never do."

"Very well then," I said, somehow unnerved. "This interview is concluded." If he'd shown any sign of budging I might have leaned back in the booth, crossed my arms authoritatively, and stared him out the door. Since he remained planted in his seat, I stood up, feeling that my last spoken words needed reinforcement.

He laid his head back into the cradle of his arms, first sliding the laminated place mat underneath. "This will protect the table surface," he said.

"That's good, practical thinking," I heard myself say as I left the booth.

It wasn't the confrontation I'd been seeking.

On the way home I shopped for breakfast, bought orange juice, milk, bagels, fresh coffee beans. I took it upstairs and unpacked it as quietly as I could in the kitchen, then removed my shoes and crept in to have a look at Miss Rush. She was peaceably asleep. I closed the door and prepared my bed on the sofa. I read a few pages of the Penguin softcover edition of Muriel Spark's *The Bachelors* before dropping off.

Before dawn, the sky like blued steel, the city silent, I was woken by a sound in the apartment, at the front door. I put on my robe and went into the kitchen. The front door was unlocked, my key in the deadbolt. I went back through the apartment; Miss Rush was gone.

I write this at dawn. I am very frightened.

4.

In an alley which ran behind a lively commercial street there sat a pair of the large trash receptacles commonly known as Dumpsters. In them accumulated the waste produced by the shops whose rear entrances shared the alley; a framer's, a soup kitchen, an antique clothing store, a donut bakery, and a photocopyist's establishment, and by the offices above those storefronts. On this street and in this alley, each day had its seasons: Spring, when complaining morning shifts opened the shops, students and workers rushed to destinations, coffee sloshing in paper cups, and in the alley, the sanitation contractors emptied containers, sorted recyclables and waste like bees pollinating garbage truck flowers; Summer, the ripened afternoons, when the workday slackened, shoppers stole long lunches from their employers, the cafes filled with students with highlighter pens, and the indigent beckoned for the change that jingled in incautious pockets, while in the alley new riches piled up; Autumn, the cooling evening, when half the shops closed, and the street was given over to prowlers and pacers, those who lingered in bookstores and dined alone in Chinese restaurants, and the indigent plundered the fatted Dumpsters for half-eaten paper bag lunches, batches of botched donuts, wearable cardboard matting and unmatched socks, and burnable wood scraps; Winter, the selfish night, when even the cafes battened down iron gates through which night-watchmen fluorescents palely flickered, the indigent built their overnight camps in doorways and under sidestreet hedges, or in wrecked cars, and the street itself was an abandoned stage.

On the morning in question the sun shone brightly, yet the air was bitingly cold. Birds twittered resentfully. When the sanitation crew arrived to wheel the two

Dumpsters out to be hydraulically lifted into their screeching, whining truck, they were met with cries of protest from within.

The men lifted the metal tops of the Dumpsters and discovered that an indigent person had lodged in each of them, a lady in one, a gentleman in the other.

"Geddoudadare," snarled the eldest sanitation engineer, a man with features like a spilled plate of stew.

The indigent lady rose from within the heap of refuse and stood blinking in the bright morning sun. She was an astonishing sight, a ruin. The colors of her skin and hair and clothes had all surrendered to gray; an archaeologist might have ventured an opinion as to their previous hue. She could have been anywhere between thirty and fifty years old, but speculation was absurd; her age had been taken from her and replaced with a timeless condition, a state. Her eyes were pitiable; horrified and horrifying; witnesses, victims, accusers.

"Where am I?" she said softly.

"Isedgeddoudadare," barked the garbage operative.

The indigent gentleman then raised himself from the other Dumpster. He was in every sense her match; to describe him would be to tax the reader's patience for things worn, drab, desolate, crestfallen, unfortunate, etc. He turned his head at the trashman's exhortation and saw his mate.

"What's the—" he began, then stopped.

"You," said the indigent lady, lifting an accusing finger at him from amidst her rags. "You did this to me."

"No," he said. "No."

"Yes!" she screamed.

"C'mon," said the burly sanitateur. He and his second began pushing the nearer container, which bore the lady, towards his truck.

She cursed at them and climbed out, with some difficulty. They only laughed at her and pushed the cart out to the street. The indigent man scrambled out of his Dumpster and brushed at his clothes, as though they could thereby be distinguished from the material in which he'd lain.

The lady flew at him, furious. "Look at us! Look what you did to me!" She whirled her limbs at him, trailing banners of rag.

He backed from her, and bumped into one of the garbagemen, who said, "Hey!"

"It's not my fault," said the indigent man.

"Yugoddagedoudahere!" said the stew-faced worker.

"What do you mean it's not your fault?" she shrieked.

Windows were sliding open in the offices above them. "Quiet down there," came a voice.

"It wouldn't happen without you," he said.

At that moment a policeman rounded the corner. He was a large man named Officer McPupkiss who even in the morning sun conveyed an aspect of night. His policeman's uniform was impeccably fitted, his brass polished, but his shoetops were exceptionally scuffed and dull. His presence stilled the combatants.

"What's the trouble?" he said.

They began talking all at once; the pair of indigents, the refuse handlers, and the disgruntled office worker leaning out of his window.

"Please," said McPupkiss, in a quiet voice which was nonetheless heard by all.

"He ruined my life!" said the indigent lady raggedly.

"Ah, yes. Shall we discuss it elsewhere?" He'd already grasped the situation. He held out his arms, almost as if he wanted to embrace the two tatterdemalions, and nodded at the disposal experts, who silently resumed their labors. The indigents followed McPupkiss out of the alley.

"He ruined my life," she said again when they were on the sidewalk.

"She ruined mine," answered the gentleman.

"I wish I could believe it was all so neat," said McPupkiss. "A life is simply *ruined;* credit for the destruction goes *here* or *here.* In my own experience things are more ambiguous."

"This is one of the exceptions," said the lady. "It's strange but not ambiguous. He fucked me over."

"She was warned," he said. "She made it happen."

"The two of you form a pretty picture," said McPupkiss. "You ought to be working together to improve your situation; instead you're obsessed with blame."

"We can't work together," she said. "Anytime we come together we create a disaster."

"Fine, go your separate ways," said the officer. "I've always thought 'We got ourselves into this mess and we can get ourselves out of it' was a laughable attitude. Many things are irreversible, and what matters is moving on. For example, a car can't reverse its progress over a cliff; it has to be abandoned by those who survive the fall, if any do."

But by the end of this speech the gray figures had fallen to blows and were no longer listening. They clutched one another like exhausted boxers, hissing and slapping, each trying to topple the other. McPupkiss chided himself for wasting his breath, grabbed them both by the back of their scruffy collars, and began smiting their hindquarters with his dingy shoes until they ran down the block and out of sight together, united again, McPupkiss thought, as they were so clearly meant to be.

5.

The village of Pupkinstein was nestled in a valley surrounded by steep woods. The villagers were a contented people except for the fear of the two monsters that lived in the woods and came into the village to fight their battles. Everyone knew that the village had been rebuilt many times after being half destroyed by the fighting of the monsters. No one living could remember the last of these battles, but that only intensified the suspicion that the next time would surely be soon.

Finally the citizens of Pupkinstein gathered in the town square to discuss the threat of the two monsters, and debate proposals for the prevention of their battles.

A group of builders said, "Let us build a wall around the perimeter of the village, with a single gate which could be fortified by volunteer soldiers."

A group of priests began laughing, and one of them said, "Don't you know that the monsters have wings? They'll flap twice and be over your wall in no time."

Since none of the builders had ever seen the monsters, they had no reply.

Then the priests spoke up and said, "We should set up temples which can be filled with offerings: food, wine, burning candles, knitted scarves, and the like. The monsters will be appeased."

Now the builders laughed, saying, "These are monsters, not jealous gods. They don't care for our appeasements. They only want to crush each other, and we're in the way."

The priests had no answer, since their holy scriptures contained no accounts of the monsters' habits.

Then the Mayor of Pupkinstein, a large, somber man, said, "We should build our own monster here in the middle of the square, a scarecrow so huge and threatening that the monsters will see it and at once be frightened back into hiding."

This plan satisfied the builders, with their love of construction, and the priests, with their fondness for symbols. So the very next morning the citizens of Pupkinstein set about constructing a gigantic figure in the square. They began by demolishing their fountain. In its place they marked out the soles of two gigantic shoes, and the builders sank foundations for the towering legs that would extend from them. Then the carpenters built frames, and the seamstresses sewed canvases, and in less than a week the two shoes were complete, and the beginnings of ankles besides. Without being aware of it, the citizens had begun to model their monster on the Mayor, who was always present as a model, whereas no one had ever seen the two monsters.

The following night it rained. Tarpaulins were thrown over the half-constructed ankles that rose from the shoes. The Mayor and the villagers retired to an alehouse to toast their labors and be sheltered from the rain. But just as the proprietor was pouring their ale, someone said, "Listen!"

Between the crash of thunder and the crackle of lightning there came a hideous bellowing from the woods at either end of the valley.

"They're coming!" the citizens said. "Too soon—our monster's not finished!"

"How bitter," said one man. "We've had a generation of peace in which to build, and yet we only started a few days ago."

"We'll always know that we tried," said the Mayor philosophically.

"Perhaps the shoes will be enough to frighten them," said the proprietor, who had always been regarded as a fool.

No one answered him. Fearing for their lives, the villagers ran to their homes and barricaded themselves behind shutters and doors, hid their children in attics and potato cellars, and snuffed out candles and lanterns that might lead an attacker to their doors. No one dared even look at the naked, miserable things that came out of the woods and into the square; no one, that is, except the Mayor. He stood in the shadow of one of the enormous shoes, rain beating on his umbrella, only dimly sensing that he was watching another world being fucked away.

6.

I live in a shadowless pale blue sea.

I am a bright pink crablike thing, some child artist's idea of an invertebrate, so badly drawn as to be laughable.

Nevertheless, I have feelings.

More than feelings. I have a mission, an obsession.

I am building a wall.

Every day I move a grain of sand. The watercolor sea washes over my back, but I protect my accumulation. I fasten each grain to the wall with my comic-book feces. (Stink lines hover above my shit, also flies which look like bow ties, though I am supposed to be underwater.)

He is on the other side. My nemesis. Someday my wall will divide the ocean, someday it will reach the surface, or the top of the page, and be called a reef. He will be on the other side. He will not be able to get to me.

My ridiculous body moves only sideways, but it is enough.

I will divide the watercolor ocean, I will make it two. We must have a world for each of us.

I move a grain. When I come to my wall, paradoxically, I am nearest him. His little pink body, practically glowing. He is watching me, watching me build.

There was a time when he tried to help, when every day for a week he added a grain to my wall. I spent every day that week removing his grain, expelling it from the wall, and no progress was made until he stopped. He understands now. My wall must be my own. We can be together in nothing. Let him build his own wall. So he watches.

My wall will take me ten thousand years to complete. I live only for the day that it is complete.

The Pupfish floats by.

The Pupfish is a fish with the features of a mournful hound dog and a policeman's cap. The Pupfish is the only creature in the sea apart from me and my pink enemy.

The Pupfish, I know, would like to scoop me up in its oversized jaws and take me away. The Pupfish thinks it can solve my problem.

But no matter how far the Pupfish took me, I would still be in the same ocean with *him*. That cannot be. There must be two oceans. So I am building a wall.

I move a grain.

I rest.

I will be free.

THE HARDENED CRIMINALS

The day we went to paint our names on the prison built of hardened criminals was the first time I had ever been there. I'd seen pictures, mostly video footage shot from a helicopter. The huge building was still as a mountain, but the camera was always in motion, as though a single angle was insufficient to convey the truth about the prison.

The overhead footage created two contradictory impressions. The prison was an accomplishment, a monument to human ingenuity, like a dam or an aircraft carrier. At the same time the prison was a disaster, something imposed by nature on the helpless city, a pit gouged by a meteorite, or a forest-fire scar.

Footage from inside the prison, of the wall, was rare.

Carl Hemphill was my best friend in junior high

school. In three years we had graduated together from video games to petty thievery, graffiti, and pot smoking. It was summer now, and we were headed for two different high schools. Knowledge that we would be drawn into separate worlds lurked indefinably in our silences.

Carl involved me in the expedition to the prison wall. He was the gadfly, moving easily between the rebel cliques that rarely attended class—spending the school day in the park outside, instead—and those still timid and obedient, like myself. Our group that day included four other boys, two of them older, dropouts from our junior high who were passing their high school years in the park. For them, I imagined, this was a visit to one of their own possible futures: they might be inside someday. For me it was not that but something else, a glimpse of a repressed past. My father was a part of the prison.

It was a secret not only from the rest of our impromptu party, but from Carl, from the entire school. If asked, I said my father had died when I was six, and that I couldn't remember him, didn't know him except in snapshots, anecdotes. The last part of the lie was true. I knew of my father, but I couldn't remember him.

To reach the devastated section that had been the center of the city we first had to cross or skirt the vast Chinese ghetto, whose edge was normally an absolute limit to our wanderings. In fact, there was a short buffer zone where on warehouse doors our graffiti overlapped with the calligraphs painted by the Chinese gangs. Courage was measured by how deep into this zone your tag still appeared, how often it obliterated the Chinese writing. Carl and one of the older boys were already rattling their spray cans. We would extend our courage today.

The trip was uneventful at first. Our nervous pack moved down side streets and alleys, through the mists of steaming sewers, favoring the commercial zone where we could retreat into some Chinese merchant's shop and not be isolated in a lot or alley. The older Chinese ignored us, or at most shook their heads. We might as well have been stray dogs. When we came to a block of warehouses or boarded shops, we found a suitable door or wall and tagged up, reproducing with spray paint those signature icons we'd laboriously perfected with ballpoint on textbook covers and desktops. Only two or three of us would tag up at a given stop before we panicked and hurried away, spray cans thrust back under our coats. We were hushed, respectful, even as we defaced the territory.

We were at a freeway overpass, through the gang zone, we thought, when they found us. Nine Chinese boys, every one of them verging on manhood the way only two in our party were. Had they been roaming in such a large pack and found us by luck, or had one or another of them (or even an older Chinese, a shopkeeper perhaps) sighted us earlier and sounded a call-to-arms? We couldn't know. They closed around us like a noose in the shadow of the overpass, and instantly there was no question of fighting or running. We would wait, petrified. They would deliver a verdict.

It was Carl who stepped forward and told them that

we were going to the prison. One of them pushed him back into our group, but the information triggered a fast-paced squabble in Chinese. We listened hard, though we couldn't understand a word.

Finally a question was posed, in English. "Why you going there?"

The oldest in our group, a dropout named Richard, surprised us by answering. "My brother's inside," he said. None of us had known.

He'd volunteered his secret in the cause of obtaining our passage. I should have chimed in now with mine. But my father wasn't a living prisoner inside, he was a part of the wall. I didn't speak.

The Chinese gang began moving us along the empty street, nudging us forward with small pushes and scoffing commands. Soon enough, though, these spurs fell away. The older boys became our silent escort, our bodyguards. In that manner we moved out of the ghetto, the zone of warehouses and cobblestone, to the edge of the old downtown.

The office blocks here had been home to squatters before being completely abandoned, and many windows still showed some temporary decoration: ragged curtains, cardboard shutters, an arrangement of broken dolls or toys on the sill. Other windows were knocked out, the frames tarnished by fire.

The Chinese boys slackened around us as the prison tower came into view. One of them pointed at it, and pushed Carl, as though to say, *If that's what you came for, go*. We hurried up, out of the noose of the gang, towards the prison. None of us dared look back to question the gift of our release. Anyway, we were hypnotized by the tower.

The surrounding buildings had been razed so that the prison stood alone on a blasted heath of concrete and earth five blocks wide, scattered with broken glass and twisted tendrils of orange steel. Venturing into this huge clearing out of the narrow streets seemed dangerously stupid, as though we were prey coming from the forest to drink at an exposed water hole. We might not have done it without the gang somewhere at our back. As it was, our steps faltered.

The tower was only ten or eleven stories tall then, but in that cleared space it already seemed tremendous. It stood unfenced, nearly a block wide, and consummately dark and malignant, the uneven surfaces absorbing the glaring winter light. We moved towards it across the concrete. I understand now that it was intended that we be able to approach it, that striking fear in young hearts was the point of the tower, but at the time I marveled that there was nothing between us and the wall of criminals, that no guards or dogs or klaxons screamed a warning to move away.

They'd been broken before being hardened. That was the first shock. I'd envisioned some clever fit, a weaving of limbs, as in an Escher print. It wasn't quite that pretty. Their legs and shoulders had been crushed into the corners of a block, like compacted garbage, and the fit was the simple, inhuman one of right angle flush against right angle. The wall bulged with crumpled limbs, squeezed so tightly together that they resembled a frieze carved in stone, and it was impossible to picture them unfolded, restored. Their heads were tucked inside the prison, so the outer wall was made of backs, folded swollen legs, feet back against buttocks, and squared shoulders.

My father had been sentenced to the wall when it was already at least eight stories high, I knew. He wasn't down here, this couldn't be him we defaced. I didn't have to think of him, I told myself. This visit had nothing to do with him.

Almost as one, and still in perfect silence, we reached out to touch the prison. It was as hard as rock but slightly warm. Scars, imperfections in the skin, all had been sealed into an impenetrable surface. We knew the bricks couldn't feel anything, yet it seemed obscene to touch them, to do more than poke once or twice to satisfy our curiosity.

Finally, we required some embarrassment to break the silence. One of the older boys said, "Get your hand off his butt, you faggot."

We laughed, and jostled one another, as the Chinese gang had jostled us, to show that we didn't care. Then the boys with spray cans drew them out.

The prison wall was already thick with graffiti from the ground to a spot perhaps six feet up, where it trailed off. There were just a few patches of flesh or tattoo visible between the trails of paint. A few uncanny tags floated above reach, where the canvas of petrified flesh was clearer. I suppose some ambitious taggers had stood on one another's shoulders, or dragged some kind of makeshift ladder across the waste.

We weren't going to manage anything like that. But our paint would be the newest, the outermost layer, at least for a while. One by one we tagged up, offering the wall the largest and most elaborated versions of our glyphs. After my turn I stepped up close to watch the paint set, the juicy electric gleam slowly fading to matte on the minutely knobby surface of hardened flesh.

Then I stepped back. From a distance of ten feet our work was already nearly invisible. I squinted into the bright sky and tried to count the floors, thinking of my father. At that height the bricks were indistinguishable. Not that I'd recognize the shape of my father's back or buttocks even up close, or undistorted by the compacting. I'm not even sure I'd have recognized his face.

A wind rose. We crossed the plain of concrete, hands in our pockets, into the shelter of the narrow streets, the high ruined offices. We were silent again, our newfound jauntiness expelled with the paint.

They were on us at the same overpass, the moment we came under its shadow. The deferred ambush was delivered now. They knocked us to the ground, displayed knives, took away our paint and money. They took Carl's watch. Each time we stood up they knocked us down again. When they let us go it was one at a time, sent running down the street, back into the Chinese commercial street alone, a display for the shopkeepers and deliverymen, who this time jeered and snickered.

I think we were grateful to them, ultimately. The

humiliation justified our never boasting about the trip to the prison wall, our hardly speaking of it back at school or in the park. At the same time, the beating served as an easy repository for the shame we felt, a shame that would otherwise have attached to our own acts, at the wall.

In fact, we six never congregated again, as though doing so would bring the moment dangerously close. I only once ever again saw the older dropout, the one whose brother was in the prison. It was during a game of touch football in the park, and he went out of his way to bully me.

Carl and I drifted apart soon after entering separate schools. I expected to know him again later. As it happened, I missed my chance.

"Stickney," the guard called, and the man on my right stepped forward.

By the time I entered the prison, it was thirty-two stories high. I was nineteen and a fool. I'd finished high school, barely, and I was living at home, telling myself I'd apply to the state college, but not doing it. I'd been up all night drinking with the worst of the high-school crowd when I was invited along as an afterthought to what became my downfall, my chance to be a bystander at my own crime. I drove a stolen car as a getaway in a bungled armored-car robbery, and my distinction was that I drove it into the door of a black-and-white, spilling a lieutenant's morning coffee and crushing his left forearm. The trial was suffused with a vague air of embarrassment. The judge didn't mention my father.

"Martell."

I'd arrived in a group of six, driven in an otherwise empty bus through underground passages to the basement of the prison, and ushered from there to a holding area. None of us were there to be hardened and built into the prison. We were all first-time offenders, meant to live inside and be frightened, warned onto the path of goodness by the plight of the bricks.

"Pierce."

We stood together, our bodies tense with fear, our thoughts desperately narrowed. The fecal odor of the prison alone overwhelmed us. The cries that echoed down, reduced to whispers. The anticipation of the faces in the wall. We turned from each other in shame of letting it show, and we prayed as they processed us and led us away that we would be assigned different cells, different floors, and never have to see one another. Better to face the sure cruelties of the experienced convicts than have our green terror mirrored.

"Deeds, Minkowitz."

I was alone. The man at the desk flickered the papers before him, but he wasn't looking at them. When he said my name, it was a question, though by elimination he should have been certain. "Nick Marra?"

"Yes," I said.

"Put him in the hole," he said to the guards who remained.

I must have aged ten years by the time they released me from that dark nightmare, though it lasted only a week. When the door first slammed, I actually felt it as a relief: that I was hidden away and alone, after preparing or failing to prepare for cellmates, initiations, territorial conflicts. I cowered down at the middle of the floor, holding my knees to my chest, feeling myself pound like one huge heart. I tried closing my eyes but they insisted on staying open, on trying to make out a hint of form in the swirling blackness. Then I heard the voices.

"Bad son of a bitch. That's all."

"—crazy angles on it, always need to play the crazy angles, that's what Lucky says—"

"C'mere. Closer. Right here, c'mon."

"Don't let him tell you what—"

"Motherfuck."

"—live like a pig in a house you can't ever go in without wanting to kill her I didn't think like that I wasn't a killer in my own mind—"

"Wanna get laid? Wanna get some?"

"Gotta get out of here, talk to Missing Persons, *man*. They got the answers."

"Henry?"

"Don't listen to him—"

They'd fallen silent for a moment as the guards tossed me into the hole, been stunned into silence perhaps by the rare glimpse of light, but they were never silent again. That was all the bricks were, anymore, voices and ears and eyes; the chips that had been jammed into their petrified brains preserved those capacities and nothing more. So they watched and talked, and the ones in the hole just talked. I learned how to plug my ears with shreds from my clothing soon enough, but it wasn't sufficient to block out the murmur. Sleeping through the talk was the first skill to master in the prison built from criminal bricks, and I mastered it alone in the dark.

Now I went to the wall and felt the criminals. Their fronts formed a glossy, encrusted whole, hands covering genitals, knees crushed into corners that were flush against blocked shoulders. I remembered that long-ago day at the wall. Then my finger slipped into a mouth.

I yelped and pulled it out. I'd felt the teeth grind, hard, and it was only luck that I wasn't bitten. The insensate lips hadn't been aware of my finger, of course. The mouth was horribly dry and rough inside, not like living flesh, but it lived in its way, grinding out words without needing to pause for breath. I reached out again, felt the eyes. Useless here in the hole, but they blinked and rolled, as though searching, like mine. The mouth I'd touched went on, "—never want to be in Tijuana with nothing to do, be fascinating for about three days and then you'd start to go crazy—" The voice plodding, exhausted.

I'd later see how few of the hardened spoke at all, how many had retreated into themselves, eyes and mouths squeezed shut. There were dead ones, too, here and everywhere in the wall. Living prisoners had killed the most annoying bricks by carving into the stony foreheads and smashing the chips that kept the brain alive. Others had malfunctioned and died on their own. But in the dark the handful of voices seemed hundreds, more than the wall of one room could possibly hold.

"C'mere, I'm over here. Christ."

I found the one that called out.

"What you do, kid?"

"Robbery," I said.

"What you do to get thrown in *here?* Shiv a hack?"

"What?"

"You knife a guard, son?"

I didn't speak. Other voices rattled and groaned around me.

"My name's Jimmy Shand," said the confiding voice. I thought of a man who'd sit on a crate in front of a gas station. "I've been in a few knife situations, I'm not ashamed of that. Why'd you get thrown in the bucket, Peewee?"

"I didn't do anything."

"You're here."

"I didn't do anything. I just got here, on the bus. They put me in here."

"Liar."

"They checked my name and threw me in here."

"Lying motherfucker. Show some respect for your *fucking* elders." He began making a sound with his mummified throat, a staccato crackling noise, as if he wanted to spit at me. I backed away to the middle of the floor, and his voice blended into the horrible, chattering mix.

I picked the corner opposite the door and away from

the wall for my toilet, and slept huddled against the door. I was woken the next morning by a cold metal tray pressing against the back of my neck as it was shoved through a slot in the door. Light flashed through the gap, blindingly bright to my deprived eyes, then disappeared. The tray slid to the floor, its contents mixing. I ate the meal without knowing what it was.

"Gimme some of that, I hear you eating, you sonovabitch."

"Leave him alone, you constipated turd."

They fed me twice a day, and those incidental shards of light were my hope, my grail. I lived huddled and waiting, quietly masturbating or gnawing my cuticles, sucking precious memories dry by overuse. I quickly stopped answering the voices, and prayed that the bricks in the walls of the ordinary cells were not so malicious and insane. Of course, by the time I was sprung, I was a little insane myself.

They dragged me out through a corridor I couldn't see for the ruthless light, and into a concrete shower, where they washed me like I was a dog. Only then was I human enough to be spoken to. "Put these on, Marra." I took the clothes and dressed.

The man waiting in the office they led me to next didn't introduce himself. He didn't have the gray deadness in his features that I already associated with prison staff.

"Sit down."

I sat.

"Your father is Floyd Marra?"

"Why?" I meant to ask why I'd been put in isolation. My voice, stilled for days, came out a croak.

"Leave the questions to us," said the man at the desk, not unkindly. "Your father is Floyd Marra?"

"Yes."

"You need a glass of water? Get him a glass of water, Graham." One of the guards went into the next room and came back with a paper cone filled with water and handed it to me. The man at the desk pursed his lips and watched me intently as I drank.

"You're a smart guy, a high-school graduate," he said.

I nodded and put the paper cone on the desk between us. He reached over and crumpled it into a ball and tossed it under the desk.

"You're going to work for us."

"What?" I still meant to ask *why*, but he had me confused. A part of me was still in the hole. Maybe some part would be always.

"You want a cigarette?" he said. The guard called Graham was smoking. I did want one, so I nodded. "Give him a cigarette, Graham. There you go."

I smoked, and trembled, and watched the man smile.

"We're putting you in with him. You're going to be our ears, Nick. There's stuff we need to know."

I haven't seen my father since I was six years old, I wanted to say. I can't remember him. "What stuff?" I said.

"You don't need to know that now. Just get acquainted, get going on the heart-to-hearts. We'll be in touch. Graham here runs your block. He'll be your regular contact. He'll let me know when you're getting somewhere."

I looked at Graham. Just a guard, a prison heavy. Unlike the man at the desk.

"Your father's near the ceiling, lefthand, beside the upper bunk. You won't have anyone in the cell with you."

"Everybody's going to think you're hot shit, a real killer," said Graham, his first words. The other guard nodded.

"Yes, well," said the man at the desk. "So there shouldn't be any problem. And Nick?"

"Yes?" I'd already covered my new clothes with sweat, though it wasn't hot.

"Don't blow this for us. I trust you understand your options. Here, stub out the coffin nail. You're not looking so good."

I lay in the lower bunk trying not to look at the wall, trying not to make out differences in the double layer of voices, those from inside my cell, from the wall, and those of the other living prisoners that echoed in the corridor beyond. Only when the lights on the block went out did I open my eyes—I was willing myself back into the claustrophobic safety of the hole. But I couldn't sleep.

I crawled into the upper bunk.

"Floyd?" I said.

In the scant light from the corridor I could see the eyes of the wall turn to me. The bodies could have been sculpture, varnished stone, but the shifting eyes and twitching mouths were alive, more alive than I wanted them to be. The surface was layered with defacements and graffiti, not the massive spray-paint boasts of the exterior but scratched-in messages, complex engravings. And then there were the smearings, shit or food, I didn't want to know.

"—horseshoe crab, that's a hell of a thing—"

"—the hardest nut in the case—"

"—ran the table, I couldn't miss, man. Guy says John's gonna beat that nigger and I say—"

The ones that cared to have an audience piped up. There were four talkers in the upper part of the wall of my cell. I'd soon get to know them all. Billy Lancing was a black man who talked about his career as a pool hustler, lucid monologues reflecting on his own cleverness and puzzling bitterly over his downfall. Ivan Detbar, who plotted breaks and worried prison hierarchies as though he were not an immobile irrelevant presence in the wall. And John Jones—that was Billy's name for him—who was insane.

The one I noticed now was the one who said, "I'm Floyd."

A muscle in my chest punched upwards against my windpipe like a fist. I couldn't speak, couldn't think. Would meeting my father trigger the buried memories? The emotion I felt was virtual emotion. I didn't know this man. I should.

I was trembling all over.

He was missing an eye. From the crushed rim of the socket it looked like it had been pried out of the hardened flesh of the wall, not lost before. And his arms, crossed over his stomach, were scored with tiny marks, as though someone had used him to count their time in the cell. But his one eye lived, examined mine, blinked sadly. "I'm Floyd," he said again.

"My name is Nick," I said, wondering if he'd recognize it, and perhaps ask my last name. He couldn't possibly recognize me. After my week in the hole I looked as far from my six-year-old self as I ever would.

"Ever see a horseshit crap, Nick?" said John Jones.

"Shut up, Jones," said Billy Lancing.

"How'd you know my name?" said my father.

"I'm Nick Marra," I said.

"How'd you know my name?" he said again.

"You're a famous fuck," said Ivan Detbar. "Word is going around. 'Floyd is the man around here.' All the young guys want to see if they can take you."

"Horseshoe crab, horseradish fish," said John Jones. "That's a hell of a thing. You ever see—"

"Shut up."

"You're Floyd Marra," I said.

"I'm Floyd."

I turned away, momentarily overcome. My father's plight overwhelmed mine. The starkness of this punishment suddenly was real to me, in a way it hadn't been in the hole. This view out over the bunk and through the bars, into the corridor, was the only view my father had seen since his hardening.

"I'm Nick Marra," I said. "Your son."

"I don't have a son."

I tried to establish our relationship. He agreed that he'd known a woman named Doris Thayer. That was my mother's name. His pocked mouth tightened and he said, "Tell me about Doris. Remind me of that."

I told him about Doris. He listened intently—or I thought he was listening intently. Whenever I paused, he asked a question to keep me on the subject. At the end he said only, "I remember the woman you mean." I waited, then he added, "I remember a few different women, you know. Some more trouble than they're worth. Doris I wouldn't mind seeing again."

Awkwardly, I said, "Do you remember a boy?"

"Cheesedog crab," said Jones. "That's a good one. They'll nip at you from under the surf—"

"You fucking loony."

"A boy?"

"Yes."

"Yes, there was a boy—" All at once my father began a rambling whispered reminiscence, about *his* father, and about himself as a boy in the Italian ghetto. I leaned back on the bunk and looked away from the wall, towards the bars and the trickle of light from the hallway as he told me of merciless beatings, mysterious nighttime uprootings from one home to another, and abandonment.

Around us the other voices from the wall babbled on, as constant as television. I was already learning to tune them out like some natural background, crickets, surf pounding. Now even my father's voice wove into the curtain around my exhausted senses. I fell asleep to the sound of his voice.

The next morning I joined the prison community. The two-tiered cafeteria called Mess Nine was a churning, teeming place, impossible not to see as a hive. Like the offices, it was on the interior, away from the living wall. I escaped notice until I took my full tray out towards the tables.

"Hey, lonely boy."

"He's not lonely, he's a psycho. Aren't you, man?"

"They're afraid of this skinny little guy, he's got to be psycho."

"Who you kill?"

I went and set my tray on an empty corner of a table and sat down, but it didn't stop. The inmate who'd latched on first ("lonely boy") followed and sat behind me.

"He needs his privacy, can't you see?" said someone else. "Let him eat and go back to his psycho cell."

"He can't socialize."

"I'll socialize him."

"He wants to fuck the wall."

"He was up late fucking the wall last night for sure. Little hung over, lonely boy?"

Fuck the wall, I came to know, was an all-purpose phrase, in constant use either as insult or as an expression of rebellion, of yearning, of ironic futility. The standing assumption was that the dry, corroded mouths would gnaw a man's penis to bloody shreds in a minute. Stories circulated of those who'd tried, of the gangs who'd forced it on a despised victim, of the willing brick somewhere in the wall who encouraged it, got it round the clock and asked for more.

I survived the meal in silence. Better for the moment to truck on my reputation as a dangerous enigma than expose it with feeble protests. The fact of my unfair treatment wouldn't inspire any more sympathy from the softer criminals than it had from Jimmy Shand, the brick in the hole. I shrugged away comments, the thrown bits of rolled-up bread, and a hand on my knee, and did more or less as they predicted by retreating to my cell. The television room, the gym, the other common spaces were challenges to be met some other day.

"Shoecat cheese!" said John Jones. "Beefshoe crab!"

"Quiet you goddamn nut!"

"If you'd seen it you wouldn't laugh," said Jones ominously.

They were expecting me in the upper bunk. My father had been listening to Billy Lancing tell an extended story about a hustle gone bad in western Kansas, while they both fended off Jones.

"Nick Marra," said my father.

I was pleased, thinking he recognized me now. But he only said, "How'd you get sent up, Marra?" and I understood that he didn't remember his own last name.

"Robbery," I said. I still responded automatically with the minimum. My crime didn't get more impressive with the addition of details.

"You're in a rush?" said Floyd.

"What?"

"You haven't got all day? You're going somewhere? Tell your story, kid."

We talked. He drew the tale of my crime and arrest out of me. He and Billy Lancing laughed when I got to the collision with the police cruiser, and Floyd said, "Fucking cop was probably jerking off with the other hand."

"He'll be telling it that way from now on," said Billy. "Won't you, Nick?"

"What?"

"Too good not to tell it like that," agreed Floyd.

And then, before I could tell him again that he was my father, he began to talk about his own crimes, and his punishments, before he was hardened. "—hadn't been sent upstairs to get the money he forgot, I woulda been killed in that crossfire like he was. 'Course my reward for living was the judge gave me all the years they wanted to give him—"

"Shit, you weren't more than a boy," said Billy.

"That's right," said Floyd. "Like this one."

"They all look like boys to me," said Billy. "Hey, man, tell him how you used to work for the prison godfather."

"Jesus, that's a long time ago," said Floyd, like he didn't want to get into it. "Long time ago . . ."

In fact he was just warming up.

The stories carried me out of myself, though I didn't exactly believe every word. I felt I'd been warned that embellishments were not only possible but likely. Floyd and Billy showed me that prison stories were myths, rendered in individual voices. What mattered were the universals, the telling.

I'd been using my story to show a connection between myself and Floyd, but the bricks weren't interested in connections. Billy and Floyd might have been accomplices in the job that got them sent up or they might never have met; either way they were now lodged catty-corner to one another forever, and the stories they told wouldn't change it, wouldn't change anything. The stories could only entertain, and get them attention from the living prisoners. Or fail to.

So I let go of trying to make Floyd admit that he was my father, for the moment. It was enough to try to understand it myself.

On the way back from dinner Lonely Boy and two others followed me back to my cell. The hall was eerily empty, every adjoining cell abandoned. I learned later that such moments were no accident, but well orchestrated. The three men twisted my arms back, pushed me into the toilet stall, out of sight of the wall, and pulled down my pants.

I will not describe them or give them names.

What they did to me took a long time.

Lonely Boy stroked the nape of my neck all through the ordeal. What they did was seldom tender, but he never stopped stroking the small hairs of my neck and talking to me. His words were all contradictions, and I soon stopped listening to them. The sound was the point anyway, a kind of cooing interspersed with jagged accusations. Rhythm and counterpoint; Lonely Boy was teaching me about my helplessness, and the music of his words was a hook to help me remember. "Little special boy, special one. Why are you the special one? What did they choose you for? They pick you out for me? They send me a lonely one? You supposed be a spy here, you want to in-fil-trate? How are you gonna spend your lonely days? You gonna think of me? I know I been thinking of you. This whole place is thinking of you. They'll kill you if I don't watch out for you. I'm your pro-tec-tor now—"

When I finally was alone I crawled into the lower bed and turned away from the wall. But I heard Ivan Detbar's voice from above. He made sure he was heard.

"You don't have to go looking to find the top dog on the floor. The top dog finds you, that's what makes him what he is. He finds you and he's not afraid."

"Shit," said Billy Lancing.

"That's who you've got to take," said Detbar. "You've got to get on him like *thunder*. There is no other way."

"Shit," said Billy again. "First thing I learned in the joint is a virgin asshole's nothing to die for. It doesn't make the list."

Floyd wasn't talking.

Graham and another guard took me into an office the next day, an airless room on the interior.

"Okay," he said.

"Okay what?"

"Are you doing what we told you?"

"Talking? You didn't tell me anything more than that."

"Don't be smart. Your father trusts you?"

"Everything's great," I said. "So why don't you tell me what this is all about." I didn't bother to tell him that Floyd didn't agree that he was my father, that we hadn't even established that after almost three days of talk.

I was feeling oddly jaunty, having grasped the depths of my situation. And I wasn't all that impressed with Graham on his own. There wasn't anything he could take away from me.

I wanted more information, and I suspected I could get it.

"There's time for that," said Graham.

"I don't think so. All this weird attention is going to get me killed. They think I'm a spy for you, or they don't know what to think. I'm not going to be alive long enough for you to use me."

I wasn't interested in telling him about the previous night. I knew enough to know that it wouldn't improve anything for me. The problem was mine alone. I didn't know whether I was ever going to confront Lonely Boy, but if I did, it would be on prison terms. My priority now was to understand what they wanted from me and my father.

"You're exaggerating the situation," said Graham.

"I'm not. Tell me what this is about or I'll ask Floyd."

Graham considered me. I imagine I looked different than when they first dragged me out of the hole. I felt different.

He made a decision. "You'll be brought back here. Don't do anything you'll regret."

The other guard took me back to my cell.

It was a few hours later that I was standing in front of the man who didn't introduce himself the first time. He didn't again. He just told me to sit down. Graham stood to one side.

"Do you know the name Carl Allen Hemphill?" asked the man.

"Carl," I said, surprised.

"Very good. Have you been speaking with your father about him?"

"What? No."

"Did you know he was a prisoner here?"

"No." I'd heard he'd been a prisoner. But I didn't know he'd been a prisoner in the prison built of human bricks. "He's here now?" Somehow I was stupid enough to yearn for an old friend inside the prison, to imagine they were offering a reunion.

"He's dead."

I received it as a small, blunt impact somewhere in my stomach. It was muffled by the distance of years since I'd seen him, and by my situation, my despair. Sure he was dead, I thought. Around here everything is dead. But why tell me?

"So?" I said.

"Listen carefully, Nick. Do you remember the unsuccessful attempt on the President's life?"

"Sure."

"The assassin, the man that was killed—that was your friend."

"Bottmore," I said, confused. "Wasn't his name Richard Bottmore, or Bottomore, something like that—"

"That wasn't his real name. His real name was Carl Allen Hemphill."

"That's crazy." I'd barely begun to struggle with the notion of Carl's having been here, his death. The assassination was too much, like being suddenly asked to consider the plight of the inhabitants of the moon. The point of this conversation, the answers I was seeking, seemed to whirl further and further out of my reach. "Why would he want to do that?"

"We'd very much like the answer to that question, Nick." He smiled at me as though he'd said enough, and thought I could take it from there. For a blind, hot second I wanted to kill him. Then he spoke again.

"He did his time quietly. Library type, loner. Nothing that was any indication. He was released five months before the attempt."

"And?"

"He had your cell."

"That's what this is about?" It seemed upside down. Was he saying that my real connection with Floyd didn't interest them, wasn't the point?

"Floyd hasn't said anything?"

"I told you no."

This time it was the man at the desk who lit a cigarette, and he didn't offer me one. I waited while he finished lighting it and arranging it in his mouth.

When he spoke again, his expression was oddly distanced. It was the first time I felt I might not have his full attention. "Hemphill left some papers behind. Very little of any value to the investigation so far. But he mentioned your father. It's one of the only interesting leads we have.

"The people I work with believe Hemphill didn't act alone. The more we dig up on his background, the more we glimpse the outlines of a conspiracy. You understand, I can't tell you any more than that or I'll be putting you in danger."

His self-congratulatory reluctance to "put me in danger" put a bad taste in my mouth. "You're crazy," I said. "Floyd doesn't know anything about that."

"Don't try to tell me my job," said the man behind the desk. "Hemphill left a list of targets. This is not a small matter. It was your father's name in his book. Not some other name. Floyd Marra."

I felt a stirring of jealousy. Carl and my father, my father who wouldn't admit he was. "Why don't you talk to Floyd yourself?"

"We tried. He played dumb."

What if he is dumb, I wanted to say. I was trying to square these bizarre revelations with the face in the wall, the brick I'd conversed with for the past three days. Trying to picture them questioning Floyd and coming away with the impression that he was holding something vital back.

"Can't bug the wall, either," said Graham. "Fuckers warn each other. Whisper messages."

"The wall doesn't like us, Nick. It doesn't cooperate. Floyd isn't stupid. He knows who he's talking to. That's why we need you."

He doesn't know who he's talking to when he's talking to me, I wanted to say.

"I'll ask him about Carl for you," I said. I knew I would, for my own reasons.

"Crabshit fish," interrupted Jones. "That's a hell of a thing."

It nearly expressed the way I felt. "He almost started a war," I said to Floyd, trying harder to make my point.

"He was a good kid," said Floyd. "Like you."

"Scared like you, too," said Ivan Detbar.

I had to remind myself that the bricks didn't see television or read newspapers, that Floyd hadn't lived in the world for over thirteen years. The President didn't mean anything to him. Not that he did to me.

"How'd you know him?" said Floyd. "Cellmates?"

It was an uncharacteristic question. It acknowledged human connections, or at least it seemed that way to me. Something knotted in my stomach. "We were in school together, junior high," I said. "He was my best friend."

"Best friend," Floyd echoed.

"After you were put here," I said, as though the framework was understood. "Otherwise you would have known him. He was around the house all the time. Mom—Doris—used to—"

"Get this cell rat," said Floyd. "Talking about the past. His mom."

"Heh," said Billy Lancing.

"That's a lot like that other one," said Ivan Detbar. "What's his name, Hemphill. He was a little soft."

"No wonder they were best friends," said Floyd. "Mom. Hey Billy, how's your *mom?*"

"Don't know," said Billy. "Been a while."

Now I hated him, though in fact he'd finally restored me to some family feeling. He'd caused me to miss Doris. She knew who I was, would remember me, and remember Carl as I wanted him remembered, as a boy. And besides, I knew her. I didn't remember my father and I was sick of pretending.

What's more, in hating him, I recalled an old feeling of trying to share in Doris's hatred of him, not in support but because I'd envied her the strength of the emotion. She'd known Floyd, she had a person to love or hate. I had nothing, I had no father. There was the void of my memories and there was this scarred brick, and between them somewhere a real man had existed, but that real man was forever inaccessible to me. I wanted to go back to Doris, I wanted the chance to tell her that I hated him now too. I felt that somehow I'd failed her in that.

I was crying, and the bricks ignored me, I thought.

"Hemphill sure got screwed, didn't he?" said Billy.

"The kid couldn't take this place," said Ivan Detbar.

"But he was a good kid," said Floyd.

"Wasn't his fault, something tripped him up bad," said Billy. "Something went down."

Through my haze of emotions—jealousy, bitterness,

desolation—I realized they were offering me a warning, and perhaps some sort of apology.

The talk of Carl made me remember my assignment.

"You guys talked a lot?" I said.

"I guess," said Floyd.

"Nothing else to do," said Billy. "Less I'm missing something. Floyd, you been holding out on me?"

"Heh," said Floyd.

"There wasn't any talk about what he was going to do when he got out?" I asked. My task might be only an absurd joke, but at the moment it was all I had.

"I don't hear you talking about what you're going to do when you get out, and you're only doing a three-year stretch," said my father.

"What?"

"That's the last thing you want to think about now, isn't it? Maybe when you get a little closer."

"I don't understand."

"That poor kid was here at the start of ten years," said Floyd. "Hey, Billy. You ever meet a guy at the start of a long stretch wants to talk about what he's gonna do when he *finishes?*"

"Not unless he's planning a break, like Detbar here. Hah."

"I'll do it, too," said Detbar. "And I ain't taking you with me, you motherfucker."

"But he got out," I said, confused. "Hemphill, I mean."

"Yeah, but all of a sudden," said Floyd. "He *thought* he was doing ten years."

"Why all of a sudden?" I said. "What happened?"

"Somebody gave him a deal. They had a job for him. Let him out if he did it."

"Yeah, but that just made him sorrier," said Billy. "He was one screwed-up cat."

"He was okay," said Floyd. "He just had to tough it out. Like Marra here."

It was as disconcerting to hear him use the last name—as though it had nothing to do with him—as it was to be linked again and again with Carl. The dead grown-up would-be assassin and the lost child friend. It drew me out of my little investigation and back to my own concerns.

I couldn't keep from trying again. "Floyd?" What I wanted was so absurdly simple.

"Uh?"

"I want to talk to you about Doris Thayer," I said. I wasn't going to use the word *mom* again soon.

"Tell me about her again."

"She was my mother, Floyd."

"I felt that way about her too," said Floyd. "Like a mother. She really was something." He wasn't being funny this time. His tone was humble. It meant something to him, just not what I wanted it to mean.

"She was really my mother, Floyd. And you're my father."

"I'm nobody's father, Marra. What do I look like?"

That wasn't a question I wanted to answer. I'd learned that I didn't even want to watch his one eye blink, his lips work to form words. I always turned slightly away. If I concentrated on his voice, he seemed more human, more real.

"Come on, Marra, tell me what you see," said Floyd.

I realized the face of the brick was creeping into my patched-together scraps of memory. For years I'd tried to imagine him in the house, to play back some buried image of him visiting, or with Doris. Now when I tried, I saw the empty socket, the flattened skull, the hideous naked stone.

I swallowed hard, gathering my nerve, and pressed on. "How long ago did you come here?"

"Been a million years."

"Million years ago the dogshit bird ruled the earth," said John Jones. "Crawled outta the water, all over the place. It's *evolutionary*."

"Like another life to me," said Floyd, ignoring him. His voice contained an element of yearning. I told myself I was getting somewhere.

"Okay," I said. "But in that other life, could you have been somebody's father?"

A shadow fell across the floor of my cell. I looked up. Lonely Boy was leaning against the bars, hanging there with his arms up, his big fingers inside and in the light, the rest of him in darkness.

"Looking for daddy?" he said.

The next day I told Graham I wanted another meeting. The man who never introduced himself was ready later that afternoon. I was getting the feeling he had a lot of time on his hands.

His expression was boredom concealing disquiet, or maybe the reverse. "Talk," he said.

"Floyd doesn't really know anything. He's never even heard of the assassination attempt. I can't even get him to focus on that."

"That's hard to believe, under the circumstances."

"Well, start believing. You have to understand, Floyd doesn't think about things that aren't right in front of him anymore. His world is—small. Immediate." Suddenly I felt that I was betraying my father, describing him like an autistic child, when what I meant was, *He's been built into a wall and he doesn't even know who I am.*

It didn't seem right that I should have to explain it to the men responsible. But the man behind the desk still inspired in me a queasy mixture of defiance and servility. All I said was, "I think I might have something for you anyway."

"Ah," he said. "Please."

I was going to tell him that he was right, there had been a conspiracy, and that Carl had been recruited from inside. An insipid fantasy ran in my mind, that he would jump up and clap me on my back, tell me I'd cracked the case, deputize me, free me. But as I opened my mouth to speak, the man across the desk leaned forward, somehow too pleased already, and I stopped. I thought involuntarily: *What I'm about to tell him, he knows.* And I didn't speak.

I have often wondered if I saved my own life in that moment. The irony is that I nearly threw it away in the next. Or rather, caused it to be thrown.

"Yes?" he said. "You were going to say?"

"Floyd remembered Carl talking about some—group,"

I said, inventing. "Some kind of underground organization."

He raised his eyebrows at this. It was not what he was expecting. It seemed to take him a moment to find his voice. "Tell me about this—organization."

"They're called the Horseshoe Crabs," I said. "I don't really know more than that. Floyd just isn't interested in politics, I guess. But anyway, that should be enough to get you started."

"The Horseshoe Crabs."

"Yes."

"An *in-prison* underground?"

"No," I said quickly. "Something from before." I was a miserable liar.

I must have been looking at the floor. I didn't even see him leave his seat and come around the desk, let alone spot the fury accumulating in his voice or expression. He was just suddenly on me, my collar in his hands, his face an inch from mine. "You're fucking with me, Nick," he said.

"No."

"I can tell. You think I can't tell when I'm being fucked by an *amateur?*" He shoved me to the floor. I knocked over a trash basket as I fell. I looked at Graham. He just stood impassively watching, a foot away but clearly beyond appeal.

"What are the Horseshoe Crabs?" said the man. "Is Floyd a Horseshoe Crab?"

"He just said the name, that Carl used it. That's all I know."

"Stand up."

I got on my feet, but my knees were trembling. Rightly, since he immediately knocked me to the floor again.

Then Graham spoke. "Not here."

"Fine," said the man, through gritted teeth. "Upstairs."

They took me in an elevator up to the top floor, hustling me ahead of them roughly, making a point now. As they ran me through corridors, Graham pushing ahead and opening gates, living inmates jeered maliciously from their cells. They made a kind of wall themselves, fixed in place and useless to me as I went by. Graham unlocked the last door and we went up a stairway to the roof and burst out into the astonishing light of the sky. It was white, gray really, but absolutely blank and endless. It was the first sky I'd seen in two weeks. I thought of how Floyd hadn't seen it in thirteen years, but I was too scared to be outraged for him.

"Grab him," the man said to Graham. "Don't let him do it himself."

The roof was a worksite; they were always adding another level, stacking newly hardened bricks to form another floor. The workers were the first-timers, the still-soft. But there was nobody here now, just the disarray of discontinued work. A heap of thin steel dowels waiting to be run through the stilled bodies, plastic barrels of solvent for melting their side surfaces together into a wall. In the middle of the roof was a pallet of new human bricks, maybe twenty-five or thirty of them, under a battened-down tarp. In the roar of the wind I could just make out the sound of their keening.

Graham and the man from behind the desk took me by my arms and walked me to the nearest edge. Crossing that open distance made me know again how huge the prison was. I kept my head down, protecting my ears from the cold whistle of the wind and my eyes from the empty sky.

The new story was two bricks high at the edge we reached. The glossy top side of the bricks had been grooved and torn with metal rasps so the bond would take. Graham held me by my arms and bent me over the short wall, just as Lonely Boy and the others had bent me over the toilet.

"Take a look," said the man.

"Looks like rain to me," said one of the nearby bricks chattily.

My view was split by a false horizon: the dark mass of the sheer face of the prison receding earthward below the dividing line, and above it the empty acres of concrete and broken glass. From the thirty-two-story height the ground sparkled like the sea viewed from an airplane.

Graham jammed me harder against the rough top of the bricks, and tilted me further towards the edge. I grunted, and watched a glob of my own drool tumble into the void.

"I hate to be fucked with," said the man. "I don't have time for that."

I made a sound that wasn't a word.

"Maybe we'll chop your father out of the wall and throw you both off," said the man. "See which hits the ground first."

I managed to think how odd it was to threaten a man in prison with the open air, the ultimate freedom. It was the reverse of the hole, all space and light. But it served their purpose just as well. Something I reflected on later was how just about anything could be turned to serve purposes like this.

"What are the Horseshoe Crabs?" he said.

I'd already forgotten how this all resulted from my idiotic gambit. "There are no Horseshoe Crabs," I gasped.

"You're lying to me."

"No."

"Throw him over, Graham."

Graham pressed me disastrous inches closer. My shirt and some of the skin underneath caught on the shredded upper surface of the wall.

"You're not telling me why I should spare you," said the man.

"What?" I said, gulping at the cold wind.

"You're not telling me why I should spare you."

"I'll tell you everything you want to know," I said.

Graham pulled me back.

"Are you lying to me again?" said the man.

"No. Let me talk to Floyd. I'll find out whatever you want."

"I want to know about the Horseshoe Crabs."

"Yes."

"I want to know anything he knows. You're my listening device, direct from him to me. I don't want any more noise in the signal. Do you understand?"

I nodded.

"Take him back, Graham. I'm going to have a cigarette."

Graham took me to my cell. I climbed into the top bunk and lay still until my trembling faded.

"The kid's getting ready to make his move," said Ivan Detbar.

"You think so?" said Floyd.

It was dinner hour. Inmates were shambling through the corridor towards Mess Nine.

My thoughts were black, but I had a small idea.

It seemed to me that one of my problems might solve the other. The way Graham had said "not here" to the man behind the desk made me think that the man's influence might not extend very far within the prison, however extensive and malignant it was in the world at large. I had never seen him command anyone besides Graham. Graham was in charge of my block, but the trip upstairs had made me remember the immensity of the prison.

My idea was simple, but it required physical bravery, not my specialty to this point. The cafeteria was the right place for it. With so many others at hand I might survive.

"Floyd," I said.

"Yeah?"

"What if you weren't going to see me anymore? Would that change anything?"

"What are you getting at?"

"Anything you'd want to say?"

"Take care, nice knowing ya," he said.

"How about 'Don't do anything I wouldn't do'?" said Billy Lancing.

Floyd and Billy laughed at that. I let them laugh. When they were done I said, "One last question, Floyd."

"Shoot."

I'd thought I was losing interest, growing numb. I guess in the long sense I was. But I still had to press him a little harder before the opportunity passed. "Did you know your father?" I asked.

"You're asking me—what? My old man?" Floyd's eye rolled, like he thought his father had appeared somewhere in the cell.

"You knew him?"

"If I could get my hands around the neck of that son of a bitch—"

"You talk big, Floyd," said Ivan. "What about when you had your chance?"

"Fuck you," said Floyd. "I was a kid. I barely knew that motherfucker."

"The Motherfuck Dog," said John Jones. "He lives under the house—"

The tears were on my face again, and without choosing to do it I was beating my fist against the wall, against Floyd's petrified body. Once, twice, then it was too painful to go on. And I don't think he noticed.

I got down from the bunk. I had another place for the fury to go, a place where it might have a use. I only had to get myself to that place before I thought twice.

Dinner was meatballs and mashed potatoes covered with steaming grayish gravy. I took two cups of black coffee aboard my tray as well. I turned out of the food line and located Lonely Boy, sitting with his seconds at a table on the far side of the crowded room. Before I could think again I headed for them.

"Hey, lonely boy, you want to sit?"

I flung the tray so it spilled on all three of them. I was counting on that to slow the other two; all my attention would be on Lonely Boy. I knew I'd lose any fight that was a contest of strategy or guile, lose it badly, that my only chance was blind instantaneous rage. So I went in with my hands instead of picking up a fork or some other weapon. For my plan to work, Lonely Boy had to live. With what I knew was in me to unleash, however, his life seemed as much at risk as mine.

They pulled us apart before very long, but I'd already gotten my hands around his throat and begun hitting his head against the table, rhythmic revenge. One of his seconds had taken a tray and lashed open my scalp with it, and my blood was running into my opponent's eyes, and my own, and mixing with the coffee on the table. The voices around us roared.

Back in the hole for the night that followed, I screamed, bled, shat. I shoved the morning tray back out as it was coming through the slot. I attacked the men that came for me. How much was pretense I can't really say. Maybe none. When they got me into the shower I calmed down somewhat. I didn't feel human, though. I felt mercenary and cold, like frozen acid.

They put six stitches in my scalp in the prison hospital and led me to another, larger office, with more file cabinets and chairs, more ashtrays. Graham was there, with two other men. One of the others did the talking.

Those others were my margin, I knew. My glint of light.

The one who spoke asked me about the fight.

"If I'm put back in the block with him, one of us will have to die," I said simply.

I could see a look of satisfaction on the face of the other of the two men, not Graham. I assumed Lonely Boy had been trouble to this man before. I assumed too that I'd done damage. I smiled back at this man, and I smiled at Graham.

Graham kept his face impassive.

The man who was talking explained to me that Lonely Boy was an established presence on block nine, that he had more support than might have been apparent—did I understand that?

"Move me upstairs," I said. "As far away as possible. If I see him again, I'll have to kill him."

The one who was talking told me that I'd likely find men like Lonely Boy wherever I went in the prison.

Nobody said the word *rape*.

"I'll never be in this position again," I said. "I can

promise you that. Nobody will ever be permitted to make the mistake he made."

The man raised his eyebrows. The other one, the smiling one, smiled. Graham sat.

"Just move me," I said.

"We don't let prisoners make our decisions for us, Mr. Marra," said Graham.

"Your unusual handling put me at a disadvantage in the situation, Mr. Graham. If you keep me on block nine, I intend to be treated like the other prisoners."

The man who had been talking turned and looked at Graham, and in that moment I knew I would be transferred.

"Unusual handling?" said the man who'd smiled. He directed the question at me, but it was Graham who spoke.

"He presents unique difficulties," he said. "His father is in the prison. In the wall. I thought it was better to address it directly."

I took a leaf from Floyd's book. It was pure improvisation, but my skills at lying were improving rapidly. "He isn't my father."

The smiling man made an inquiring face.

"He knew my mother, I guess. But she told me later he wasn't my father. He's just some guy. Just another brick to me."

The smiling man smiled at Graham. "This doesn't seem to me to require special treatment."

"I had the impression—" Graham began.

The smiling man laughed. "Apparently mistaken, Graham."

Graham laughed along.

Graham never spoke to me again, though I lived in fear of some reprisal. I would see him moving through the corridors with the men in charge of my block or other blocks and think he was about to point a finger at me and say, "Marra, come with me," but he never did. I don't think he cared enormously. It might have been some relief to him to be able to say to the man behind the desk that I'd slipped away. Graham was a man with a difficult job and dealing with the man behind the desk was clearly not an easy part of it.

I never saw the man behind the desk again.

He was a sadist and an idiot. The two were not mutually exclusive, I understood after that day on the roof. The agency or service he worked for had assigned him the task of tracing a conspiracy he was a member of himself. Sending me in to question my father was just ritual activity. He might have been curious to know whether Hemphill had talked about what was happening to him, but he wasn't worried. He hadn't even bothered to wire the cell, or he'd have know how I came up with *horseshoe crabs*. Until I'd panicked him, triggered his paranoia with that bluff, he was just making a show of activity by torturing me. And keeping himself entertained, I suppose, killing time on an absurd assignment.

The only deeper explanation was that I'd become a

kind of stand-in for Carl, the other young prisoner they'd had in their grasp. He'd been theirs, for a time, and then he twisted loose, became history. I don't know if what he did was a disastrous perversion of their plans, or whether it served them, but I sensed that either way they experienced a loss. The mechanism of control was more precious than any outcome. I'd become the new instrument, the new site where control was enacted. Until I broke the spell.

As for Carl himself, I hadn't learned much about the tortured prisoner and would-be assassin, and I didn't have any interest in trying to learn more. The image of my thirteen-year-old friend had been obliterated without anything taking its place. I didn't object. He was just a ghost now, and there were plenty of more substantial ghosts available, in the wall.

I became another prisoner in a cell, living out my hours, hoarding my grudges, protecting my back. I spent days in the weight room, years in the television room. I told lies to make the time pass. The rest of my story was no different from anyone else's, so in the telling I made it as different as I could. I learned to use the phrase *fuck the wall*, though like a million other cowards I never tried it.

I didn't see my father again until a week before I left the prison, when I was granted a minute in my old cell.

Billy Lancing was still the same. He looked me over when I came in and said, "Marra?"

"Yeah."

"I remember you. Where'd you go?"

"Upstairs."

"Well, I remember you."

I climbed up into the top bunk.

Ivan Detbar was dead, his eyes stilled. I recognized it instantly by now. John Jones was still raving, but more quietly, not looking for an audience anymore.

My father was still alive, if that's the word for it, but someone had pried out his other eye, splintering the stony bridge of his nose in the process.

His mouth was moving, but nothing was coming out.

"Floyd's not good," said Billy.

I went over and put my hand on him. He couldn't feel it, of course. I was touching my father, but it didn't matter to either of us.

I wondered if it was Graham or the man behind the desk who'd removed the eye, in some offhand act of revenge. It could as easily have been a living prisoner, someone in that top bunk who'd taken offense at too much attention, or at some joke.

Floyd, like Billy, had listened fairly well. That was the only real difference between him and the hundreds of other bricks I'd met by that time. What had happened between him and Carl was absurdly simple, but the man behind the desk was puzzled, because it wasn't supposed to happen to an assassin-in-training, or to a human brick. They'd become friends. Floyd had expressed his dim, blundering sympathy, and Carl had listened, and been drawn out of his fear.

Which was more or less all Floyd had done with me.

Had he pretended not to know me, pretended not to make the connection between my stories, my family history, and his? I'd stopped wondering pretty quickly. I had more immediate problems, which was part of his point, I think, if he was making one.

Bricks only face one direction.

I let my hand slip from the wall, and left the cell.

SLEEPY PEOPLE

He was no danger to her. Judith Map felt that immediately. He lay on the porch, one arm flung out across her doormat, obscuring the word WELCOME. She'd come home late from work. The street was silent, apart from crickets chirping and a far-off siren. She could see his chest rise and fall calmly. She turned her key in the door and stepped past him.

Inside, she switched on the porch light, and looked at him through the glass pane at the top of the door. He wore jeans and workboots, and a tee-shirt which read QUICK'S LITTLE ALASKA. It was the name of the bar at the corner where her street met Schermerhorn Avenue, three blocks away. It was called Little Alaska because of the air conditioning.

A car pulled into a drive up the street, headlights flaring over the porch where he lay. Another of her neighbors coming home. The street led nowhere, and the only cars that went past were cars that belonged to houses there. Nobody on her street walked except Judith. But the man on the porch must have walked, or been carried. From the bar, she guessed.

She opened the door and lifted his arms and shoulders from underneath and dragged him across the threshold. His head lolled. The carpet at the entry bunched under his back, so that she had to nudge it away with her toe. She grunted, heard her own rough breath. His was still calm. She draped his arms over his stomach, and stepped out onto the porch. No one was watching. She shut the door.

She dragged him a little farther into the room, to the space between the sofa and the coffee table. She felt a little trickle of sweat under her arms. It was enough, she'd moved him enough. She went to the kitchen and filled a glass with water. When she went back in to look at him she was struck by the beauty of his features at rest. She felt she understood him. Though she didn't understand how he had gotten to her porch.

She'd heard about the sleepy people, but she'd never met one before.

She climbed over the back of the sofa and sat with her legs crossed and peered down at him. Her heart was beating fast. She wasn't frightened. She wondered if she should bring him a blanket, then remembered that the sleepy people conserved energy, kept themselves warm. He'd been on the porch, after all. Though really this was the kind of night where it was as warm outdoors as in.

A perfectly calm night, as if it had settled itself around
his sleeping body. She was the only thing agitated, her
breath unsteady. But she wasn't frightened.

Should she move him back to the porch? He might
have wanted to be there. He fit nicely between the couch
and the coffee table, though. She climbed over the back
again, and went to her bedroom door. From that vantage
he was completely out of sight. What if someone were
looking for him? It would be someone from the bar, from
Little Alaska. They might have left him here just because
they couldn't carry him anymore, intending to come
back. Certainly her neighbors wouldn't leave a sleepy
man on her porch. But the people in the bar, the militia,
never left the bar. She tangled again in the mystery of
his arrival on her porch.

It didn't matter. She was suddenly exhausted. She pic-
tured herself stretched out on the sofa, alongside him but
perched above. It was absurd, she decided, and thrust it
aside. She went into the bedroom and locked the door,
quickly. That too was absurd; she might as well have left
him on the porch. It was as though she wanted to abdi-
cate the house to him and reduce her own space to the
single room.

She unlocked the door, and left it ajar. She could see
the back of the sofa from her bed. She could hear him
breathe.

She didn't dream, but woke thinking of him. She got
out of bed to check; he was still there. His arm was
threaded through the legs of the coffee table. She pic-

tured him flinging his arms, gesticulating in the night. Otherwise he lay there exactly as she'd left him. She went to the kitchen and made herself coffee.

When she was ready for work she lifted his shoulders again and dragged him around the other side of the sofa, and back out to the porch. She didn't want to lock him inside. What else she wanted wasn't clear, but she shouldn't lock him inside. *Her back grew strong from moving him daily,* she imagined reading in an eighteenth-century novel. His boots clunked, one after another, over the doorjamb. She propped his head and shoulders slightly, just because it seemed righter for day-time. Anyone could see him from the street.

There were only two other people left in her office, Tom and Eva. There had been six people working there when she started, two years before. It was telephone work. They were collecting information. The information was highly specific: the price of carpets and hardware, the cost of garbage collection and plumbing repair. The rent board had hired them to study the legitimacy of an appeal by the commission of landlords for a cost-related increase in fixed rents. She conducted phone interviews with suppliers, repairmen, and landlords picked at random. They weren't necessarily the landlords who'd requested the increase, and they didn't always understand the questions she asked.

Halfway through the morning she called Eva's cubicle instead of the next number on her list.

"A sleepy man came to my house," she said.

"Sleeping?" said Eva.

"He's sleeping, yes. But sleepy, also. One of the sleepy people."

"Do you have any houseplants?" said Eva, whispering.

"Yes."

"They make plants grow," said Eva. "If you put them in the same room. Also sharpen razor blades."

"Really?"

"That's all I know. I better go, I've got a call."

"Thanks," said Judith.

"Sure. I think you have to put the plants pretty close to them."

"Okay."

She went back to work. She knew that Eva and Tom spoke on the phone between their cubicles all the time. Tom and Eva were in love, she guessed. They never spoke in front of her.

She walked home a little early. He was still there, propped beside the door where she'd left him. She realized she'd been holding her breath. The evening sun cast the whole porch in yellow glaze, and the sleepy man seemed to her like a diver figurine resting at the bottom of a golden aquarium. She almost didn't want to intrude. But she went past him, let herself in, dropped her keys on the sofa. There was half a casserole in the refrigerator; she moved it to the oven.

She poured herself a glass of wine to go with the leftovers, and sat drinking and just nibbling, poking at the food. Through the window the porch framed a sunset that glowed and died like an ember. The street was very quiet. He was still outside, his head just below the window frame.

A dog barked. It was night. She thought of how it wasn't safe to leave him out all night. There were the people that roamed making trouble, the dinosaurs. They sometimes found this street, though it led nowhere particular, though it was just one of so many residential streets. She'd heard them, and seen her neighbors' torn-up lawns, wrecked mailboxes. A sleepy person would be a natural target for the dinosaurs.

Every sleepy person should have someone to take care of them, she thought. That seemed simple enough.

She went out and lifted his shoulders and dragged him inside. This time she got him up onto the sofa, first sitting him against it, then hoisting him up like a baby into a car seat, finally swinging his legs up so that he turned and sank against the pillows. She closed the curtains and got her wineglass and brought it over and sat with him, perching her buttocks on the lip of cushion left free. The margin wasn't enough, and she slid down to the floor between the sofa and the coffee table. She'd taken his place.

She emptied her glass and put it on the coffee table. Outside, the dog barked again.

She turned in the little coffin-like space and was faced with his middle. His Little Alaska tee-shirt had bunched up where she'd gripped him under his shoulders. His stomach was almost black with hair. It whorled in a dev-

ilish vee in and out of his navel and into his jeans. She
was very close, having turned there. She propped herself
with her elbows on the coffee table. He wasn't fat but the
jeans were tight on his hips, and there was a pinkish
imprint of seam where they pinched his flesh. His fly was
fastened with steel buttons. She undid the first. She could
smell him a little. Her mouth tasted like wine.

The buttons had worn out their buttonholes. She only
had to nudge them apart. His penis was beating slightly,
like it had a little heart of its own. She covered it with
her hand, then put her lips to her knuckles. His hair tick-
led her nose. Under her hand his penis was twitching,
growing in little throbs. His chest rose and fell as steadily
as before.

She pushed the backing cushions off the sofa to make
room to fit her knee, and moved his arms up above his
head, so that he resembled some sculpture she'd seen, a
saint or slave carved in marble. But with stubble. Saint
Stubble of Little Alaska, she thought. His erection was
taut against his stomach now, the dewy pink head nestled in his black hair.

She slipped out of her underwear and clambered on
top, then reached down and placed him with her hand.
She was very wet. He sighed. She imagined that he was
pretending to be asleep. But he wasn't, really. She moved
slowly, keeping him inside. The backs of her thighs were
a little cold.

She brought herself to orgasm, bracing her other hand
against his collarbone, not hurrying. She pitched for-

ward. He grunted gently. Outside the dog was barking. She slid to the side and then, knees a bit tangled in her stockings and skirt, to the floor below him again.

She daubed at them both with her underwear, and buttoned him up. She stood and pulled her skirt up and it was as if nothing had happened, except her smeared underwear was on the floor and she felt a coolness and a trickling on the inside of her thighs. She ran a bath. Then she went out to him again and arranged his tee-shirt so it covered his stomach, and fit his arms back at his sides.

Something was wrong. The more she restored him, the deader he looked, as if she were a mortician. She moved him with difficulty to the easy chair, which was an improvement. It seemed to put more of an end to the affair. Then, a little guiltily, as though it should have been the first thing she'd done on coming home, she gathered the houseplants. There were four of them, a fern, a spiderplant, a tall thing that was some kind of succulent, with fat, fleshy plumes, and a small fist-like cactus with white wisps of hair instead of spines. She arrayed them near his chair.

He slept on. She got into the bath.

When she got home from work the next day, the plants already seemed bigger, and the fern, the most flexible of the four, was definitely bent towards him, as if in the direction of sunlight. His position was changed too, his head tipped forward, chin on his chest, and his arms were folded. It gave him a decisive, even obstinate look.

She put her things on the sofa and went into the kitchen.

After dinner she put on her coat again and went out onto the porch. The street was quiet. It was a cold night. It looked safe. She closed the door.

Perhaps the people in the bar would know something about the sleepy man.

Quick's Little Alaska was a perfect cube, like a children's block that had been disguised with scribbles of neon and daubs of graffiti and surrounded with Dumpsters and parked or abandoned cars so it could pass as a building. The cars on Schermerhorn Avenue raced by, oblivious. Judith herself didn't know anyone with a car anymore. Eva and Tom walked all the way downtown to work, like she did. Judith suspected the people inside Quick's, the militia, hadn't driven their cars, if they had cars, for a long time. The cars around the bar didn't look like they'd been started in a while. They all had cat footprints on the windshields and hoods.

It was chilly inside, as advertised. Everyone at the bar turned when she stepped through the door. Farther inside, at the cluster of tables, nobody seemed particularly interested. She recognized some of the faces, others were new. She took a deep breath and went to the bar.

The music playing was slurred and slow, a voice and a trumpet winding down like an uncranked engine.

The man working the bar was one she remembered from the last time she'd come in, years ago. He was the son of Quick, the owner. His hair was red, like his father's. He moved over to where she stood and cleared away

277

an empty bottle. He obviously remembered her too. "What can I do you for, Judith?" he said. "Looking for someone?"

"Not exactly," she said. She knew that Quick's son meant someone in particular: John, who had been Judith's husband once. John was sitting in the back of the bar, at one of the tables. He was part of the militia now. He was a general. Judith tried not to look his way.

"Do you sell tee-shirts?" she said.

In answer Quick's son reached underneath the bar and pulled out a shirt identical to the one the sleepy man wore.

"Yes, that's it," she said.

"You want one?"

"No. There's a man—he had one. I was wondering if you knew him."

Quick's son didn't answer, but the man beside her at the bar turned and said, "Where'd you see him?"

He had a beard and was wearing a sweater with leather patches and the kind of hat she imagined men wore on fishing boats.

"He was sleeping on my porch," she said.

The bearded man raised his eyebrow and said, "Give the lady a drink, Red."

"She didn't order anything," said Quick's son.

"I don't need anything," Judith said. "Do you know the man, the one who was sleeping?"

The bearded man raised a finger and said, "Lieutenant?"

A woman a seat away from him rested her elbow on

the bar and peered at him and Judith over the top of her half-glasses.

"Lady's looking for Danny-boy," said the bearded man.

"I'm not looking for him," Judith said quickly. "I wanted to know if he came from here." *Danny-boy*, she thought. If that was his name, if they meant the same person.

"Sure, sure," said the older woman. "We understand what you mean. Danny-boy giving you trouble?"

"No," said Judith. "So he was here? He lived in the bar?"

"He's Absent without Leave," said the bearded man. "It sounds like you have information concerning his whereabouts." He took a large finishing swallow of his drink. "Another like that, Red," he said to Quick's son, who was leaning on his side of the bar. "And don't listen in on privileged communication."

"Okay, okay," said Quick's son.

"Danny-boy's not in any trouble, is he?" said the older woman, removing her half-glasses. They were strung around her neck by a red cord and rested crookedly in her cleavage.

"No," said Judith again, a little confused. If anything, she was getting him into trouble by coming here.

"Sounds like he's found himself a woman," said the bearded man.

"Sergeant, we don't presume anything around here," said the older woman, the lieutenant. "We operate on the basis of verifiable fact."

Quick's son was still leaning in from his side of the bar, listening. They'd attracted another listener, too, a man with a cane, but no limp. He had hawk-like eyes and a gigantic nose. He stepped over and hung his cane on the bar.

"One of our scouts has been contacted, Admiral," said the woman, moving her eyebrows significantly.

The admiral turned and looked sharply at Judith, then reached out and pinched her chin. Judith jerked her head away. "Excellent disguise," said the man.

"Not her," said the lieutenant. "She's a civilian volunteer."

"Scout, that's a good one," said the sergeant. "Dannyboy couldn't scout the inside of his eyelids."

Judith didn't like agreeing with the abrasive sergeant, but she did want them to understand. "He's sleepy," she said.

"Who isn't?" said the admiral. "I'm interested in his findings, not his feelings." He turned and scowled across the bar. "Scotch, Quick."

Quick's son hurried to his bottles. Two other members of the militia joined them from the tables at the back of the room. A young woman in overalls, with a crewcut, and John, who had long ago been Judith's husband. "Hello, Judith," John said.

"General Map," said the admiral. "Hail."

"You joining our merry band?" John said to Judith, ignoring the admiral.

"I was just—I just had a question," said Judith.

"She's playing Betsy Crocker to a Benedict Arnold," said the sergeant sneeringly.

"Don't you mean Betsy *Ross?*" said the lieutenant.

Quick's son put a whiskey on the bar in front of the admiral, then opened two bottles of beer and handed them to the woman in overalls, who passed one to John. Quick's son still hadn't refilled the sergeant's glass, Judith noticed.

"Danny-boy?" said John to the lieutenant. She nodded sagely.

"He's taken up position on a porch," said the admiral, and then added, "As per my orders," and shot a fierce look at the sergeant.

Judith opened her mouth to say that he wasn't actually on the porch anymore, that he'd been moved inside. But she didn't speak.

"So what's the problem?" said John, his eyes on Judith.

"Communication is poor-to-nonexistent," said the admiral, with a hard look in his eyes.

"Snoring, however, is highly satisfactory," japed the sergeant.

"Admiral, why don't you buy the young lady a drink?" said the lieutenant. "I hate to see her empty-handed."

"It's fine," said Judith.

"Make it a round for the house," said the sergeant. "That's the only way I'll ever get a drink around here."

"We'll reestablish communication when we need to," said John to the admiral. "For the time being let's leave Danny-boy where he is. Deep in mufti."

The woman in overalls suddenly laughed.

"In mufti?" said the sergeant puzzledly.

"A round for the house," said John. "I'm buying."

"Mighty white of you, General," said the lieutenant. But John was already headed back to his table.

"Mighty white of you, General," echoed the sergeant in a mocking whine.

"Young lady, I wonder if perhaps you would accompany me to a booth?" said the admiral to Judith.

"No thank you," she said. "I have to go."

In another day the cactus had grown extra knobs, on the side that faced him. Almost like tumors, she thought. The needle-fur over the new growth was downy, like a baby's first hair. It was overweighted on that side now, and nearly tipping its pot. She turned it so the new growth faced away from him.

The other three had proliferated too. The spiderplant had cast new trailers over his ankle, and the fern and the succulent were both turned towards him, and thicker and shinier on his side. He was like King Arthur, she thought. The land, the crops, grew when he was well and died when he was sick. Or was it the other way? King Midas, maybe that was righter. Golden touch. She wanted him to have a title or rank, like the others from the bar. Danny-boy didn't seem enough.

Porch King. Arthur Midas, Porch King. Maybe she should move him out to the porch again.

Instead she moved the plants all a little farther away, then stood back and looked. She was embarrassed for him, somehow, in a cozy chair surrounded by the eager foliage. It was too feminine, not really kingly at all, let alone military. She thought of the famous painting of the Midwestern farmer parting the cattails to find the nude sleeping there. He was still as inappropriate, as unexpected as that. The plants seemed to make it worse.

If she took him and the plants out together to the porch, they would be camouflage, not decoration. But it was too cold; the fern would die. And she wanted him inside. So she took them away to their original spots in the house. They'd basked enough, and what was happening to the cactus didn't necessarily seem so healthy anyway. Denuded of the plants he looked dead again, but she had an idea.

In the closet was her television, on a rolling metal stand. She didn't watch it anymore. It had gone from all news about militias forming and dinosaurs to replaying old shows that weren't about anything at all. She rolled it out of the closet to a spot in front of his chair and plugged it in, set the volume low, and stepped behind it to watch him. Perfect. He was transformed, restored. The flickering glow seemed to animate his features. It reminded her of when she found him, that first day, on the porch.

She went to the closet and took out a large cardboard mailing tube. It was still marked with stamps and stickers. She put one end in his lap and pointed the other across his shoulder, and arranged his arms around it as though it were a rifle. She tipped his head forward a bit so he seemed more attentive. If the dinosaurs looked in her window, they would see him keeping watch, waiting. Though it was hard to see it really as a rifle; they would think he was holding a bazooka, a flame thrower. Or a cardboard tube.

Finished, she knelt and let her head rest against his knee briefly. His breathing was soft and steady, as always. He was a good sleeper, she thought. He was getting good sleep. She touched his thigh. It felt nice. But that part of their relationship had to wait, she decided. He shouldn't be undressed now, she shouldn't be thinking of that.

"He made the plants grow."

She'd just learned that in one shop 70-watt lightbulbs were selling for two dollars and fifty cents apiece, while in another shop, a few blocks away from the first, they cost almost ten dollars. Then she'd called Eva.

"They all do that, I told you."

"Do you—have you known a sleepy person?"

"Well—" Eva giggled.

Out of the corner of her eye Judith saw Tom go from his cubicle to the door of Eva's. "Just a sec," said Eva.

Judith could make out their talk, though Eva must have had her hand over the mouthpiece. "Who's on the phone?" said Tom.

"It's Judith. We're talking."

"Hurry up, I want to go to lunch."

Eva came back on the line. "I have to go," she said.

When she got home, Judith saw that the new growths

on the cactus had sagged, like little deflated balloons. The hair on them was thin and disordered. She brought the cactus back into the living room and put it on the floor at his feet, in front of the television.

That night from her bedroom, just as she was drifting off to the sound of the voices on the television, she heard him pad to the bathroom and pee. The sound of his urine falling into the little pool went on forever, and the tone rose, as if he were filling the bowl completely. Finally it stopped, and there came the sound of the faucet, then a slapping and slurping noise that she decided meant he was drinking from his cupped hands. He left the bathroom without flushing the toilet.

In the morning she saw he'd gotten to his chair and retaken the tube into his arms, though he was holding it more like a pillow than a rifle, hugging it to his chest, his grizzled cheek resting against it. A little stream of drool was soaked into the cardboard. She restored the tube to rifle position, then turned the television off for the day.

The cactus had already reinflated nicely.

At work she found that her phone couldn't be used to call the other cubicles anymore.

They arrived while she was brushing her teeth before bed. She was in a robe. It was a warm night. His television was on now, a reassuring monotone of chatter. They broke the front window with a rock from the yard. When she came out of the bathroom to look, someone had a foot through the broken window, tangling in the blind, and someone else was pounding on the front door. She opened it, and they came at her.

It was a group of dinosaurs, five of them, three male and two female. They looked young, younger than dinosaurs looked in the news. She wondered if any of them were even twenty. The first two through the door grabbed her by the arms. One pulled her wet toothbrush from her hand and threw it under the table. The last stepped in and closed the door.

"Drop it," one of them yelled. His hair was fluffed into an enormous Afro, and he wore a pumpkin-colored satin jacket with a fluted waist and sleeves. He poked a small knife toward the sleepy man and said again, "Drop it." Another dinosaur, a teenage girl, dashed forward and jerked the cardboard tube out of the sleepy man's arms, releasing it to clatter to the floor beside his chair.

"He's asleep," said Judith.

Keeping the knife at waist-level, the dinosaur with the Afro squinted at the sleepy man. "Sure he is," he said. "Be rough with her. We'll see how he likes that."

"What?" said the teenage girl.

"Be rough with her," said the one with the Afro. "Don't make me tell you twice."

They threw Judith back against the sofa. Her robe was flung open, revealing her body to them. She was wearing panties, nothing else. She was conscious of her appendectomy scar. The teenage girl took the knife and perched at the other end, on the arm of the sofa. "Sit still," she said.

"Search for stuff," said the dinosaur with the Afro to the others.

"What stuff?" said one of the other dinosaurs.

"Shut up," said the dinosaur with the Afro. "You know what I mean."

The dinosaurs began tearing up the house, two in the bedroom, two in the kitchen. They cleared cabinets with a sweeping arm, dumped every drawer and container on the floor, then tipped each piece of furniture onto its front, away from the wall. It didn't seem to Judith that they were really searching for anything, more like a ritual destruction. Even for that it was halfhearted.

The dinosaur with the Afro came out of her bedroom with both hands full of stuffing. They'd slashed her bed. He tossed the handfuls, and the stuffing scattered in clumps over Judith and the sofa. She pulled her robe closed.

"We've been watching you," he said, sneering.

Judith didn't say anything. The other dinosaurs came out and stood gathered there in front of her.

"We watch everyone," the dinosaur said after a moment, as though he'd decided he didn't want her to feel special after all.

"On this street?" said Judith. She wasn't sure she understood what he meant.

"We've never been here before. You'd know if we'd been here, believe me." The other dinosaurs laughed. One of them was poking at the sleepy man, checking his pockets and under the cushions of his chair.

"What did you see?" she asked him.

"You live like robots," he said. "Don't ask me any more questions."

One of the dinosaurs stepped up and pulled her hair and poked her gently in the eye. "Sorry," he said. Judith covered her eye with her hand. Another of the dinosaurs tuned the television to a station playing music, and turned the volume up so loud that the throb of the bass line was like an elephant's footsteps muffled in static.

"Hold her," said the dinosaur with the Afro. The girl on the sofa and the boy who'd poked Judith took her arms now and pinned her back against the cushions.

"What are you doing?" said Judith, frightened.

"Quiet." The one giving the orders pulled a roll of duct tape from his jacket. Judith thought: $12.99. He ripped a short patch of tape from the roll and pasted it across her mouth and, inadvertently, her nose. She could breathe through only one nostril. Suddenly all of her attention was devoted to the need to continue breathing.

The leader pulled open her robe and tore away her panties. They were old and ripped easily. He hurled the rent garment at the sleepy man, and it spread like a butterfly across his stomach and the arm of his chair. "Wake him up," said the leader. "Make him watch."

The sleepy man's head was to one side, his jaw slack. His right arm was still curled up beside his shoulder where it had held the cardboard tube. Judith wondered if they could sense the peacefulness that came from him. She saw in the corner of her vision that someone had knocked over the cactus, and it lay beside its pot in a sprawl of pebbles and dirt. She tried to struggle, but her arms were pinned back.

"Wake him up," said the leader again. He unfastened his belt and knelt between Judith's legs on the sofa. He didn't have an erection.

Judith tried to say, "He's asleep" but couldn't make a sound, and the effort drained her of air, so she had to focus on breathing again. Her entire head felt hot with blood, and her body felt cold and numb. The dinosaur's hand was on her chest, pressing her down as she tried to breathe. She imagined that her head was bright red and her body white and empty, sagging like the deflated growths of the cactus. She couldn't feel her body, just her bright hot head and the burning hand of the dinosaur against her chest.

"Wake him."

She saw that one of the dinosaurs, the eye poker, was slapping at the sleepy man now. Another was behind him, lifting the back of his chair, then jolting it down on the floor. She could barely hear the sounds over the noise of the television.

"Fuck, man."

"Is he dead?"

"Dead to the world."

He's only sleeping, thought Judith.

The leader made a disgusted sound and awkwardly got himself free of the sofa and the tangle of Judith's legs and robe. Judith felt his handprint fade from her chest. He went to the sleepy man and lifted his right eyelid, carefully, like a doctor. The other dinosaurs all watched. Then he buckled his belt and buttoned his pants. The television still blared, but it was the only sound. The girl released Judith's arm. Judith tugged the duct tape away from her nose. One of the dinosaurs that had been trying to wake the sleepy man was in the kitchen now, eating something. Another was in the bathroom, brushing her teeth with Judith's toothbrush. Judith pulled her robe closed.

The leader picked up the mailing tube and broke it easily over his knee. The halves didn't separate, but remained bound by a flexible curl of cardboard. The dinosaur who'd been in the kitchen emerged, chewing, and holding a big piece of bread. The leader slapped it out of his hand, and it landed on the sleepy man's lap, with the panties.

"Let's get out of here," he said.

"Can I take a shower?" said the tooth-brushing one from the bathroom.

Judith tore the patch of tape clear of her mouth. "It's okay," she said.

"Shut up," said the leader, pointing at her, but his heart definitely wasn't in it.

Judith cleaned up the mess and put everything that wasn't broken back in its place. She repotted the cactus, which didn't seem any the worse for wear, and put it on the kitchen windowsill where it had been before. Let the new growth take care of itself one way or the other, she thought. She didn't really need a bigger cactus.

Then she moved him from upright in the chair to supine on the sofa. She realized now how much better that was, how much less pretentious. She considered putting him out on the porch, but that seemed a little extreme. What happened wasn't his fault. The television went back into the closet; she didn't know who she was fooling with that one. She missed falling asleep to the sound of his breathing anyway.

At work the next morning she was alone in the office, wondering what had happened to Tom and Eva, and whether she would always be alone here now, when she thought to check a calendar and discovered it was Saturday. She wasn't supposed to be at work.

The militia came the following day. It had been raining through the night, and the air smelled washed. The sky was gray. They massed on her porch, admiral, lieutenant, sergeant, general, and others. They all wore baseball caps or hunting hats. Quick's son was along, carrying a pair of sagging duffel bags. Perhaps he'd been deputized, Judith thought. If that was the word for it. They knocked on her door, and when she came out, it was the admiral who addressed her. He carried a walking stick, and he gestured with the end of it.

"They raped you, didn't they?" he said.

"Not really," she said.

"Brave girl," said the admiral, shaking his head. Then he raised his stick and turned to the others. "They must be stopped," he declared.

"I don't think they're around," Judith said. "They went away."

"We'll find them," said the admiral.

"They can feel us breathing down their necks," said the sergeant, chuckling.

Judith had heard of this, of militias going mobile all of a sudden.

"We've come for Danny-boy," said the lieutenant. There was a note of sympathy in her voice, but Judith couldn't read her eyes, which were shaded with a green acetate insert behind her glasses.

"He's asleep," said Judith.

"R and R is over," said the sergeant.

"Besides, his mission's accomplished," said the admiral. "This position's no longer useful—it's *behind* us."

How did you know it was in front of you before? Judith wondered. But the sergeant and Quick's son were already past her and inside. They went to the sofa and took him by his arms, the sergeant saying, "Now is the time for all good men—"

John, Judith's former husband, stood a little behind the others, on the porch steps. The younger woman in the overalls stood with him. Judith looked at him. Suppressing a smile, he held out his hands and said, "It's true, Judith. A good scout has to stay ahead."

"I don't think he came here to scout," she said.

The sergeant and Quick's son had him up and walking, sort of. His head was drooped forward, and Judith could see that if they let go, he'd crumple. Yet he was

planting one foot after another, moving forward. She felt
a little proud, oddly enough. They got him through the
door and across the porch, where John and the younger
woman helped him down the steps and held him while
Quick's son retook his duffel bags. No one but Quick's
son had to carry any luggage, which testified to his low
status within the militia. If he could even be said to be a
part of it, Judith corrected. The sleepy man might only
be a scout, but he was obviously crucial to them.

The admiral poked the end of his walking stick at the
mat in front of her door. "What's this?"

The sergeant turned his head. "It says welcome," he
said.

"That's hardly advisable," said the admiral.

The sergeant lifted the mat. "Might make a heck of a
chest protector," he said, sizing it across his stomach.
"May I?"

"Go ahead," said Judith.

The sergeant tucked the edge of the mat into his belt,
so it projected like a section of cone from his waist, ter-
minating at chin level. "Hey hey!" he said, beaming.

"We're off, then," said the lieutenant, moving aside to
let the admiral use the steps. She clasped Judith's hand
in both of hers. "For everything, thanks." Judith nodded,
and the lieutenant turned away.

John and the younger woman had walked the sleepy
man out to the curb. The rest of the militia trickled
across the yard and bunched around them. Several of
them put a hand out to help support the sleepy man, and

they began to advance along the pavement. The sleepy man looked conspicuous among them without a hat, Judith thought. She hoped they'd find him one.

She stood and watched them from the porch. Soon they were at the end of the block, just a little black knot headed into the mist. She couldn't make out the sleepy man, couldn't distinguish any of them. God help him, she thought, then corrected it to, God help *them*. But that wasn't right either. God *bless* them? God bless us all? Just before they were completely out of sight she narrowed it to a curt *God bless,* as though someone had only sneezed.

FOL

JUN 2 5 2024

CPSIA information can be obtained
at www.ICGtesting.com
Printed in the USA
LVHW041500241220
675096LV00009B/1317

9 780156 032483